H

Was

My Man

First

Also by Nancey Flowers

A Fool's Paradise
Shattered Vessels
No Strings Attached
Twilight Moods (contributor)
I Didn't Work This Hard Just to Get Married (contributor)
Morning, Noon & Night (editor)

Also by Courtney Parker

Runnin' Game
Twilight Moods (contributor)
T.O.'s Finding Fitness (coauthor)

He
Was
My Man
First

Nancey Flowers and
Courtney Parker

ST. MARTIN'S GRIFFIN
New York

This is a work of fiction. All of the characters, organizations, and events portrayed in this novel are either products of the authors' imaginations or are used fictitiously.

HE WAS MY MAN FIRST. Copyright © 2011 by Nancey Flowers and Courtney Parker. All rights reserved. Printed in the United States of America. For information, address St. Martin's Press, 175 Fifth Avenue, New York, N.Y. 10010.

www.stmartins.com

LIBRARY OF CONGRESS CATALOGING-IN-PUBLICATION DATA

Flowers, Nancey.
  He was my man first / Nancey Flowers and Courtney Parker.—1st ed.
    p. cm.
  ISBN 978-0-312-67849-4
  1. African Americans—Fiction.   2. Triangles (Interpersonal relations)—
Fiction.   I. Parker, Courtney.   II. Title.
  PS3606.L6838H4 2011
  813'.6—dc22

2010040376

First Edition: March 2011

10 9 8 7 6 5 4 3 2 1

To any woman who has ever been in love,
desires love, or has lost love . . .
this book is for you.

1 Corinthians 13:4-8, "true love never fails."

Blessings, Courtney & Nancey.

Acknowledgments

Thank you to my family: my mother, Leonia; my sister, LaCreasa; my brother, Jay; and my daughter, Caley. I love you. To my agent, Joe Regal: You are the best thing that has ever happened to my career. To Kristel Crews: Thanks for "everything"! To all my friends: Thank you for giving life to every story I could ever think to tell. To the man who makes me believe in happily-ever-after, I'm excited to see how our story unfolds. To Nancey Flowers: Thanks for your patience, endurance, and friendship throughout this entire process. To Kevin Hunter, thank you for everything you did to help push this project forward. To Hilary Teeman and the entire staff at St. Martin's Press, a million thanks for your help on this project. Finally, to my Creator and Heavenly Father, I am better because You are my God.

In His Love,
Courtney

If everyone were as fortunate to have a mother like mine, they'd be blessed. I have to thank God for having Mama Rose in my corner. You are one of the strongest women I know, and if I've never told you this before, Mom, you are my shero! I love you beyond measure.

To my wonderful family: Maxine McIntosh, Marcia McIntosh, Diane Flowers, Andrea Flowers, Orane Haughton, Aisha Flowers, Prince Wint, Mama Paula, Mama Una, and the rest of you who continue to offer me encouraging words and love: thank you!

To my husband, Michael Harris, who is my biggest supporter and fan: Thanks for everything that you do. You are my rock.

Big love to all of my friends who continue to inspire me by being the smart, ambitious, and unyielding women they are: Majida Abdul-Karim, Tracy Green, Leone Williams, Yvette Hayward, Courtney Parker, Dawn Green, Aleshia Harmon, Chandra Sparks Taylor, and Hyacinth Carbon. My good friends Jermine Benton, Beverly Smith, and Patricia Harris: thanks for listening to my stories on a daily basis.

A special thank-you to the readers; fans; book clubs; United Sisters; online literary groups; distributors; street vendors; retailers; online booksellers; and a host of others who have been instrumental in helping my literary career blossom. I appreciate you more than you know.

Last but not least, Kevin Hunter . . . you made this all possible. Thank you!

Nancey

He
Was
My Man
First

1

◁◈▷

My Man

It's 2:06 A.M. My stomach has been uneasy for the past two hours and a rash of goose bumps have taken residence on my caramel skin. I've been up since midnight wondering where my man is and when he's coming home. There's no acceptable excuse that he could possibly proffer for being out this late on a work night and not calling. I've already taken the initiative of contacting his mother in the event that there was a family emergency and she confirmed that everything is copasetic. Calling his friends is pointless, since I know they'll cover for him. As much as I hate to admit it, I know he's with another woman.

Rich and I have been together for nine years and have been engaged for three of those years. I'm the one wearing the two-carat, princess-cut diamond and platinum engagement ring on my finger. Rich and I go back many, many years and he was my man first and will always be *my man*. My friends always say, "Valentine, cut Rich off. He ain't nuthin' but a dog." But they'll never understand our relationship and our commitment to one another.

Those other girls that he used to kick it with on the side weren't nothing serious. I understand that men cheat and those women out there who think their men don't cheat, are only fooling themselves. If the notion that your man ain't sticking his dick in some other chick helps you sleep better at night, then good for you. I like to keep it real!

Richard Washington and I met when I was seventeen years old and he was eighteen. I was messing with this drug dealer named Colombo, who had Lafayette Gardens and Marcy Projects on lock. I was Colombo's number one chick and life was real good with us, but whenever things went wrong with his game I got the short end of the stick or the thick end of the belt, literally. Colombo was known for his quick temper and being violent. Nevertheless, my options were limited.

My father pulled a Houdini and disappeared when I was ten years old. Three years later, my mother was robbed and stabbed to death on her way home from work, leaving me with her younger sister, my aunt Zenobia.

Aunt Zenobia spent much of her time trying to tackle baby daddy number three. It didn't seem to matter that baby daddies number one and two pissed on her and left. Aunt Zenobia hunted men for sport and was determined to find her big payday. She barely raised her own two children, CJ and Shaquetta, and definitely didn't want to be bothered with another mouth to feed. I figured adding me to the picture made it difficult for her to pin down another man. Especially since the majority of the men who visited Aunt Zenobia flirted with me behind her back. Yeah, I had barely entered my teens, but my body was very shapely, which made me look mature for my age. Aunt Zenobia was wise on these men, and though she never raised the issue with me, I knew it annoyed her. Either way, I didn't stick around very long, and by fifteen I was living the life with Colombo.

Rich was one of Colombo's many runners. Colombo operated out of an apartment in LG projects, but we didn't live there. Colombo was a follower of Biggie Smalls's "Ten Crack Commandments" rule number five: *never sell no crack where you rest at. I don't care if they want a ounce, tell 'em bounce.*

I had seen Rich at the headquarters, and we would make small talk, but Colombo didn't like me associating with the hired help. Although I handled the bookkeeping, I knew more than anything I was his dime piece. However, if he ever caught someone admiring me for too long that could've caused trouble. Therefore, I kept communication to a minimum. Rich was different though, whenever he came around, he carried himself with respect. His territory and money were always on point and when his business was complete he left. Rich wasn't like the other runners who sucked up to Colombo, hung around idly, and made excuses for coming up shortchanged. He's the kind of brother that you can carry to the club one night and a black-tie affair the next. At six feet, two inches, with burnt caramel skin, sensuous lips, silky eyebrows, and lustrous hair to match, Rich put male models to shame. So even though I didn't say much, my eyes must have said a million words. Whenever Rich came by my heart would flutter and it didn't help that he was always so nice. All of Colombo's workers were polite to me because I was his girl. Most of them even had the nerve to proposition me on the low, but I knew better than to ever mess with any of his men. If Colombo ever found out they were disrespecting him he would have popped their dumb asses, but I kept my mouth shut. I could handle myself.

Colombo and I had a bittersweet relationship. The sweet side was he wined and dined me and bought me anything my heart desired. He spared no expense, because he loved to show me off. After all, I was young, sexy, and hot and Colombo knew that if we split the next big-time hustler would be on standby. He paraded me around like a queen. However, he also had a dark side. He was very controlling and abusive to me and his employees. You never knew what or who was going to set him off. He could be in a room with fifty people and even if he never spoke a word to you, he could recollect the outfit you wore, your hair and eye color, amongst other details that the average person may overlook. His memory was remarkable—he could recall numbers, dates, places, and incidents that at the time may have seemed insignificant, but down the line may have had a major impact on his decision to do business with someone. Colombo didn't take unnecessary chances with his operation and trusted his team to have similar values and common sense. Unfortunately, that wasn't always the case.

Chief was one of Colombo's front men. Chief met with this cat that was a regular, but on this particular day the guy was accompanied by two friends who were trying to leave the parking lot without paying for the merchandise. Chief panicked and ran into the building, returned with his Glock, and fired shots at the truck that they were riding in, killing two of the men instantly. The third guy managed to escape. Needless to say this messed up Colombo's entire game because not only was it on his turf, but it was right in front of the building that he operated out of. Things were chaotic and I tried to calm Colombo down. He was moving around in circles like a windup toy without direction. I knew this was bad, and to make matters worse there was still one guy on the loose and Chief was so messed up over the ordeal he couldn't even give a simple description. Colombo got so pissed with Chief that he beat him to the point where I had to intervene. One of Chief's eyes was already swollen shut and if Colombo did the same thing to the other eye Chief definitely wouldn't be able to identify the survivor. Colombo thought I was taking up for Chief and started beating me like a rag doll. By the time he was done, I knew he had broken my arm, a few ribs, and it felt like I was breathing under water. I didn't even want to see a mirror. It was a madhouse and Colombo took Chief, his crew, and the rest of his mess and left me in it.

Rich heard about the mishap with Chief and the shooting in the parking lot. When he arrived at the apartment the only thing left of Colombo and his crew was me. I was much too weak to do anything other than remain still and wait for the police to find me, but that never happened. Instead, Rich came and rescued me. He picked me up and took me to his apartment, which was only two buildings over from where Colombo operated. When things cooled down and the cops left the scene, Rich drove me to the hospital. In the ER we learned I had a punctured lung, fractured ribs, and a broken arm and they admitted me.

Rich visited every day and when I was discharged, he carried me to his house and nursed me back to health. Rich doted on me day and night making sure that I was comfortable. He prepared my meals, fed me, and made sure I took my meds. It felt so good to finally have someone care for me the way Rich did that I hadn't given Colombo a second thought. Then it dawned on me that if he found out who I was staying with he would certainly kill us. However, Rich allayed my fears when he informed me that Colombo, Chief, and six of his boys were killed the same night he nearly pummeled me to death. The entire exchange was a setup and those cats had been looking for a way to take Colombo and his crew out, though they hadn't anticipated losing two of their soldiers. However, once they were able to take Colombo off his turf, it was on.

After that fiasco, I knew it was time to get out of the drug game. I barely escaped with my life and understood I had been given a second chance. At the time, Rich lived with his mother and younger sister. Almost immediately they became the family I had longed for and Rich the man of my dreams.

One night while Rich and I were up talking about getting out of the projects, I learned that he had aspirations that didn't include being a drug dealer. And with each thought and word that he spoke, I was always somewhere at the beginning, middle, or end of each sentence. Rich had dreams of becoming the next big fashion designer and I, surprisingly, was his muse. Buried beneath his bed he had a big black sketchbook of urban clothing designs that he had drawn and to my amazement every female sketch was patterned after me. No one knew about his ambitions except me and I urged him to pursue his dreams. I pointed out that most of the biggest designers were men: Ralph Lauren, Tommy Hilfiger, Calvin Klein, and Giorgio Armani. Rich deserved better, and so did I. And even though we only had our dreams and a little bit of money stashed away I knew together we could definitely have something strong.

At my encouragement, Rich enrolled in the Katharine Gibbs school of fashion design. While attending school, he was able to secure a job in the mailroom at Jorge Jacobs, which was one of the hottest up-and-coming fashion houses. I also returned to school, but I had to get my GED first. It didn't take long, especially since Rich was my motivation. Since we didn't know anything about financial aid, Rich paid my tuition and I earned my degree in office administration at Katharine Gibbs as well. Now I'm a highly paid office manager. A lot has changed since Rich and I first hooked up, for better and for worse.

The better was that we were partners and relied on each other to survive mentally and physically. We worked hard and together we managed to save our money and move out of the 'hood. Rich and I still live in Brooklyn, but we recently purchased a two-bedroom condo in Clinton Hill. The worse is Rich's affinity for women. Unfortunately those same rugged good looks, charm, and magnetism that attracted me to Rich are the things that attract other women to him. And since Rich is a born hustler, women are just part of his hustle.

The thing is chicks think that because I'm petite and my name is Valentine, that I'm some sweet, dainty, docile person they can take advantage of. News flash: just because my name is associated with true love and romance does not mean I'm touchy-feely or sentimental. The dictionary defines Valentine's Day as a day for the exchange of tokens of affection and if you rub this Valentine the wrong way, I will affectionately kick your ass. Those same chicks that mistake me for a pushover or think they're putting one over on me—after I find out they've been pushing up on my man usually find my foot connected to their ass.

My mother—may she rest in peace—was very sentimental and decided to name me after the day on which I was born. The fact that our surname is Daye added to the appeal. However, growing up on the fast streets of Brooklyn, I learned that although my name fascinated people, the kids in my 'hood would often pick fights with me because of it. Therefore, from very early on I didn't take any shots, maintained skin as thick as Kevlar, and could kick ass like the Karate Kid.

The first trick to enter the picture was Qwanisha. Rich and I were going through our first major crisis in the relationship: money. At the time, the jobs we had barely paid us any real dough. At least not the kind of money we were used to. Colombo had always kept my pockets padded and Rich managed to stack his cash, but that was dwindling to nothing and neither of us was used to living paycheck to paycheck. We argued about any- and everything, and started drifting apart.

Qwanisha was best described as a 'hood rat that I had to squash, because rodents deserved to be terminated. I heard from a friend of a friend that Rich was messing around with some girl. I approached him about it, but he craftily changed the subject and began caressing my breasts and nibbling on my ear. Rich knew I couldn't resist his touch then or now. After a few more minutes of foreplay, we ended up screwing right on the kitchen countertop. Although I didn't broach the subject again that night, Qwanisha never left my mind.

After about two months of nonsense and a few nights of Rich not coming home, I had to put that garbage to an end. The look of surprise on Qwanisha's face when I knocked at her door and asked for my man was a Kodak moment. It wasn't until I punched that trick square in her face that she snapped back to reality and Rich came to the door, looked at Qwanisha, and took me home. Rich obviously didn't care enough about her to stick around and he never commented on my clocking her either, because I know without a doubt he'd do the same for me. We never discussed that night and things returned to normal for about two years. Then there was Chantal. She didn't hang around for long and I made sure of that. The one thing I wasn't going to tolerate was my man catching feelings for these tricks. That wasn't going to happen and as far as his cheating goes, this is one habit that I'm going to make sure Rich breaks.

Now there's some new chick named Vanessa. Her number has

appeared on his cell phone on numerous occasions and whenever she calls he leaves the room. If it were purely business, there would be no reason for him to leave. Rich has conducted business calls from home in the past, and never has he felt the need to visit another room. Additionally, he's been doing a lot of overtime, which probably comes from his new responsibilities. However, he seems distracted and distant and when he comes home the first thing he does is rush to take a shower. Now my man has always been into hygiene, but of late it's been almost compulsive.

Rich never admitted when he was messing around in the past and he wasn't going to start now, but I knew something was going on between them. Vanessa wasn't on the same level as the hoochies from Rich's past. She's a bourgeois chick who works at Jorge Jacobs with Rich, so they deal with each other regularly. I can't get a whole lot of information from anyone because she isn't in my network of friends. So for once I feel handicapped because I can't just go to his office and beat this ho down the way I want to. The majority of Rich's coworkers know that we are an item, so I'm more than positive this home wrecker knows everything there is to know about me. Still she appears to be pursuing my man. For once, I actually feel threatened by this woman named Vanessa.

It's now three o'clock and I'm still wide awake. Rich slipped in a half hour ago, which makes that the third time this month. Yeah, a sistah gotta keep track of her man and his habits. For the past few weeks I've been mulling over my present predicament in our relationship and as I look at Rich, now sleeping peacefully, I know that sacrifices must be made. Our relationship means everything to me and I will stop at nothing to allow no man or woman to pull asunder all that we've built.

2

But He's My Man Now!

Although her mouth was occupied at the moment, Vanessa's mind raced with exciting thoughts of Richard. They had just been together the night before, but after having worked together for weeks on the presentation he had led this morning, Vanessa was proud of the job he'd done today on their behalf. Of course he deserved a little midday mouth-to-head reward for a job well done. And she was more than happy to give him that reward. Vanessa had been looking for a way up the corporate ladder for years now. Her stagnant director of business affairs and strategic marketing position had long worn out its welcome, and she wanted nothing more than an opportunity at the vice president position that would soon be up for grabs. When Richard was brought in a year ago to serve as co-director alongside Vanessa, she assumed the worst. It didn't matter that she was overqualified for her job or that her family was well connected, she always suspected that her male-dominated office would never allow a woman of color to hold a higher position than a male at the same professional level. Part of the reason they even hired her in the first place was because of who she was, taking little to no notice of what she was actually doing. With Vanessa on board, her company was assured that New York's finest was always either in Jorge Jacobs designs or at a Jorge Jacobs event. In Vanessa's mind, since corporate America had no problem using her to fill quotas and maintain good standings with the diversity actions groups, she too would have no problem using anyone to get what she wanted.

"Oh baby, you're the best!" Richard moaned as Vanessa continued to stroke his penis with her tongue.

"You like that, don't you?" she teased. "Savor it . . . won't happen very often." Vanessa curled her tongue and moved her lips faster against his taut skin, causing him to cum.

"I don't know what I'm gonna do with you."

"The question is what am I going to do with you?" Vanessa asked as she walked over to her desk and wiped her mouth with Richard's handkerchief. "This is truly just the beginning. Our bosses have made it clear we're up for the same spot. Rather than compete against each other, I figured I'd help you out." Vanessa cringed at her own words yet continued. "I'll help you make VP then serve as your official first lady. Doing whatever I have to and for you, to ensure my spot."

"I got you, you know that, right?"

Vanessa reached for the bottle of Scope she kept in her desk, took a swig, swooshed, and spit it out in her trash can. "Speaking of doing whatever we can for each other, have you left *that* woman yet?"

Vanessa could see the irritation on Richard's face. She couldn't understand why a man with such a prestigious future insisted on dwelling in an obviously hideous past, especially with a woman that clearly was stuck in that state. The nerve of Richard to continue to even entertain his longtime girlfriend, Valentine, annoyed her. Why anyone would want to be with someone whose name was Valentine Daye was beyond her. What kind of ghetto mother would name their child Valentine, especially since their last name was Daye? From what Richard stated, her mother wanted her name to reflect the love inside her . . . Vanessa chuckled a bit to herself. *She should have loved her enough to give her a real name.*

"It's complicated, babe. Val and I go way back. It's just a timing thing; that's it. Val is not like you, Vanessa. You're polished, refined, and sophisticated. She's from the street and capable of street mentality things. I don't need her bringing that kind of drama to you. Not now, not with everything we've got going on."

"So, your going home to her every night is a way of protecting me?"

"Yeah, it is."

Vanessa rolled her eyes. It was clear she wasn't buying his excuse for one minute but she did like that he was giving her one. Richard's little loyalty story about how she was there for him in the early days was becoming redundant and, even more, unimportant to Vanessa. This girl from his past clearly had nothing on her, which made her more determined than ever. Even if Valentine had been there first, Vanessa knew she was here now, and to her now was all that mattered.

"I'm not afraid of her." Vanessa reached for his tie. "You don't have to stay there. Am I not everything you want?"

"I didn't say that, but—"

"But, nothing. Sooner or later you're going to have to let her go. Now I've been patient with you, have I not?" Vanessa stroked her tongue seductively against his lips. "And I've listened to your story of loyalty long enough, but I'm your future, baby, and the plans I have for us don't include company." Vanessa unbuttoned the top few buttons of her purple silk blouse after locking the door to her office. "Now I expect you to handle this. I'll give you a little more time, before assuming you need my help."

Her blouse fell to the floor. Her skirt and hose followed. All that remained was a caramel-coated Vanessa in a black lace La Perla bra and thong. "It's time you returned the favor," she whispered while leaning back against her desk spreading her legs. "Let me show you why you need me and not her."

Vanessa could tell Richard couldn't resist her as he slid his legs out of his pants, which were already bagged around his ankles. He buried his head between her thighs, licking and sucking the wetness of her center dry. As a lover, Richard mastered the art of oral pleasure. He devoured her like a scoop of ice cream on a cone, sparing not even a drop of her goodness. Though Vanessa may have thought and acted like a woman when it came to Richard, she had sex like a man. Her goal was clear from the start where Richard was concerned, especially since they were fighting for the same promotion: she'd keep her friends close and her enemies even closer. Since it seemed certain that Richard was in for the VP position, she'd make sure she was sleeping with the enemy.

Vanessa pulled his shirt off and sucked at his neck. She clawed at his back and chest, ensuring the remains and evidence of their lovemaking. It was a gift she so graciously chose to send Richard home to Valentine with. If nothing else, Vanessa needed Valentine to know that they had been together. Despite Valentine and Richard's lengthy past, Vanessa didn't plan on going anywhere. Vanessa thrived on competition in every area of her life. The plot for promotion may have been what stirred her, yet the thought of taking Richard from Valentine was definitely an added ingredient. She would fight for what she wanted, expecting nothing less than a victory.

If Valentine wanted Richard half as bad as she did, then may the best woman win! But as it stood, with his tongue knee-deep in her vagina, victory was already hers.

Vanessa exited the ladies' room refreshed and headed back to her office. Nothing beat a little midday loving, especially when no one else in the office had a clue as to what was going on. Although they hadn't been sleeping together for more than a month now, Vanessa knew she would have Richard eating out of the palm of her hand the minute he came to the executive floor over a year ago. It took her that long to feel him out and deem him worthy of her good love and generosity. Vanessa never did anything that didn't benefit her and Richard was no exception. The minute she established him as her corporate guinea pig, it was on.

Much to her surprise, Richard moved her. His rough-around-the-edges persona intrigued and excited Vanessa. Richard was just smart enough to welcome the grooming from the major partners and naïve enough to fall prey to her charms, in order for her to get where she wanted to go.

After pulling Richard's file, Vanessa discovered that although he was a graduate from the Katharine Gibbs school of fashion design and clearly Jorge Jacobs's excuse for keeping well within the affirmative action guidelines for hiring, Richard was a borderline fashion genius. Despite his lack of any true education, his quick-study approach to the job, coupled with his good looks, charm, and sexy personality made him a bona fide threat to Vanessa. Richard was the full package. The partners always appreciated the perspective of one of their own over a female voice anyhow, and made no apologies about it. Manipulating her way from the inside wasn't Vanessa's problem, it was the more she got to know Richard and the more often they had sex. Richard was getting to her in a way she never expected. The roller coaster of emotions from day to day hadn't been a part of her initial plan. So much of who he was and wasn't, attracted her. Vanessa loved the fact that Richard wasn't the protégé of one her parents' friends. With Vanessa's father, Justice William Montgomery Knight, being the only black Supreme Court judge for the state of New York and her mother, Cornelia Elaine Mitchell-Knight, heiress to the Soul Shine Corporation, Vanessa was always being paired with the traditional Who's Who. Richard served as a healthy change, with the added bonus of pissing off her overbearing, perfectionist, snob of a mother.

"A bachelor with honors from NYU and a master's in global fashion management from the Fashion Institute of Technology, not to mention a year of studying in Paris, and here you are gallivanting with some reject flunky from a design school no one's ever heard of," her mother taunted.

"This is why I stopped talking about my male interest to you, Mother. Always the skeptic."

"You could have your choice of proper, more prominent suitors and you choose that man? Nessa, you're breaking my heart."

This was something Vanessa knew to be untrue. The only thing that broke her mother's heart was her mother not being able to control her daughter's life. And if screwing Richard day in and day out helped Vanessa to define her independence, then she would just call Richard her Plymouth Rock.

"Ms. Knight, there is an urgent message from your mother. She'd like you to call her ASAP. I've put a fresh cup of coffee on your desk, as well as left your other messages."

"Speak of the devil," Vanessa said aloud.

"Excuse me, Ms. Knight?"

Vanessa shook her head and smiled at her assistant, Cynthia. Nearly twice her age, Vanessa wondered why Cynthia never aspired to do more than be someone's secretary.

Though Vanessa was accustomed to barking orders to the hired help, she always managed to show Cynthia respect. "Thank you, Cynthia. Please hold my other calls. If I know my mother, this will take a while." Vanessa smiled then turned back to Cynthia. "Better yet, interrupt me in exactly two minutes."

Vanessa entered her office and closed the door behind her. She had, by far, the most beautiful office in the entire building, all compliments of her parents. When the time came to decorate her quaint corner office, Vanessa insisted that she incur the cost of the décor. If she was going to work there indefinitely, she would have to design her office to her liking, not based on what her employers would allow her to spend.

Vanessa curled her back into her coffee-colored leather chair and smiled. Just minutes before, during her and Richard's second romp in the office, he had her legs straddled on each arm of that very chair. She craved him . . . and was determined to have her appetite completely fulfilled.

The only deterrent was Richard's 'hood rat girlfriend, Valentine. And even though Vanessa wasn't exactly sure where things were headed with Richard, what she did know was that Valentine wouldn't be the reason that "it" didn't. Vanessa had always been taught to believe in fairy tales so even if Richard proved to be yet another frog she'd have to kiss, she knew that she'd do whatever she had to professionally and personally to get to her happily-ever-after.

3

❧

Fatal Attraction

Her smell permeates the air long before she decides to sit directly in front of our pew. I've never seen her, but I am 100 percent positive the woman who just came into our place of worship is Vanessa—the same trick who had ruined my weekend plans with Rich.

Every Sunday, Rich accompanies me to church, because after our fiasco nine years ago, I wanted to put our lives on the right track with God. Rich and I always sit in the third row from the front of the church, and during service to show our union, we always hold hands. The only time we don't is if one of us has to go to the restroom or attend a separate activity.

Once he realizes Vanessa is sitting in front of us, Rich's palm becomes moist and he slips his hand away from mine. This signal, though I'm sure unintentional, serves as confirmation that this trollop who wore entirely too much makeup, dressed in a champagne-colored two-piece suit, and played out Chanel No. 5 is indeed Vanessa.

My heart begins to swell beneath my chest and in that moment I think I'm experiencing a mini-stroke. It dawns on me to resume breathing, but I am furious. How dare this woman take it upon herself to visit our church? I know good and damn well Rich didn't invite her—especially after that stunt she pulled making him work late Friday and all day Saturday. We had plans for the weekend. WFAT, the radio station where I'm employed, had their annual Grown and Sexy weekend cruise. It was going to be the boat ride of a lifetime and Rich and I had been looking forward to it for months. The station booked some of the hottest neo-soul artists: Jaheim, Angie Stone, Jazmine Sullivan, Erykah Badu, and Anthony Hamilton. It was going to be a very intimate concert, seeing as the Seven Seas Cruiser only had a passenger capacity of four hundred and ninety. Since I was in middle management, I received a standard room for free, but I paid additional money for the upgrade. Then Friday, the very day we were scheduled to leave, Rich called me from the office to tell me he had to work late that night and he also had to work on Saturday. That witch Vanessa wasn't giving him any slack and he was working his ass off to move up to vice president. We had to forfeit our trip. I was so upset that when I got home from work, I took two sedatives and was knocked out cold until morning. I wasn't mad at Rich because it was out of his control, but I was upset that we pissed away three hundred dollars and couldn't get a refund because of the short notice.

Since Vanessa entered the scene, our world has been shaken like a one-liter bottle of soda. Once you remove the top the explosion is inevitable. I was doing all I could to avoid the drama, but I believe Vanessa enjoyed wielding her little magic wand. If this witch would fly away on the broom she rode in on, things would go back to normal between Rich and me. Of late, Rich hasn't been behaving rationally, and though I'm patient because I believe in the concept of standing by your man, a sistah will have to eventually put her foot down—and anywhere else it's needed.

I need to calm down. I can feel myself about to detonate and it takes every ounce within to restrain myself. After all, we are in church and surely this isn't the time or place to kick her ass. The irony is the message Pastor McCash chose to deliver is "The Purpose of Marriage and the Perils Within." And Vanessa is definitely a peril.

In my mind, Vanessa is either real dumb, or too bold for her own good. What point could she possibly be trying to prove by coming to *our* church? This trick is crazy. And if Rich doesn't see that now, he needs to open his eyes and recognize.

Church had always been the one place that I found solace and it held some of my fondest memories. As a child my mother and I attended regularly. Even after her death I tried to maintain my attendance, but living in the fast lane doesn't leave much room for church. Still I knew in my heart one day I'd return. In the beginning of our relationship, Rich gave me fever about coming to church. We quarreled until I couldn't argue anymore. Then one Sunday he finally gave in, got dressed, and attended service with me. To my surprise, I never had to argue with him again about coming to church. He serves as the assistant coach for the summer youth basketball program and even purchases their uniforms. Rich serves as a positive role model and I'm proud of his work within the church. The only problem is I don't know what appeals to Rich more: God, helping the kids, or the women, since this was where he met and hooked up with Chantal, who is no longer a member.

I take a quick glance at Rich. A stranger would think he was in deep thought or prayer with his head bowed and eyes shut, but I know better. I love Rich with my heart and soul, but when we get home I'm certainly going to find out what's really going on between these two. That's if I can make it to the apartment, because I'm about two seconds from asking him to step outside. The only thing saving Rich from my wrath right now is these nosy church people. I don't want to run the risk of having anyone accidentally overhearing our business, especially since my last debacle. It took a while for me to recover from when I drop-kicked Chantal at the church picnic two years earlier.

Normally I'm so involved with the word that I never pay attention to the time. However, frustration is setting in and I'm anxious for service to be over. I glance at my watch and see there is only another half an hour before the collection plate is passed around, and then Pastor McCash will give his benediction. However, temptation is getting the best of me, as I wring my hands to save myself from reaching out and strangling Vanessa from behind. She keeps flinging her hair all over the place, and I'm sure that mess is a weave. Vanessa's presence isn't allowing me to focus and enjoy the word. The good thing is that Pastor McCash always records his orations and sells them on CDs, so I can always purchase a copy later.

Rich surprises me by resting his moist hand on my bare thigh. Immediately, my thoughts wander to the night before, when Rich and I had made love so great that I was still feeling the aftershocks. When he came home from his workout, I had some scented candles burning along with a nice bath in the Jacuzzi for us to relax in. I rested between his athletic, muscular thighs and gave him a nice leg rub as we discussed our plans for the upcoming week. Rich rubbed the tension away from my back as well as a couple of other areas. When his very talented hands moved to my breasts, I knew the games had officially begun. He rubbed my nipples until they became erect and slid me up toward his chest until my breasts were in his mouth. Rich loved my ass, and without effort he palmed and kneaded my cheeks. The sensation between my legs soon became unbearable, but Rich has always been big on foreplay, so when he was done nursing on my ample bosom he buried his head between my recently shaved honey pot. He lapped my clitoris over and over until my bud rose. His expert tongue probed my insides, and I drifted into a state of half-consciousness. I got carried away by the sensation of pleasure as his fingertips began grazing my nipples. I grasped the side of the Jacuzzi to steady myself, but my hands slipped from the wetness. I decided to relax and enjoy my man. My eyes were tightly shut as I concentrated on the intensity of the moment. It had been a while since Rich had last feasted on my honey pot. Rich hadn't excited me this much in a long time, and I could feel a climax building. I didn't want to cum before him; the experience felt heightened when he was in me and we climaxed simultaneously. The level of pleasure was that much better, so I pulled myself away from him and stepped out of the Jacuzzi, still a little soapy and dripping wet in all the right places. Rich immediately got up and followed me to the bedroom with his thick, hard penis, like a heated bar of steel. I didn't want to do it on the bed, I wanted to sex him on the nearby chair. I had tied a sash around the seat because I liked to secure his hands to the back as I had my way with him. Rich appreciated that I was so dominating and always willing to do new things. The one thing that never dulled in our relationship was the sex. Between the shoes, scarves, wigs, and toys, we had it all and did most everything.

When he took a seat, I stroked and rubbed his penis as it

throbbed and moved involuntarily from my touch. Raising my legs I mounted him and wrapped my arms around his neck. Slowly I lowered myself slightly, rocking back and forth to draw his thickness along the entire length of my slit. I lowered myself again, burying him into my wetness while tightening the grip of my thighs. The feeling that ran through me felt like an electric current. It felt so good that I cried out and Rich moaned. I leaned forward and offered Rich my lips. He accepted my invitation and began probing the inside of my mouth, then he nibbled my lips. I could feel his penis as it pulsated. He unfastened his hands and held my waist firmly and began thrusting in and out of my sex, each stroke bringing us higher toward the pinnacle of sexual ecstasy. I felt myself about to cum, and I didn't hold back. Rich was all too familiar with my body language and knew I was about to release, which excited him even more. Eventually our orgasms overcame us and we came simultaneously.

"Will everyone please rise as we sing, 'O Lord You're My Everything,'" Pastor McCash says, pulling me from my reverie. My mind had drifted for some time, because I realize church will soon let out. And the song selection makes me aware that it's time to give our tithes and offerings.

The offering basket starts going around and when it comes to our row, I nudge Rich who has remained seated. The one thing that Rich and I always do is pay our tithes and offerings. From the moment I was able to pay the full 10 percent, I made sure I never skimped. And since our church membership is only about three hundred and fifty people, it is even more important to me that I contribute as much as I can. Pastor McCash isn't one of those preachers that talks smack, he doesn't pocket the money, and he isn't flashy. In my eyes he is a very humble man and I respect the work he does in the community. After the song we return to our seats and Pastor McCash makes an altar call and asks if any-one wants to come to the front for a special prayer or to turn his or her life over to the Lord. Then suddenly one of the deacons comes to the front, which is unusual because he is asking for Pas-tor McCash's immediate attention. The pastor excuses himself for a moment and the church deacon takes over in his absence.

Due to the disturbance, the assistant pastor is unable to main-tain order in the church. Everyone starts whispering and ques-tioning what could possibly be so important that they needed to pull Pastor McCash away. Even the first lady looks a little per-plexed. When the pastor returns to the pulpit, he clears his throat and begins.

"Today, we want to ask our visitors to please stand." Everyone turns to see who the visitors are. Vanessa stands alone. Vanessa turns around and flashes a one-hundred-watt smile at Rich then smirks at me. Rich immediately focuses his energies on fixing a tie that doesn't need fixing, and even though I am staring dead at him, he refuses to give me eye contact. Instead of getting angry, I repeat Psalm 23 over and over in my head.

"People, as I stand here today, we would like to welcome Ms. Vanessa Knight to our church. Ms. Knight has given a generous and I do mean generous contribution to Praise the Lord Minis-tries." Pastor McCash extends his arms for a hug and she happily obliges. Vanessa turns quickly to look at me with a malicious smile. When she removes herself from Pastor McCash's embrace she smiles at the congregation who are still clapping as if she is their savior instead of God. Vanessa then goes on to say a few words, and I begin to hum "O Lord You're My Everything" to myself. When I see Pastor McCash return to the pulpit, I tune back in.

"Church, today we welcome Ms. Knight to join our congrega-tion if she doesn't already have a church home. Members, can I get a praise the Lord." And as is our custom everyone chants, "Praise the Lord." It is almost unanimous; everyone wants her to join with the exception of me. I want this bitch dead!

Time moves as if it is on its own schedule and I'm happy when Pastor McCash says the benediction and service is over. As Vanessa is collecting her purse, I see Pastor McCash pull her to the side. I truly hope he isn't going to push the issue about her joining again.

Rich and I linger for two minutes as a few church brothers and sisters approach us in the aisle for greetings. As we make our way toward the exit, a small welcoming committee circles Vanessa. She's playing it up big time, and I can see she loves every minute of it. When Rich and I walk by, I make sure his arm hugs my waist and I even plaster a smile on my face as we stop to briefly greet Pastor McCash and his wife. Even though we stand directly in front of Pastor McCash, he is gazing over at Vanessa who stands only a few feet away, and Mrs. McCash elbows him to regain his attention.

"Oh, Sister Valentine Daye and Brother Richard Washington, it's always a pleasure to see you two. When I chose today's sermon I had you two lovebirds in mind. You know you all are one of my favorite couples, and you'll become my number one couple when you decide to tie the knot before the eyes of the Lord. Praise the Lord," he says and Mrs. McCash concurs by repeating praise the Lord.

"Pastor McCash, you know Richard and I are engaged." I smile.

"I know, but it's been a while now that I've been seeing that beautiful diamond ring caressing your finger. I still look forward to the day I'll preside over your nuptials."

Richard flexes his shoulders and clears his throat. "Pastor McCash, man, you know Val and I just purchased a nice little condo and we're getting our act together financially. We want to be able to do a few more things and then we're gonna start saving for the wedding, but don't worry. It's gonna happen in like the next year or two. I ain't gonna keep my woman waiting forever." Rich looks at me, smiles, and kisses my ring finger.

"That's right," Mrs. McCash says. "You don't want to lose a good thing by keeping your lady waiting too long. More importantly, God needs to bless this union."

"I know, Mrs. McCash," I say, smiling.

We say our good-byes and just as we are about to walk off, Vanessa saunters over. She makes eye contact with Rich and smiles. I look at Rich, who tries to pretend he doesn't see Vanessa. I move closer into his embrace and we keep it moving. Then without notice she calls his name, and though he doesn't turn around I can feel his body tense.

"Richard," Vanessa says, pausing for effect, "I look forward to seeing you at work tomorrow." And without another word she walks off.

4

~∂~

Something to Shout About!

"No, Mother, I told you, I already have plans." Vanessa placed her lip gloss into her purse then got out of her car. She looked around the somewhat empty lot in search of Richard's car. Once she spotted it she smiled while fastening the last button to her Chanel champagne-colored suit. She opted to wear the matching pants, despite that she deemed the skirt more fitting for the occasion.

"Listen, Mother, I realize I haven't been to service with you and Daddy in over a month, but today is simply not the day to rectify my absence. I have a very pressing engagement to attend to this morning, so not even you can talk me out of it."

"Well, will you at least come by the house for dinner, this evening! Maybe you could bring that Richard character you've been so wrapped up in."

"I'm working on it, Mother, now I really must go. Smooches."

Vanessa switched off her phone before heading into the rinky-dink church. It had been years since she'd been to Brooklyn, and from what she could see, she quickly remembered why she'd kept her distance. If it weren't for Richard, she would probably never visit Brooklyn. She thought it was cute how Richard always suggested restaurants there instead of in the city. He said it was his way of "keeping it real." She, on the other hand, vowed to keep it rich, and stay away from the stench of poverty, like this hole-in-the-wall church she was about to enter.

The curiosity of finally seeing Valentine was getting the best of her, so it was only natural she make it her business to see what all the hoopla was about. Because Vanessa was a woman of character, she thought it appropriate to face her competition on what would otherwise be her best-dressed day. Yet from the looks of the neighborhood and the building, Vanessa definitely felt as though she wasted an outfit. Still her anticipation was high with regards to what to expect inside and without further delay she was about to find out.

"Praise the Lord, oh praise Him," the minister shouted as she opened the doors to the church.

This is going to be easier than I thought. Vanessa smiled as she spotted Richard from behind. The shape of his broad shoulders in the DKNY suit she'd just purchased for him gave her chills. *See, he was thinking of me,* Vanessa thought.

Vanessa felt all eyes on her as she made her way down the center aisle. *How bold do I really want to be?* She smirked as she talked herself through her plan of action, making her way to their aisle then opting to sit in the row directly in front of them. She took a long pause before sitting, hoping to allow this short hair–wearing wannabe Toni Braxton an opportunity to get a good glimpse at who was going to take Richard away from her. She slung her lengthy mane to and fro allowing her vanilla-scented shampoo to envelop both their senses. With one final fling, she turned her face toward them, allowing Valentine to witness her flawlessly made-up face and give her an opportunity to place her purse down. With a devious smirk she tossed her blue-black, silky straight—thanks to her Creole grandfather—hair back into place.

Vanessa knew Richard wasn't the only one having a fit, but by the way he snatched his hand from Valentine's grasp upon laying eyes on her, she knew God was good.

"Can the church praise the Lord, for the visitor that just came in?"

"Praise the Lord," they all murmured.

"May we welcome you to the house of the Lord. I am Pastor McCash and I just wanna say thank you for your presence here at our service this Sunday morning."

Vanessa gave a polite smile as she tried hard to understand what this idiot of a preacher had just said. *Are you freaking kidding me, did he just say Pastor McCash?* Vanessa tried to keep from laughing. This had to be a joke. The thought of her beloved Richard having to be subjected to such a place bothered her. Only the truly low class would come to a church like this. *Wait, did he just wink at me?* Vanessa raised a brow, reaching for her Bible with hopes to shield her obviously overwhelming beauty from this fool of a preacher.

As she endured minutes of agonizing shouting and hundreds of mispronounced words, she was actually extremely grateful for her tardiness. Good thing for her that she'd missed the sermon, Vanessa could only imagine what that must've been like. As the church prepared for their offering, Vanessa sensed Valentine's eyes burning a hole through her back. She wondered if Valentine knew who she was and laughed at the thought of who she would soon know her to be.

"Now, chuuuuuuuurch," Pastor McCash interrupted. "I'm axing you to look deep within yoselves and give as the good Lord has so blessed you, amen." Vanessa knew she had to give abundantly with hopes that this preacher would take some classes on how to speak.

With the final stroke of her pen, she placed a check for twenty-five-hundred dollars into the collection plate. She never imagined her act of kindness would stir up such a commotion until she was asked by Pastor McCash to come forward and be thanked properly for her generosity. Vanessa immediately took advantage of the opportunity to stand before Valentine and the entire congregation for her much-needed recognition.

"Ms. Vanessa Knight, we here at the Praise the Lord Ministries Baptist Church would like to thank you for such a generous offering."

Vanessa squirmed from his grasp, hoping to move her ass just far enough away from the reach of his hand yet she couldn't manage the escape.

"We'd like to welcome you to join our church, as an honorary member if you're in search of a church home. I'd surely like to be your partner, I mean pastor."

The church clapped enthusiastically. Vanessa smiled again, locking her eyes on Richard who was trying hard to avoid eye contact with anyone. "Well, Pastor, I would be honored. However, I don't get to these parts much. When I heard about your little church and how wonderful your members and messages were, I had to come see for myself." She directed her attention from Richard to Valentine. Just as she was about to continue, she paused, noticing that Pastor McCash's hand went from her ass to her waist as he clutched her close to his side.

"Well aaaaaaaaaaaaaaamen and alright. Now, choir, as I try to

---

get wit." He coughed. "I mean witness to Ms. Knight, sing for us, 'Blessed in the City.'" As his mic went down, Vanessa felt a bulge in his pants go up. Pastor McCash mumbled as he scooted her closer to the pulpit, "Um, Ms. Vanessa, do you know any of our members?"

Vanessa looked down at his hand then uncomfortably back to the crowd. "Why yes, I know one of your members extremely well." She tried to smile, and then managed to once she got a glimpse of Valentine who was straining to see and hear what was going on. She yelled, "Richard has been an extreme blessing and has made quite an impact on my life. I guess you could say I owe a lot to the Praise the Lord Ministries Baptist Church. So this offering was just my way of saying thank you."

Vanessa could see the sweat bouncing off Richard's forehead, and the anger fuming from Valentine's face. *It's working*, she thought to herself until she felt Pastor McCash's hand return to her behind.

"I can't hear you, the choir's too loud, but if it's possible I'd like to thank you personally after the benediction."

Vanessa's frustration grew as she damn near had to fight herself away from Pastor McCash. When the music stopped Vanessa realized she was still on display.

"Praise the Lord, chuuurch."

"Praise the Lord," the congregation shouted.

"Now after I give the benediction, I'd like you members to come up here and shake Sister Vanessa's hand. What a blessing she and her extremely generous offering have been for our church today. Praise the Lord. Praise the Lord."

Once the church let out, Vanessa shook hands with a few members before witnessing Valentine and Richard rush for the exit. She quickly excused herself from the conversation of a burly woman and hurried after them. As she made her way to the front steps of the church, she called out to Richard who'd just made it to his car.

She approached him, leaning forward, exposing a little cleavage and said aloud, "Richard, I look forward to seeing you at work tomorrow." She bit her bottom lip, tossed yet another devilish smile in Valentine's direction, and walked away. Valentine had nothing on her, she didn't even have to look back to know how her presence at their church affected Valentine; her silence was deadly. She could only imagine that there would be no after-church loving going on this Sunday, so in her mind her mission was definitely accomplished!

5

❧

Fess up!

"Who the hell was that bitch at church today?" I ask. The silence during the ride home nearly killed me. My intentions were to tread on the subject lightly, but the more I thought about Vanessa, the more heated I became. "And I warn you, Rich, don't play stupid, because the trick knew your damn name."

Rich doesn't answer. He merely walks toward our bedroom stripping off his clothes along the way. I am right on his heels following him, because he is going to give me a freaking answer, today!

"Well?" I ask again and he finally turns around to look in my direction.

"Do you mean . . . Vanessa?" he asks innocently.

"Yesssss, I mean Vanesssssa." I say her name like I have a bad taste in my mouth.

"She's my coworker at the job. I've told you about her before."

"And why did this coworker decide to visit our church? Didn't that trick have another church she could contaminate?"

"Baby, why are you overreacting? I didn't even acknowledge her and I can't control the people that choose to visit our church. It's not like I invited her, if that's what you're insinuating."

"First of all I'm not overreacting and if I were, I'd be justified seeing as this is the same woman that caused us to miss our trip! Vanessa is the issue. What the hell did she mean by 'Richard, I look forward to seeing you at work tomorrow'? What was that all about?"

"Just what she said, she'll see me at work. Now did you see me do anything wrong? Val, you are making a big deal out of nothing. Besides, Vanessa's like one of the boys at the office. We're cool. She's teaching me the ropes about corporate America and introducing me to all the right people in the industry." Rich proceeds to hang his necktie on the tie rack as I lean against the doorway watching his every move.

"Cool? Is that the new word for screwing?"

"Val, on the real, you are tripping. I'm telling you, Vanessa is only a friend. There is nothing going on between us. She believes I have potential and with her help I can branch off and start my own fashion empire. You know that's all I've ever dreamt about."

"Friend my ass! If she's a friend, why the hell didn't you introduce me to her after service? I know all of your other so-called friends."

"My funny Valentine, she's just somebody I work with and shouldn't be a threat to you."

Rich reaches for my hand as he exits the closet, but I pull away. There is a tug-of-war with my emotions. On the one hand, I'm not in the mood for his gentle caress. I don't want his big soft hands to throw me into a sexual frenzy, but on the other, I live for our moments of making up. His eyes study my facial expression and he backs off.

"Rich, you are a damn liar. You were acting mighty strange from the moment she sat down in front of us flinging her hair like a damn fool and don't deny it. First, you let go of my hand, and don't think I didn't notice that. Then you started sweating and whatnot, and the freaking AC was on full blast."

"Val, you need to relax," Rich says. I can tell he is losing his patience as he makes a motion to stand. His six-foot stature hovers over my small frame.

"What? Are you taking up for her now?" I stand directly beneath him with my arms folded across my chest. Rich is a head taller than me. We are close enough for me to feel the heat radiate from his body and I can see his muscles flex with his every move.

"You know what, Val? This right here is getting real tired. You always tripping and making assumptions. It ain't even about taking up for nobody. I work with Vanessa and I have to see her every day whether you like it or not. So I don't need any drama at my place of business. I can't have you playing with my job. I worked too damn hard for my position at Jorge Jacobs and the last thing I need is some mess like this to go down."

Rich is visibly shaken. He is opening and closing drawers, fussing with the clothes, but not taking anything out. Apparently fed up, he finally gets up from the bed and returns to the closet. When he reappears he has on sweats, his new sneakers, and a T-shirt. His look reminds me of the Rich that rescued me back in my days with Colombo. The Rich that used to rush home to make love to me, make me giggle like a schoolgirl, and do anything to make me happy. Damn, I thought he looked good earlier in that new suit he was rocking, but he looks even better now. Still, I am mad and I can't allow his manliness to get to me.

"Rich, all I'm saying is if that Vanessa chick oversteps her boundaries again like she did today, she won't be walking away with a smug look on her face. She better have her dentist on call, because she'll be shitting teeth outta her ass."

"You need to grow up and stop bullying people with your little self."

"Grow up? If you stopped messing around I wouldn't have to keep putting my foot in people's asses. You feel me? She deserves to have her ass kicked for making us miss out on the cruise. You probably told her about our plans and she decided to make you work late on purpose. That bourgeois chick ain't slick."

"Val, I'm out," Rich says, waving me off with his hand as if I were insignificant. "I'm not hanging around for this. All I wanted was a chill day at home to relax with you, but you messed that up. I don't know what time I'll be home. Eat without me."

Hot liquid flows down my cheeks after Rich leaves our apartment. I never felt as threatened as I do today. Rich never brushed me off like this before and this really bothers me.

In the past when Rich was messing with all of those other chicks, I knew it was really just about the sex. Boning was one thing, but catching feelings for a chick was an entirely different story. Rich lying is nothing new. He always lied when he messed around but eventually he would get sloppy and I'd have to slap, punch, or kick a ho. But this time, he was calm. Normally we would go at it until I was blue in the face and eventually he would pull me to him and wrap me in his embrace. This was Rich's way of saying he had messed up and that other chick was history. The words were left unsaid, but the meaning was clear. However, this time there was no kissing, hugging, or loving. Even though I brushed him off, he didn't even attempt to come after me a second time and this was a first. I can't recall a time when he left without us making love and this is confirmation that something is definitely awry.

In truth, I can't pinpoint exactly when our relationship began to spin out of control. The first few years were blissful. We took weekend excursions to Atlantic City and even went to the Poconos for the annual ski summit. Nothing mattered. All we cared about at the time was us and we enjoyed every moment by pleasuring each other day and night. Rich fawned over me with gifts, trips, love, and affection. There was no doubt in my mind that he loved me and only me. There was no Qwanisha or Chantal. Our main focus was getting our act together so we could move out of those miserable projects.

After the incident with Colombo, I lived with Rich and his family. He took me in when I had no place to turn. For the first time in a long time, I finally felt safe and at ease. Rich's mom, his sister Lindsey, and I got along amicably. They were truly a dream come true and the closest thing I'd had to a real family since the passing of my mother. Rich's mother was hardworking and very nurturing and Lindsey was the little sister I never had. However, Rich and I weren't afforded much privacy and though they made me feel very much at home, I felt awkward. Lindsey was sixteen when I moved in and I didn't really feel it set a good example for Rich to have his girlfriend living in his mother's home. I also didn't want to wear out my welcome.

Fortunately, it wasn't long before we completed school and managed to land jobs at our present places of employment. We quickly rented our first one-bedroom apartment in Crown Heights, Brooklyn. We were well on our way to the road of freedom and prosperity. We had recently purchased our own condo, and got engaged. Rich and I have come too far for me to ruin everything over mere speculation.

Rich is right, I can't approach Vanessa the way I had those other females in the past. He does work with her, which I despise. He tells me that she's setting up meetings for him and they've been engaging with potential investors for his endeavors, thus the late-night dinner meetings. In general, I know he enjoys working for Jorge Jacobs, because he doesn't stop talking about the new responsibilities he's been assigned. He's even more excited about his personal venture, RichWear. I know how much starting his own fashion line means to Rich and I don't want to risk him losing out on that opportunity because of my rage. I don't want to sacrifice the lifestyle we were finally able to afford. A year ago when he received his promotion, he upgraded his Toyota 4Runner for a Lexus GS 430 and this year for my birthday he bought me a Nissan Murano. Though I told Rich I really didn't need a car, he insisted that it made him feel better knowing that I had a reliable means of transportation. Over the years, he's treated me to diamond bracelets, earrings, and necklaces. We've both worked hard to attain this lifestyle and I'll be damned if I allow some stray woman to come in and terrorize the house that Valentine built.

The phone chime brings me out of my reverie. I don't really feel like speaking to anyone and decide to let the answering machine pick up.

"Val, are you home? Val, it's your aunt Zenobia. Well, anyway, I was trying to get your attention in church today, but you and that sucka Rich left so quick I didn't even get the chance to say hi. *Guurlll*, did you see that hoochie up in church—"

"Aunt Zenobia, I'm here." I grab the phone reluctantly. If I hadn't answered she would've left one of her crazy-ass lengthy messages on the machine.

"What the hell, you screening your calls now? You knew that it was me."

"Aunt Z, I was changing my clothes and didn't get to the phone in time. Damn, why you always gotta make a mountain out of a molehill? If I didn't wanna speak to you, I wouldn't have picked up at all."

"Oh, so it's like that now. All right, I see how you treat family."

This woman has the nerve to talk about family, I think to myself. My aunt didn't give a damn about me while I was living under her roof and cared even less when I left. Now she wants to show her ass. I wasn't about to address her crude remark, because truthfully there were bigger, smellier, and slimier fish to fry.

"Did you call to argue with me, because I'm not in the mood," I quipped.

"No, I didn't call to argue. Just to chitchat. I ain't seen you in a minute."

"Well, I'm in church every Sunday. You're the one that comes once in a blue."

"Whatever," she said, smacking her lips. "You left before I could introduce you to my new friend, J-Boogie."

"J-Boogie?" I ask. My voice filled with surprise and skepticism. Who the hell went around calling themselves J-Boogie other than some wannabe rapper or drug dealer? "And just how old is J-Boogie?"

"Girl, old enough." Aunt Zenobia chuckles, ignoring the disdain in my voice. "Anyway, he's fine as hell, hung like a doggone donkey, got a good job, and I can train this one. This boy here is a keeper. Matter of fact, he didn't even turn his head when that floozy stepped up to the podium with Pastor McCash. She had all of them other fools drooling and wagging their tails. If I was you, I'd watch out for my man, Rich."

Little does she know how close to the truth she is, but I refuse to let on that Rich already knows and works with this floozy.

"Aunt Z, no disrespect, but you're not me. Rich and I are fine. We've been together for nine years now."

"Yeah, and you'd think y'all would be married by now. Sheee-iiiit, that ring has been on your finger for what, three years? By the way, is your ass fertile? After all these years, you should've had at least one kid by that man." She continued without allowing me a word in edgewise. "Anyway, all I'm saying is you know Rich's history. Anytime a pretty face with a big butt and a smile joins the church, Rich loses his damn mind."

"Auntie, thanks for your concern, but we're doing quite fine. As a matter of fact we'll be setting a date for the wedding real soon, so look out for your invitation. Listen, I have to go, my other line is beeping," I lie, rushing to get off the phone. This conversation was depressing me even further and going nowhere fast.

"Okay, but next month Shaquetta is having her twenty-first birthday party in the big community center at Marcy Projects, and I want y'all to come so you can meet J-Boogie, all right?"

"Yeah, if I'm free I'll come. Bye." I hang up before she can utter another word.

"If I was you, I'd watch out for my man, Rich." My head spins as Aunt Zenobia's words continue to bombard my thoughts. I pace up and down the apartment, wiping my wet face. I'm tired of the tears, because crying isn't my thing. I head to the bathroom to wash my face. As I walk past the chest of drawers I notice a pair of cuff links with Rich's initials engraved in them, RW. Now as long as I've known Rich, he has never, ever worn cuff links; much less a pair with his initials. He wouldn't take the time to get something like this done. This isn't Rich's style, which leads me to believe these items were purchased by Vanessa. I immediately

pick them up and carry them to the kitchen to find the torch we used to light the grill at summer barbecues. I lay the cuff links on the tiled countertop and flick the lighter, aiming it at the cuff links until they began to char. When they are damaged beyond repair, my mind races back to the suit that he wore to church this afternoon. The suit had turned up around the same time as the cuff links. I run into the closet and yank the suit off the hanger and find the large scissors and go to work. Before the evening is over, I have cut up three more suits that I'm sure Rich acquired through Vanessa. The suits look like I have run them through a paper shredder and I have left the heap of scrapped material in the entrance to our bedroom. I want him to know that he isn't smarter than me and if that witch continues to cross me I will cut her shit up just like I did those suits.

6

So What!

Vanessa knew that little church incident was costing Richard dearly. "So what, serves him right for still being with her," Vanessa voiced aloud. Vanessa stood nearly naked with the exception of her neutral-colored thong, admiring herself. Although her relationship with Richard at the moment was merely sexual, she could tell he was playing perfectly into her plans. The only thing she didn't factor into the equation was Valentine Daye.

Vanessa wasn't sure what was changing as it related to Richard. Ordinarily she wouldn't have cared about Richard's life or feelings, remaining focused only on her goal of corporate advancement. She definitely wouldn't have shown up at his church to cause a stir nor would she have allowed herself to be seduced by a man she was supposed to be seducing. Yet Richard appealed to her in a unique way. He was smart, extremely charming, drop-dead gorgeous, and someone she quickly decided she didn't want to share, even under the circumstances.

Vanessa went to her room-length walk-in closet and hung her

suit up. She went to the casual side of the closet to select her favorite dark denim True Religion jeans with her Dolce & Gabanna baby tee. She didn't really feel like going out, however, she had promised her mother she'd come to the house for dinner after church. Vanessa reached for her phone and dialed her parents' house.

"Knights' residence, may I help you?"

"Hi, Loretta, is my mother around?"

"Ms. Vanessa, how are you?"

Vanessa sighed from annoyance. "Not really interested in having idle chitchat. Is my mother there?"

Loretta's silence indicated that she had gone to get her mother. And moments later her mother was on the phone.

"Darling, is everything okay? Loretta said you were short with her."

"Mother, I barely want to talk to you, let alone chitchat with the help."

"I'm not amused."

"Mother, I'm joking. Apologize to Loretta for me, I've just had a not-so-pleasant morning and don't feel like talking, that's all. Besides, I don't want to be disrespectful to her, she practically raised me."

"I'll let her know. You are coming to dinner, aren't you? We're preparing your favorite, smoked salmon with a butter-cream sauce and asparagus."

Vanessa thought how delicious the meal would be. Not only did that sound wonderful, but right about now she was starving. "Mother, dinner is casual today. I'll come as long as I don't have to dress up. I know you, you'll try and use this as an opportunity to invite one of your society friends and their single sons over, trying to set me up."

"If you would just direct your attention to Stephen instead of that Richard character . . ."

"Mother . . ."

"If you ask me, Vanessa, I don't know how much longer Stephen's going to put up with you. Two years now, your father and I introduce you to him and what do you do? You string him along. He's a lawyer. His mother and I play tennis together. Really, darling, what is your problem?"

"That's the problem, you and Daddy trying to plan my life."

"Oh, Vanessa, what's wrong with us helping you out? It's not like you're going out of your way to get yourself married."

"So, you suggest that I marry Stephen, even though I don't love him?"

"All I'm saying is Stephen is a good man. He comes from a good family. If you're not careful, you may lose him to someone else."

"Me, lose him?" Vanessa quizzed.

"You're not—"

"Mother!" Vanessa sternly interrupted. "Just as sure as I called you, I'll hang up and order in."

"Okay, honey. Come however you want. Just come. Your father and I are dying to see you. You don't make it out here as often as we'd like. When do you think you'll be here?"

"Well if I leave now, I could possibly make it there by three-thirty."

"I'll make sure dinner is waiting. See you soon."

Vanessa hung up the phone and reached for her powder-pink leather-and-mink bomber. Soon all the pieces to her puzzle of a life would be in order, and with Richard in the picture, she'd quiet the mouth that mattered most . . . her mother's. She thought about Stephen and realized she'd avoided him for more than a week now. He was definitely due a call, but her head, heart, and energy just weren't into him. Maybe it was the challenge of Richard that moved her. And that movement didn't exist with Stephen. He was a good man, and on paper he was an ideal catch. With Stephen, she could continue with the high-class, society life that she was accustomed to, clean-cut and carefree. Stephen was safe and for once she didn't want to be who she knew she was. With Richard, there was a certain edge that she couldn't shake. He was exciting and Vanessa needed the excitement.

Vanessa dialed Richard's cell and immediately got his voice mail. Although her message was work related, she hoped he'd pick up. Vanessa took a deep sigh before hanging up. She didn't know if she really wanted Richard or if she was more determined to just take him from Valentine.

"I can't take this," she said, slamming her fist against the steering wheel. Just as her anger rose through her body, her phone rang. She flipped her phone before checking to even see who it was. "What!"

"You called?"

It was Richard. Vanessa smiled, calming herself.

"I take it you didn't check your message. I was reminding you about our board meeting tomorrow," Vanessa purred.

"Was that it?"

She knew he was upset. "Did there need to be something more?"

"Well . . ." He hesitated. "Sounds like you're driving."

"Yeah, I'm headed to dinner at my parents'. Care to join me?"

"I wish I could, but your little episode at church this morning caused a lot of drama."

"That's what happens when you associate with trash. Eventually it's bound to stink. Society people don't have to deal with such drama. The invitation is open for now but trust me, Richard, my patience is wearing thin. I won't be the other woman much longer. I want my man to be just that, mine."

"Vanessa, I didn't know what to think when we hooked up, but I've got to admit, I've fallen . . . hard. Give me a little more time to work this thing out with Val. I'll make it up to you, I promise."

"You better. Listen, I've got another call, gotta go."

"That better not be another man." Richard's voice reeked of jealousy.

"As if you're really in a position to say anything, while laying up there with that woman. Get it together then maybe I'll answer those kinds of questions."

Vanessa hung up the phone and smiled. "Check and mate." She had Richard exactly where she wanted him.

Vanessa slipped onto her Napa leather chaise and lay down. The evening air, though cold, felt good in her overly heated apartment. She'd forgotten to turn down the thermostat when she left for her parents', so by the time she made it back home her apartment felt like hell. She could have sworn she saw Satan chilling on her couch when she walked through the door it was so hot.

A chill covered Vanessa's body after moments of sitting in front of the cool air from the window. She rose to close the window just as her cell phone rang. She glanced over at the clock on the wall. The only person who could be calling her at this hour on her cell phone was Richard. Because of Richard's current circumstances, Vanessa didn't allow him to have her home phone number. She was a stickler on rules—if she couldn't call him at home, he damn sure couldn't call her at her house. She took her time walking to the phone.

"I knew it was you," she said after verifying her caller ID.

"Then why did it take you so long to answer?"

"Why should I hurry? Were you going somewhere?" Vanessa's tone was soft yet sarcastic.

"I had to get out of the house." He sounded drained.

"Why?" she said with a smirk. "Ole girl getting on your nerves?"

Vanessa was taken aback my Richard's hesitation. Something told her there was something wrong.

"Richard, is everything okay?"

"No, everything's not okay. I've been driving around for hours. . . . I just . . ." He paused. "Ness, can I just come by? I really need to see you." His words were low, barely understandable. "I just want to be with you right now. Is that cool?"

Vanessa felt warmth cover her now extremely chilled body. His tone was extremely personal and endearing. "Um yeah, that's cool. I'll see you soon."

As she flipped her phone shut, she hurried to the window to close it. She could tell something major had gone down between Valentine and Richard because he'd never called her Ness before and certainly had never come across so vulnerable.

For a moment Vanessa felt herself soften. She tried to mask her emotions with a motive but couldn't pretend that what she was feeling for Richard wasn't real. No matter what drama had transpired between him and Val, as co-director it was her responsibility to make sure she did whatever she had to in order for him to be in top form at their board meeting the next day. It was never Richard's style to stay the night, so she wondered what the evening would bring about. At some point she knew he would have to leave and return home to Valentine. However, as long as he was there with her, she'd make sure that even when he went home, he'd wish he'd never left the comfort she'd provided.

Vanessa slipped her silk rose-colored robe around her body and began lighting candles throughout her apartment. She wanted to make sure the atmosphere was inviting. Even though she considered Richard a fixer-upper kind of man, she'd invested so much into making him a classic find, that she'd be damned if Valentine got to drive her well-restored vehicle anywhere. She was going to be there with Richard for the smooth ride into corporate bliss. And even though there might have been some bumps along the way, Valentine wasn't going to ruin their ultimate destination of happiness.

7

❧

Out All Night

This negro has the nerve to try and creep in at a few minutes before five in the morning. Rich is definitely out of his mind, because he hasn't done anything stupid like this since I stepped to him at that trick Qwanisha's house back in the day. Barring death of a family member or close friend, nothing could justify his twelve-hour disappearing act.

After destroying Rich's suits and a few other items that I knew he wasn't responsible for purchasing I wandered around our apartment aimlessly. My mind couldn't erase all of the messed-up thoughts and the conversation that Rich and I had before he walked out of here yesterday afternoon. I didn't understand why he would try to play me like this and for that trick. It was me who encouraged Rich to follow his passion and pursue a career in fashion. I was the one who enrolled us in school so we could get our degrees. I was his biggest cheerleader and now this priss bitch steps onto the scene and he loses his flipping mind.

The bedroom door is still open, because I left the mountain of clothes right there in the threshold. It is my intent that he realize just how serious I am about him accepting gifts from this woman or any other, for that matter.

His footsteps are getting closer and I know it will be only moments before he walks into our bedroom. He tries to quietly place the house keys on the sofa table, but there are too many on the ring and they clank together. It sounds like he is removing his jacket and returning it to the coat closet, but I hear something else rustling. His attempts at trying to be quiet are pathetic. Now he is heading to our room. Rich's estimated time of arrival will be in five, four, three, two . . .

"What the hell," Rich says as he stumbles into the room, tripping over the shredded heap of his belongings.

I use this opportunity to quickly turn on the lamp on the nightstand at my side of the bed. My arms are folded across my chest as I sit upright with my back against the headboard. This is the position I have been in for the last two hours.

When the light switches on, surprise shines all over Rich's face. He thought he was going to be able to sneak in and act like his ass had been here all along, which made me realize that he was just as crazy as that witch in church today.

"Val, what the hell is all of this stuff in the doorway?" Rich asks as he tries to regain his composure.

"No, the question is, where have you been?"

"What do you mean, where have I been? Where have I been?" He repeats himself like a parakeet and then begins to study the items on the ground. He turns his full attention to the pile and sifts through it to check the damage. Rich holds article after article in the air as he sifts through the mess and nods his head like he is upset. But I know he is just trying to avoid answering me. As far as I'm concerned Rich had had all night and morning for that matter to rehearse some answers.

"Rich, I didn't freaking stu-stutter. You come rolling up in here at a quarter to five in the morning, so I need to know where you're coming from."

"I needed to blow off some steam. Get away from all this unnecessary drama. That's where I've been." The waver in his voice makes him sound guilty.

"Rich, you must think I'm stupid, but you better wise up and stop trying to play me." I step out of bed and walk to where Rich is standing.

"Val, you're tripping and why in the world did you cut up my suits? Are you crazy? Do you know how much these joints cost?"

"No crazier than you trying to step up in here one hour before the sun returns from China! And as far as how much those suits cost, I'm not concerned, because you didn't buy nary one of them." I'm practically in his face and then it dawns on me that Rich smells like vanilla. I sniff again, making it obvious for him to figure out what I am doing.

"Okay, you don't want to tell me where you've been. Take out your dick." Rich doesn't know what the hell I have up my sleeve, but he knows something isn't right and he pulls away. However, I am faster than he is and slide his boxers down and grab a hold of his dick. Rich pushes me away and I lose my grasp, but my fury won't allow me to go down like that. I lunge at him, yanking at his dick, and since he isn't hard it's easier to hold on to. I quickly bend down to smell his dick. I get a good whiff and just like I thought, his dick smells much closer to shower fresh than sweaty stank. By the time Rich pulls away it was too late. His swift-jerk motion causes me to lose my grip and I land on my side on the floor. I'm not in pain, but the tears are burning my eyes and there's nothing I can do to stop them or the pain that's wringing my heart and sapping all of the life out of me.

"Why Rich? Why?" I ask between sobs. "Why are you doing this to me? What did I do to deserve this?"

"Val, stop crying and get up off the floor. Baby, come here. I don't know why you're making all this fuss," Rich says, reaching for my hand.

My body rocks back and forth as I try to calm myself down. I don't want him to lay a hand on me. I don't want Rich's nasty-ass hands to touch or console me, so when he reaches out to me, I draw back. But Rich knows he is guilty and continues his attempt at getting me off the ground.

"Don't touch me, Rich. Don't put those nasty hands on me, because I know where they've been."

"The only place my hands have been is on a basketball and while I was at the court, my boy stopped by with an extra ticket to the Knicks game and we bounced. That's why I don't smell all sweaty," Rich said unconvincingly.

"Rich . . . you are such a liar. If you can't tell me the truth, get out of my sight."

"Baby, I'm telling you the truth this time. On my word that's what happened." He stoops down to the ground to talk to me. "You gotta have more trust in me. Why you trippin' so hard? Cutting up my clothes and trashing my stuff like that."

"Rich, I'm so tired of the lies," I snivel. "I'm exhausted and I can't keep fighting over you like this. It's either me or that high siddity slut you're laying up with, but I'm tired."

"Baby, stop talking crazy," Rich says as he strokes my hair into place. I don't resist him. My body aches and my heart is sore from years of anguish. Rich lifts me and carries my dead weight back to bed. "Wait right here," he says and rushes back out to the living room.

When Rich returns he is carrying something in his hand. My vision is slightly blurred from a fresh set of tears and Rich hands me some tissue to wipe my face.

"See, I told you I was at the game," Rich says, extending his hand as he shows me the game ticket, which displays yesterday's date, row, seat assignment, price, bar code and the team that they played against. "Baby, you may have thought that I was guilty in the past, but you have to know that I love you. It's always been about me and you, and there's no question that my queen is and always will be you. No one can hold a candle to you, much less come between us. You see this ring on your finger?" He holds my hand before his face and kisses my fingers one by one. "You are the woman that I'm going to marry. You are the woman that my heart desires. Val, you are my first and only love. Believe that!"

Rich holds me in his embrace and my tears continue to flow. I'm not crying because his words touch me or because of his un-relenting confession of love. These tears are because Rich talks a good game, and I know he is runnin' game on me. Here I am allowing him to sweet talk me even though I know there are sev-eral hours in between the game and his arrival at home that are still left unaccounted for. According to the ticket the game started at 8 P.M., which meant it was over at eleven at best. Yeah, he loves me and I love him even more, but I'm no fool. There are still questions running rampant in my head and I know he is get-ting over, but I can't prove it—at least not tonight. Nevertheless, he will slip up again, and next time, I'll be ready.

8

Speaking of the Devil

"It sounds like that chick could scare the devil out of hell," my best friend Gina replies after I tell her about our uninvited visitor at church. I don't dare tell her that Rich also had the nerve to spend the night out, because I'd really never hear the end of it.

"Well, what she better recognize is that the devil doesn't scare that easily and the devil knows how to make hell even hotter. Can that bitch handle the heat? Cuz you know I can bring it!" I respond. However, inside I am pissed off. This Vanessa chick is really getting under my skin, especially after yesterday.

"Well, I've got to say you're much better than me. I can't believe you didn't jump up and slap that hussy."

I can't help but laugh, because I was that close to clocking Vanessa right in her grille. I could care less that she is taller than me. A few inches don't mean anything to me.

"Trust me, Gina . . . I wanted to."

"But?" she asks.

"But? What do you mean, but? Gina, I was in church. You

don't expect me to act uncivil in the house of God, do you? I mean really, give me some credit."

"That didn't stop you from drop-kicking Chantal at the church picnic two years ago. When you caught her trying to serve Rich a plate of food and he was debating whether or not he should accept it."

"Please, you know she was wrong. She ain't have no reason to be fixing my man a plate of food. What she needed to do was find herself someone who wanted her ass," I say while filing the last few folders my boss had put on my desk earlier.

"Well, Rich wasn't objecting and as far as I know—"

"Gina, don't even go there, okay? I don't need the lectures."

"Okay, fine. You won't get a lecture today. So how did she look?"

"First of all she had on so much makeup you would need a chisel to break through to her skin." Both of us bust out laughing. "She was a'ight looking, but she wasn't all that. You know one of them hi-yella rich snobby-looking hoochies."

"For real. Damn, well you don't need no makeup for your beauty to shine."

"I know that's right," I say with a smile.

"So what did you say to him?" Gina asks.

"Oh, I ripped into his ass. I asked him who she was."

"And what did he say? Did he deny knowing her?"

"No, he said she was just a friend."

"That's some ole Biz Markie stuff." Gina breaks into song. *"But you say she's just a friend."*

"Oh, how very original. You substituted the word *he* for *she*. I'm glad you think this is a joke," I say, trying to sound upset, but I manage to laugh instead.

"Val, this whole thing is a joke. You surely don't seem to take

Rich's antics seriously. It's just one big merry-go-round with y'all constantly spinning in circles and ending up in the same old spot. I get nauseous every time you tell me about Rich's tired games."

"This is not a game."

"Well, you are going to have to put your foot down and give that man an ultimatum. How much longer are you going to put up with his trifling ways?"

"Girl, Rich is my man and will always be my man. These women are the trifling ones."

"Val, even if the women are throwing themselves at Rich, he doesn't have to respond by screwing them. You can't keep blaming them. Rich has to take responsibility for his actions and you need to stop acting like he's the victim. He's been proven guilty a number of times."

"Gina, forget you!"

Gina and I have a lot of history together and she is the only one of my friends who can talk out her face to me and it's cool. It isn't one of those stories where I was getting jumped and she saved me or vice versa. We didn't steal from candy stores together or bully people. We were just friends from grade school and our mothers had been friends. We lived in the same housing community and have always looked out for each other. If I didn't have, which was often after my mother died and before I hooked up with Colombo, my girl Gina supplied me with whatever she had. She would give me her last and I'd do the same. It was unsaid, but we both knew the deal. Gina is five-six and I'm five-three, but aside from that we bear a slight resemblance and wear the same size clothing. Gina looks more like Halle Berry, and I look more like Toni Braxton. Still our personalities are like yin and yang. Gina hated when I was dating Colombo, because of his trade, and the fact that he occasionally beat my ass didn't help. I saw Colombo as my way out of the ghetto—a means to an end. When I left my aunt's house I stayed with Gina for a few weeks, but the space was too cramped. It was only two bedrooms and Gina has a sister, a brother, and a cousin June Bug who liked feeling up on me at night. I didn't enjoy these sexual assaults, and at the time I didn't want to tell Gina that her cousin June Bug was a pervert, so when Colombo entered the picture it was my way out.

Here we are more than a decade later and Gina still hates my man. Colombo, I could understand, because of the drugs and the danger that came along with the business. I'm not even gonna front, there were days that I wanted to walk away from Colombo and his association, but I didn't have any place to turn. I was stuck between the life and Colombo's fist. On the contrary, Rich is an entirely different story. For one he's never used me as his punching bag. There were times in the past where we got into heated discussions and I was so used to fighting with Colombo that I expected the same from Rich, but he never touched me. Rich has a big heart and is always willing to help others. When we grocery shop, he always picks up a bag or two for his mother and there's rarely a time that he'll shop and not pick up a little something for me. He's very affectionate, caring, kind, humble, smart, maintains a positive attitude, and he has his life together. Rich is in a good position at his job and like the Jeffersons he's moving on up—slowly, but surely. He wants me to be his wife and I definitely want him to be my husband. We've been through tougher times and I'm in this for the long haul. Besides, we started this journey together and his career is finally on the rise. You don't come this far and then say screw it and walk out. How do you leave the man that you helped groom after years of labor, only for the next woman to reap the benefits? And Rich has had my back from the beginning. There were times life had proven to be more than I could bear and Rich talked me off the ledge, figuratively. Rich has always been my bedrock. I hear what Gina is saying, but it just ain't happening. It's not that serious and this too shall pass. We have a genuine love for each other and a bond that is unbreakable.

What my girl Gina has to understand is that everybody's life isn't surrounded by a white picket fence. I admire Gina, because she's always been a go-getter. She didn't use the projects as an excuse. As soon as she graduated from high school she went to college, but ended up pregnant by her sophomore year. Gina had to take a job as a receptionist at a law firm. This ended up being a good thing, because she eventually became a paralegal making stupid dough and now she attends John Jay College part-time completing her bachelor's degree. Afterward, she plans to go to law school. And quite honestly, I don't doubt her for a minute, because Gina is happily married to her baby daddy, Oscar. In my freakiest nightmares I never thought my girl would've gotten pregnant, much less marry Oscar the nerd, but that man worships the toilet seat she rests her funky ass on.

Don't get me wrong, Oscar's a nice person, but he's definitely not the pick of the litter since he's a little on the chunky side and that's being polite. The thing is Gina is pretty. No, she's gorgeous and has never had a problem turning heads, so when she hooked up with Oscar it seemed strange. But they are a happy family living in a nice four-bedroom house in Lefferts Gardens. Oscar knows that he has a trophy wife, and treats her like a queen, doing everything to make sure she is always happy. So I guess her fairy tale came true.

"All I'm saying is that I don't know why you put up with his nonsense. That man should be kissing the ground you walk on, but instead he does nothing but give you fever. How many women does this make now?" Gina inquires.

"Gina, I don't know. All men have affairs," I say, not wanting to admit to the actual number, and it is almost as if she were reading my thoughts.

"Val, I don't believe that to be true, but what are you going to do for the rest of your life? Kick every woman's ass that Rich screws? I mean come on, Val. You are beautiful and smart. You've got the bomb job at WFAT and you make good money. You've got your business together and can handle your own, but when it comes to Rich, you lose your damn mind."

I listen as Gina rants, and accept her compliments and slights with a grain of salt. We go through this every time Rich messes up, but it wasn't always this way.

"Gina, leaving Rich really is not an option. We are getting married and we're going to build a family together. We have history and he's always been there for me when times were tough." I pull the vase of yellow roses with the red tint that Rich had had delivered to my office this morning to my nose. The arrangement of flowers is beautiful. He always knows how to romance me. Of course this time the flowers are to get back in my good graces, but he does this quite often. Rich never forgets an anniversary or birthday and he always gets me flowers on the anniversary of my mother's death. He knows this day is especially difficult for me and that flowers help brighten my day.

"Well, history sure has a way of repeating itself when it comes to you and Rich, because he just keeps on humping whoever he wants and you keep kicking these girls' asses and taking him back.

The day you realize Rich is really at fault and not those women is the day you'll wake up and leave his sorry butt."

I am growing tired of this conversation. She said no lectures and here she is going on and on. Gina is being more like a mother today than a friend and my mother is in her grave. I need to end this conversation. Just then, my call-waiting beeps.

"Gina, hon, I gotta go. Somebody in the office is in need of my assistance."

"All right, but call me tonight and if you want to pack a bag and chill at my place for a few days you are more than welcome. You haven't seen your goddaughter in a minute now anyway."

"You lying heifer. I saw Ashley this past weekend. Anyway, thanks for the offer. We'll talk."

I click over to the blinking line.

"Hello, this is Val," I answer.

"Val, hey girl. You have another flower delivery at the front desk," the receptionist says. I can hear a playful lilt in Kristina's voice.

"Okay, I'll be right out."

I scoot my chair away from my desk, leaving the confines of my area. I have pictures of Boris Kodjoe, Chris Webber, and Will Smith hanging in my space. My model, ballplayer, and actor; the best threesome a girl could have.

On my way to the reception desk I was stopped—no, attacked—by one of our sales directors, Ronald—a tall, deep, dark chocolate glass of milk. Ron remind me of Tyson Beckford—body and all, but his lips aren't quite as exaggerated. He jumps in my path and grabs me by my wrist. Ron, aka Ready Ron, is known as a player, but I am the only one he constantly tries to push up on in the office. Still it was known that he got around. Since WFAT is the leading urban radio station, we receive a lot of complimentary tickets to parties and concerts and Ron brings a different date to every one of these events.

"Hey beautiful," he says.

"Hi Ron," I say, pulling my arm away from his grip.

"So, when are you and me gonna hook up?" This question was asked of me every other day, and honestly if I wasn't with Rich, I probably would have dropped the draws long ago—even though I'm not in favor of office affairs.

"Never," I say with a smile.

"You'll break one of these days, because you need a real man. That bruh Rich don't have what it takes to keep you happy. You think I don't know Rich done messed up again." Ron pulls me by the arm to whisper in my ear. "The only time you get flowers is when he messes up."

His warm breath sends thrills up my spine and makes my nipples pucker. I quickly ease away.

I was surprised at his assumption, and though Rich bought me flowers as an apology that isn't always the case. "Ron, my man doesn't need a reason to buy me flowers and if anything, you should take a couple of pointers. Anyway, what do you know about being a real man, when you can't keep a woman longer than I keep a pair of panty hose?" I ask.

"Maybe you'd be able to keep those stockings longer if you cut them toenails down. See, that's what I'm talking about. Your man is not even pampering you properly. I'd be clipping those cute little nails for you every week along with a good foot massage."

All I can do is laugh and he does too. Ron's comment doesn't even deserve a response.

"Ron, I'll see you later."

"At my place or yours?"

"You do know this is bordering on sexual harassment, right?"
I ask.

"Are you going to write me up or report me?" he jokes.

"I will if you don't leave me alone." I quickly walk off, but I can
feel his eyes watching my ass as I saunter away. If I were a few inches
taller my swagger could give those runway models a run for their
money along with a few lessons.

As I approach the front desk, I can hear Kristina talking loudly
with whoever was on the phone, bragging about the party she
had attended over the weekend. When she sees me, she attempts
to cut the conversation short.

"Girl, I gotta go, but we'll definitely speak later, because you
know I gave that nucka my number."

I wait patiently as Kristina wraps up her call.

"Girl, hell yeah he called, but that ain't even the icing on the
cake."

I clear my throat and run my fingers through my tresses.

"Lisa, for real, I gotta go." There is a pregnant pause. "Okay,
like around six-thirty when I get home. Later," she says, finally
hanging up the phone.

"Kristina, I hope you are not up here running your mouth all
day long instead of answering the phones."

"Val, I'm doing my job."

"Okay, because you know I like you and all that, but you can't
be up here chilling on the phone all the time. You are paid to answer the phones, not make personal calls."

Kristina's face tells me she is pissed off, but I don't really give a
damn. She lives on the phone and I have gotten a few complaints

from the sales team that she hasn't been responsive enough and needs to take better messages. Kristina is a nice girl, but just like the last receptionist I had to report who eventually got fired, I will do the same to her. The job is not hard. I used to be the one who would relieve the other receptionists until we had sense enough to hire an office assistant who substitutes for Kristina during the lunch hour.

"Are those my flowers over there?" I ask, pointing at a bouquet behind her head.

"Yeah, those are them. They smell real good too," Kristina says, returning to her normal self. "So, Val, what are you guys celebrating? Is it your anniversary?"

"No," I respond as I slip behind her desk to retrieve my flowers. I stoop down to smell the vibrant array. Kristina is right, these flowers smell like some type of hyped-up air freshener.

"Damn, girl. You got that man whipped. He's sending you flowers for no special reason—just because! I need me a man like Rich."

Kristina is cool and all, but I wasn't going to allow her to step a foot into my real world, so I have to front like everything was good.

"Girl, don't worry, Mr. Right will come your way soon enough. Rich and I didn't happen overnight. Good relationships take a lot of time and compromise."

"Yeah, true . . . true. But Val, you got it all. I mean Rich is fine, he's got a phat job at Jorge Jacobs, making bank . . . I'm sure. Y'all live in a nice neighborhood, you flossing the crazy rock on your ring finger and Rich still knows how to romance a chick. Now that's hot."

Kristina made my relationship with Rich sound like some

storybook tale, and she was almost right. I do have everything, but there is still that nasty little thorn in my side called Vanessa. Once we get rid of that prickly shrub, my life with Rich will once again smell like a bed of roses!

9

❧

The Man of the Hour

Vanessa couldn't believe her eyes as Richard strolled into the office wearing a hideous, olive-green, apparently dated, nontailored suit. She was shocked that Richard wasn't his normal dapper self. Although not much could make Richard look bad, this suit was clearly trying to work the "C" right out the word *chic*.

Vanessa buzzed her secretary, "Cynthia, I need you to get me Sergio on the phone ASAP."

Vanessa looked at the clock. *At least he arrived early, so there's still time to correct this crime of fashion.*

"Mr. Sanchez is on line one," Cynthia buzzed through to Vanessa's office.

"Thank you." She pushed the button to accept the call. "Sergio, I need you to work a miracle, please tell me you are in town."

"Jes chica, I'm actually at Barneys pulling some things for a photo shoot for this new young diva. I'm tellin' ju these little chicas think dat just because they can sing, they supposed to be able to look like Janet Jackson. I'm like, chile you no look like Joseph Jackson let alone Janet Jackson, 'cause even Janet Jackson barely knows what Janet Jackson looks like, ju know what I'm saying?"

"Sergio, could you tear away from that for just a moment, run to the men's department, and buy a fierce dark-colored suit for Richard? You already know his size. Get a Gucci, Hugo Boss, or DKNY. Anything! You know what I like to see my men in. We have a board meeting in less than an hour and the man of the hour looks like a GQ reject. I'll send a car to Barneys right now to pick up the suit. Leave it with the driver and charge it to my personal account. Oh, and by the way, I'm going to need shoes, socks, and a fabulous tie. If you saw Richard right now, you'd know why. He looks like a walking fashion faux pas. Do you think you can handle it?"

"Oh honey, I'm already on it. I'll have that suit there to you in ten, complete with all the right accessories."

"Make sure to get yourself a little something wonderful via me, spare no expense." She paused, remembering who she was talking to and corrected herself. "However don't get too carried away."

"Oh chile, thank you, I've been eyeing these fab Gucci loafers and some Prada mules."

"Get them both. Just please get that suit to me pronto."

"Thank you, mija. It'll be there right away."

Vanessa rose from her desk and walked out the door to Cynthia's area.

"Cynthia, send a company car over to Barneys. Instruct the driver to wait out front for Sergio. He'll be bringing some bags to the car that I'll need him to bring back to me. Let me know the minute he gets here. Time is of the essence, so please get a move on."

Vanessa returned to her desk to relax. She could feel a small migraine headache and she needed to settle down. *What in the world was Richard thinking?* Vanessa thought quietly to herself. *How could he possibly represent Jorge Jacobs looking like that?*

She opened her top desk drawer and reached for her bottle of Advil, popped two pills, and took a swig of bottled water to wash it down. If Richard kept pulling stupid shenanigans like this, he could jeopardize everything.

Within moments there was a knock at the door. Vanessa pulled herself together before opening the door. She knew Sergio could work miracles, but he wasn't that quick, Vanessa thought.

"Come in," Vanessa replied to the incessant knocking.

Cynthia frantically rushed inside and closed the door behind her.

"What in the world is wrong with you?" Vanessa asked, busying herself with the presentation for the upcoming meeting.

"Mr. Etienne Jorge, Claude Jacobs, and the other members have arrived. I already set up the conference room, but I know that you're waiting for Mr. Sanchez. What should I do?"

Damn, I don't need this right now, Vanessa thought as she rubbed her temples.

"Cynthia, let's not lose our cool. They're a little early, so relax. Just go into the conference room and be a good host. I know you already made sure the food arrangement is set up nicely, and the laptop is fine, right?"

"Yes, to all of the above."

"Well, send the tech guy in there to double check, so everything will run smoothly and keep an ear out for the delivery from

Sergio. As soon as it arrives, take the items directly to Richard's office. Pronto!"

"No problem."

"Oh, and if Mr. Jorge or Mr. Jacobs asks of my whereabouts, tell them that you overheard me on the phone with a client. That should keep them for a while."

"Okay," Cynthia said and dashed out just as quickly as she had entered.

What now? Vanessa asked herself as the phone rang. "Vanessa Knight. How may I help you?" Vanessa dreaded answering her own phone, but she knew Cynthia was off doing the chores she had just ordered.

"Hello, beautiful."

"Daddy, to what do I owe the pleasure of this call?"

"Hi pumpkin, your mother and I wanted to remind you about the charity benefit event that we're hosting in conjunction with the United African American College Program next week."

"Ugh . . . is that the thing for the less fortunate?"

"If you're referring to the African American College Endowment the answer is yes. We expect you to be there and Dr. Marshall has been inquiring about you. I believe he wants you to accompany him. Or perhaps you could bring Stephen. It would look quite good and you know there'll be a ton of press coverage."

"Daddy, I'm quite capable of finding my own date, but thank you for your assistance. Besides, Dr. Marshall is a tad square and too uptight for my tastes and Stephen and I . . ." she hesitated, "are going through something right now."

"Fine, but don't bother bringing any riffraff to this event. We do not need any embarrassment. Your mother has told me about this guy you met in the projects."

"Daddy, he works at my office and he's not from the projects."
Anymore at least, Vanessa thought.

Vanessa's father grumbled. "In which department? The mail-room?"

"God no! Richard Washington is an *executive* just like me. He just needs a little polishing is all."

"Your brother is bringing London as his date. It seems that the two of them are hitting it off well. Now she comes from the proper lineage."

"Daddy, that's great, but I'm preparing for an important meeting with Mr. Jorge and Mr. Jacobs, so I must go."

"Good luck. We'll see you this Sunday for dinner."

The last thing Vanessa needed was for her parents to set her up with another tight ass. Sure they had money, but as the heiress to her family's fortune, money wasn't an issue. Besides, Vanessa already knew who would be accompanying her and they would definitely make a grand entrance.

The knock at the door distracted Vanessa from her thoughts.

"Come in."

Vanessa watched as Richard sauntered in still wearing that thing he referred to as a suit. Within seconds, Cynthia followed with a garment and large Barneys bag in tow.

"Great. Thank you, Cynthia. That will be all," Vanessa said as she took the packages from her. "Richard, these are for you. We don't have time to waste, so instead of going back to your office to change, feel free to freshen up in my office bathroom. The last thing we want Mr. Jorge and Mr. Jacobs to see is this fashion disaster you call a suit. If you're giving the last half of this presentation and I the first, there is no way you're following me looking like that."

Before walking off, Vanessa placed a sweet sensual kiss on

Richard's lips and smoothed her hand over his crotch, knowing she would get an immediate rise out of him.

"Chop, chop!"

"And in conclusion, this new line will cater to the urban community. The revenue to be earned is substantial. The inner-city youth are already experimenting with our brand, but we should capitalize on it and create this particular line to cater to their buying needs. If you have any doubt, it has been reported by leading economists that the buying power of African Americans increased by a hundred and twenty-seven percent over the past fourteen years from three hundred eighteen billion to seven hundred and twenty-three billion dollars. In another five years that figure is expected to increase to nine hundred fifty billion. Of that forty-five billion will be spent on apparel. Let's not waste any more time allowing our competitors to have the edge over us."

Vanessa's heart beat with pride. Together, they had nailed it. She knew Richard could do it, especially with her help. It was in that moment that Vanessa realized that maybe she was going about Richard in all the wrong ways. Instead of her usual way of getting what she wanted from Richard, she now had an actual desire to help him.

As he finished his speech, Vanessa led the room in applause.

"Bravo." Vanessa smiled.

"*Fantastique!* Mr. Washington and Ms. Knight," Mr. Jorge praised.

"*Merveilleux.* So, when do we get started?" Mr. Jacobs said light-heartedly as he patted Richard on his back. His thick French accent coated every word.

"Mr. Jorge and Mr. Jacobs, Richard and I have been working

diligently with the design team on a fall line and we'd like to unveil it at the upcoming Magic Trade Show in Vegas," Vanessa boasted as she took her place beside Richard.

"Ms. Knight, we can always depend on you to think ahead. Very good," Mr. Jacobs commended.

"Thank you."

"Mr. Washington, there are big things in your future here at Jorge Jacobs. We are looking forward to the unveiling of this new line you speak of. We would also like to see the preliminary figures and bottom-line revenue. You will have for us, yes?"

"Yes, I'm working on those numbers for you now and you can expect to receive them by the end of next week."

"Good work," Mr. Jorge stated as he and Mr. Jacobs shook hands with Richard. The other board members shook Richard's hand as well before exiting the room.

"Thank you and I know you'll like the projections we're working on."

When everyone had left the room, Vanessa locked the door to the conference room and hopped on the table.

"I told you if you play along with me, I'd help you get to the top."

"And I'll forever be grateful," Richard said, loosening his tie.

"How grateful?" Vanessa asked as she parted her legs and hiked up her skirt, revealing her soft center.

"Real, real grateful." Richard smiled when he noticed that Vanessa wasn't wearing any panties.

"Well, I'm waiting." Vanessa opened her legs, tilted her pelvis up and leaned her body back. Within seconds Richard's face and tongue covered her vagina with long, wet, slurp-like kisses. She smiled as he pleased her orally, wondering if an actual relationship with him was even possible. She knew that with each day that passed her feelings for him were growing more real. In her attempt to control everything, one key component had been neglected: her heart. She wondered if it was too late, if there was any way to stop and step back from it all now. But as he sucked and chewed on the tip of her clit, she knew it was too late. Richard wasn't the only one who had fallen. Surprisingly, Vanessa had fallen too.

10

All I Need to Get By

I didn't know if I should laugh or cry, but I was only a minute away from taking Vanessa out of her misery.

It's been a whole week and things still haven't returned back to normal between Rich and me. If anything, things have gotten worse and I'm beginning to lose control. I'm backed up from lack of dick and Rich was getting bolder in his actions with Vanessa.

Rich smelled like sweet vanilla. He owned Burberry by Burberry, Drakkar Noir, and Polo Blue by Ralph Lauren. However, I could smell the faint fragrance of vanilla on him as we lay in bed every night—not touching. We don't have anything vanilla scented in the house—soap, body oil, incense, nothing. Up until now I used to like the smell of vanilla, but it quickly became the most repulsive smell, making me want to vomit.

No matter what has happened in the past, Rich and I always managed to make some kind of contact during the night and by morning our legs would be intertwined. Before leaving for work we would make love like there was no tomorrow and then we'd rush home from our jobs to do it all over again. But this time a whole week went by and we barely exchanged more than a few words. Our chats were more like, "Do we have any more tooth-paste?" to which I would answer, "Look beneath the sink."

Basic conversations with no substance is the best way to de-scribe the way we've been behaving. We are acting like roommates instead of lovers or two people who intend to spend the rest of their lives together. And trust me when I say Rich and I are definitely going to be spending the rest of our lives together. This right here is just a phase.

It's Friday night and I don't feel like going home to the same stale situation, so I copped two concert tickets for me and Gina to go see my girl Alicia Keys at SOB's.

During my lunch break I hopped over to Macy's on Thirty-fourth Street and purchased the hottest BCBG outfit. It cost me a grip, but I was gonna look hot to death. I planned to turn a few heads, but that's as far as it was gonna go.

The plan is to go to Gina's house to freshen up and change, so I can avoid bumping into Rich, because to be honest right now I'm really not feeling him.

Gina's husband Oscar greets me at the door when I arrive. He has on an apron and reminds me of a black Chef Boyardee, and whatever he is cooking is giving me second thoughts about going anywhere other than their kitchen. The man can cook and has a belly to prove it.

"Hey, Oscar, how're you doing?" I ask as he closes the door behind me.

"I'm as good as can be. I was just cooking some dinner for my lovely wife, but it looks like it's just me and my baby girl tonight."

"Sorry, Oscar. I didn't mean to ruin your plans. If Gina had told me that you two were dining in together, I would've made other plans," I say, knowing damn good and well that I still would have dragged Gina to the show with me. Besides, Gina loves Alicia Keys just as much as me, so it wouldn't have taken too much to persuade her to come along.

"No, it's okay. My cooking was just spur of the moment. We didn't make any real plans or anything, so don't worry about it."

"Okay. So where is my girl Gina at?" I asked, looking around their spacious living room.

"She's upstairs getting all dolled up. Make sure you look out for her tonight, I don't want any of these gangster thug men trying to steal my wife."

"Oscar, you don't ever have to worry about that, because Gina only has eyes for you." And that is the truth!

When I get upstairs Gina is tending to Ashley's hair, while Ashley works on her homework. I give Ashley a quick hug and then head to the guest bedroom to get dressed.

SOB's is packed wall-to-wall with men of all flavors. I thought Alicia's fan base was mainly women, but the men are definitely representing tonight. My eyes quickly scan the room for familiar faces from work. I knew that a few people from the job had copped tickets that were supposed to be given to fans who called in to the station during the top-ten at ten or if they heard a particular artist or song. It depended on the disc jockey, but either way I knew at least five heads that didn't belong were up in SOB's profiling. I immediately spot Kristina and another coworker, Diane. Diane works in the accounts receivable department and is someone that I often hang out with in the office. They are at the bar drinking, talking, and chilling. I tap Gina on the shoulder; she takes my lead and follows me to the other side of the room.

We stand behind Diane and Kristina's bar stools before deciding to get a table near the stage and people watch until the show begins. We discuss the women parading around in outrageous barely-there outfits, crazy hairstyles, ugly shoes, too much jewelry, and a bunch of other stuff. Then I begin to notice how desperate these women are behaving as they hike their already short skirts even higher, grinding into these men's crotches, allowing themselves to be felt up by strangers and it makes me think of Vanessa. She is a decent-looking woman and can probably have any man that she wants, but instead she is intent on going after my man.

My mood quickly became sour as I thought about Rich cheating around on me with Vanessa. Before I know it, I am on my fourth drink and I'm not known for holding my liquor.

Alicia Keys is grooving on the piano, her voice is tight, the band is jamming, and the crowd sways to the rhythm and as much as I try to front like I am enjoying myself, I'm not. After a few more songs, Alicia is replaced by a deejay, and the music is banging as they play old-school tunes.

Diane, Kristina, and Gina are all on the dance floor having a good time as I sit at the table drinking and sulking, sulking and drinking. I am ready to go home, but everybody is having such a good time that I don't want to be a busta and stop everybody else's fun and I'm not up to taking the train home alone.

My eyes are closed, the glass is still half full as it sways in my hand and the liquid swishes from one side to the other. I dread the night as it is coming to an end, because I don't feel like going home to the nonsense I've been dealing with all week long. Suddenly there is a light tap on my shoulder taking me away from my thoughts. Through blurred vision I see that it is Ron. After staring at him for a few seconds he takes a seat at one of the empty chairs across from me.

"Having a good time?" he asks, taking my available hand into his and slowly massaging my fingers. I was too drained mentally and physically to fight him.

"Yeah, I'm cool," I answer. "Where's your date?" I ask, trying to give him a hint to leave me the hell alone.

"Actually, I didn't bring a date tonight. I carried one of my clients who loves Alicia Keys, but after the show she decided to leave. So I put her in a cab after Alicia's performance."

I take another swig, nearly emptying my glass, but I start feeling a little lightheaded and place the drink down.

"Are you all right?" Ron questions trying to look dead into my eyes, but I quickly turn my head so he won't see the look of sadness in my eyes.

"I'm cool," I lie.

Ron grabs both of my hands and tries to make me get up.

"Come on, beautiful, let's dance. I think they're playing our song."

"Ron, we don't have a song. You and I don't have anything," I slur.

I try to resist, but to no avail and eventually I just get up and join him. By the time we hit the dance floor the song has changed to Mary J. Blige and Method Man's "You're All I Need to Get By," and this *is* my joint. Whenever Rich and I went to a club or a party and they played this song we would jam hard, so when Method began spitting his lines, I close my eyes and dance as if Ron were Rich. The song after that is hot, as well as the next, and the next. Before long Ron and I are pressed up on each other like all the other hoochies dancing with men who are more about getting their free feels. I can feel his hardness bulging through his slacks and we have been dancing for so long I feel it throb a few times. I try to ignore it, but Ron's dick is too hard to overlook.

"I like the way you dance," Ron whispers in my ear while Jaheim sang "Put that Woman First." "Val, why you be frontin' on a brotha? You know I'm really feeling you, right?" Ron says, which immediately brings me back to reality. Now I'll be the first to admit that Ron is making me feel real good as he holds me close. I haven't allowed another man to rub up on me since Rich and I became an item. My honey pot was definitely hungering for some attention, especially since Rich ain't licked or stuck his fat dick in me all week, but what Ron was suggesting couldn't even happen.

"Ron, stop playing," I say, creating a little distance between us. I look up into his eyes and have to avert my gaze, because he is looking good. *Damn*, I think to myself. "You know I got a man. Why you keep coming at me like that?"

"You got a man . . . then where he at? If he was so concerned about you, he'd be here with you tonight. You wouldn't be up in SOB's with your girl, Gina. Yeah, I saw you enter the spot with Gina earlier. I also saw you over there drinking, looking like you want to be anywhere but here."

The alcohol is definitely wearing off and my senses are quickly coming back, because on the real I am about to punch Ron right in his slick-talking mouth. This man doesn't know me like that and I was getting tired of him passing judgment on me and Rich. I step away from Ron and we are no longer touching, because I definitely need to make myself clear.

"Let me tell you something, and you get this straight." My hands are planted firmly on my hips as my neck snaps left and right and my voice elevates so he can hear me over the music.

"Don't you ever worry about where my man is at! I chose to come here tonight with my girl. You have never ever heard or seen me crying about my man, and that's because he knows how to handle his business. My relationship with Rich is infallible, so I suggest you step the hell off. If you continue to make advances toward me at work I will file a suit against you so fast, you'll wish you never met me. You may think you're the man, but as far as I'm concerned, you ain't special!"

"Val, I'm not trying to disrespect you and I ain't looking for no mess at the job either, so you don't have to worry about me stepping to you at work. But one of these days you'll open your eyes and realize that that man you with ain't shit and don't say I ain't told you so. Cuz as much as you want to deny it, I know things ain't right between y'all. The signs are all there. You moping, drinking, and hanging with your girls instead of your man and all those damn flowers he's sending begging for forgiveness for whatever screwup he did last. I only hope that by the time you wake up from that deep-ass slumber a man is still waiting around for you." He presses two fingers to his lips and kisses them before saying "Peace."

Ron walks off and leaves me standing there alone, and I am too stunned to move. Everybody else is still on the dance floor having a good ole time, oblivious to what has just gone down.

I am furious. Ron has a lot of nerve making that last comment and he really got under my skin. His ego is inflated like a mutha! All those girls he messes with were gassing his head and making him think that he is irresistible. True the brotha looks good, but as far as I am concerned, my man looks even better. I don't even know why I allowed Ron a second of my time. He isn't worth the energy.

Slowly I make my way back over to our table. Gina has returned and is nursing her drink.

"Hey, girl," she said. "You having a good time? I saw you out there getting your groove on with Ron," she says, laughing and nudging me in the side.

"Yeah, I'm good." I don't want my funky mood to ruin Gina's good time. I can always tell her what went down between me and Ron tomorrow. I glance at my watch and see that it is a quarter to one. I'm about ready to go home.

"You ready?" Gina asks me as she looks in her miniature mirror and applies a fresh coat of lipstick.

Those words are music to my ears. I'm glad that I don't have to make the suggestion first.

"Yeah, I'm ready."

"Cool, maybe if I'm lucky, Oscar will still be up waiting for me and we can do the nasty."

"Ugh," I say as I make a face and giggle. The last thing I want is a visual of Gina and Oscar. That was too much information.

"Val please, you wish your man could lay pipe like my husband."

"Gina, I'll take your word for it."

We put our jackets on and exit the club. As the cool night air sweeps across my face I inhale deeply. I try to exhale all of the negative thoughts before heading home. The one thing that I know for sure is that my tomorrow had to be better than my today.

11

❧

Who's Been Sleeping in My Bed?

The ride home is painful as we listen to John Legend talk about
"Ordinary People." It almost feels like he is singing that song on
behalf of Rich and his sorry ass. *It seems like we argue every day*
and *I know I misbehaved.* Though right now, that's a huge under-
statement. Rich has royally screwed up this time around, because
Val won't take a backseat for noooooo BITCH!

"Val, girl, what is up with you? I said we're here."

"What?"

"You must be doing some serious thinking, because I said your
name three times before you even answered once. Are you okay?"
Gina asks.

"I'm good. Or at least I'm about to be good. I just got some serious issues to handle with my man."

"I hear that. Well, let a sistah know if you need me to come
upstairs and whoop some ass, because you know I'll do it," Gina
says, laughing.

I open the door and step out of the car. I know Gina means well, but at this time and place, I can't find the humor.

"I'll holla if I need you for anything," I reply as I slam the door.

Gina waits for me to enter my building before she peels off and I am a little bit envious. Oscar never puts Gina through the things that Rich puts me through month after month, year after year. I was starting to feel like Rich's doormat. He walks all over me, comes, goes, and wipes his dirty-ass feet all over making me feel dirty and worthless. Why can't I find someone that cherishes me the way Oscar does Gina? Tears sting my eyes as I enter the elevator and push the button for my floor.

Before entering the apartment I wipe my eyes from the few tears I managed to shed on the way up. Crying seems to be a favorite pastime these last few weeks and I always said that I wasn't going to be one of those weepy women crying over their man. Yet here I was crying over Rich's sorry butt. Maybe Ron isn't such a bad choice and I should consider giving him a chance. The only problem is that I'm not a big fan of getting involved with coworkers, because if the shit started to stink, everyone else in the office would start to smell it and the last thing I wanted was everybody in my business.

When I enter the house, the first thing to hit my nose is the smell of my favorite scented oil, Ecstasy. The table is set for two and I can see the candles have been lit, because they are melted partway. An open bottle of wine is chilling in a bucket and a glass has been used. My curiosity is piqued. As I walk farther into the apartment I can hear Luther Vandross crooning, "A House Is Not a Home" and the light from the bedroom creeps through the crevice.

What the? I know this man didn't lose his mind and bring that skank up in our house? He has to have better sense than that. Now Rich has gone too far and tonight will be his lucky and possibly last night on this earth.

I lay my keys and purse on the sofa table and head into the kitchen to get the butcher knife, which I had sharpened a few days earlier. The silver blade gleams as I hold it before me while walking back in the direction of the bedroom. Luther's song ends and is replaced by soft moaning. Then I hear Rich's voice, a slapping sound, and more moans mixed in with grunts. *Oh hell no,* I think to myself, *this muthafucka is not disrespecting me by bringing this broad to our house.* This tramp was going to feel a lot more than my size-seven shoe in her behind, because as far as I'm concerned she's trespassing and trespassers usually get shot. Unfortunately, I don't have a gun.

For a moment I think about calling Gina so she can turn around and help me give this hoochie a good old-fashioned beat down, but this situation is embarrassing enough. Gina knows the majority of the things that went down between Rich and me, but she doesn't need to see it firsthand. And at the end of the day, I don't feel like hearing her famous last words, yet again.

My heart races so fast that I just know it would jump out of my chest and open the bedroom door for me. Just before getting to the door, I stop and say a quick prayer. I want to receive forgiveness before committing any murderous acts. God knows my heart and He knows that I am at my wit's end. This type of stuff would drive any sistah out of her mind.

When I turn the knob, I brace myself to expect the worst. But I damn sure wasn't expecting to witness what I see. Rich is lying on the bed butt naked and he didn't notice me enter the room. He is so engrossed with handling his business and I am so caught up in watching him that I don't draw away his attention. I become a voyeur gazing at Rich while he slowly and methodically strokes himself and watches a DVD that we made together a few months back. The moaning and spanking I heard earlier was us on the video.

My body heaves a sigh of relief, but my heart continues to race. I drop the meat cleaver, which hits the floor with a thud and Rich switches his attention from the screen to me. My lips ache for his touch, because it definitely has been a while since he broke me off some.

Rich wags his finger for me to come to him and I happily oblige and a piece of clothing is removed with each step.

His love juices cover the head of his penis, making it smooth and sticky to the touch. I replace Rich's hand with my mouth and allow my tongue ring to massage his dick. Within moments, Rich pulls my legs onto the bed so he can bury his head between my slickness. Now I'm facing the television and have a clear view of Rich on the video and I become so aroused.

Rich doesn't waste any time pulling me onto his dick and I ride him backward. The full length of his shaft is entering me and it's both painful and blissful. If I have to endure this all night I would, but then Rich bends me over and is banging me with force, causing his big soft balls to rub against my clit. I feel myself losing it again. Rich spoons me and holds my breasts as they jiggle. My nipples harden under his touch and he softly caresses them.

"I'm cumming," I scream.

"Wait . . . wait for me," Rich exclaims. "I'm . . . I'm . . . oh umm.

V . . ." Rich's body jerks. Soon after his body slumps on mine and his full weight lays on top of me.

Eventually Rich rolls over and pulls me into his embrace. It feels so good to be in his arms like this again. I can't believe I was tripping earlier. What would make me think that Rich would be stupid enough to bring some ho into our house? I spy the knife on the floor and feel like a complete fool. I want to pick it up before Rich spots it. I don't feel like having to explain why I entered the bedroom with a butcher knife.

"What took you so long to get home?" Rich asks.

"I went to SOB's with Gina."

"Word! Who performed?"

"Alicia Keys. She was nice on the keys and the mic tonight."

"Damn, and you couldn't bring your man?" Rich asks as he slaps my ass for effect.

Smiling to myself, I don't respond immediately. I choose to marinate in the moment and enjoy the sting of Rich's palm against my ass. He knows this is a major turn-on for me.

"What, you not gonna answer?" Rich slaps my ass two consecutive times.

"Don't start nothing you can't fulfill," I state.

"Oh, and you know I can tear this up a second and third time. So the question is can you handle what I'm fixin' to give yo ass?"

"Negro pleez!"

"A'ight," Rich says and I feel him rise to the occasion again.

"I'm surprised you have the strength." As soon as the words leave my mouth I regret them. If I want everything to stay good with us it would be best if I didn't stir the pot in the wrong direction.

"What is that supposed to mean?" Rich asks.

"Nothing," I answer quickly, sorry I ever opened my mouth.

"Nah, don't give me that. You definitely meant something."

I want badly to retract my statement and set things right between us again. There really is no point in arguing, because it would only put a larger wedge between us and the last thing I need is to push him into another woman's arms. Especially that trick Vanessa's arms. "Why can't we just go back to lovemaking? I don't want to argue anymore. What's important is that you're here with me. Okay?"

Rich is still looking at me strange, but I see the fire of rage in his eyes dying down as my words douse out the flames.

"You lucky I don't feel like arguing either," Rich replies. "I came home all early and whatnot to see my woman and you wasn't even here to celebrate with me."

"Celebrate what?" I ask, rubbing my hand slowly across his chest and snuggling my head in the crook of his arm.

"It's a little premature, but word on the street is that I may get promoted to vice president."

My squinty eyes become wide and my heart races with each word that spills out of Rich's mouth. I can't believe that my man is about to make vice president. I knew he could do it and I'm going to be right in the passenger seat when it happens too.

"Stop lying," I say as I sit up to look into his face.

"Now why would I lie about something like that?"

"I'm just saying? Damn, that's hot, baby. This is what you've wanted all your life and you know you can do this, right?"

"No doubt and Vanessa has been holding my hand the entire way."

"What?" Rich's use of *Vanessa* and *holding* in the same sentence doesn't sit well with me.

"Stop trippin'. I told you from the go there was nothing going on between me and her. She's like a big sister to me. From day one all she's tried to do is school a brotha on the ins and outs of da business. That's it," Rich says.

"School you, huh? Is that what they call it now?" Absolutely amazing. I can't believe Rich is going to lay here while I'm in his arms and flat-out lie.

"Val, I'm telling you ain't nuthin' going on between me and ole gurrl. Remember, it's only a few of us at Jorge Jacobs, so we have to look out for each other. You are my world and don't you ever forget that," he says, nudging my chin.

"Rich, just some words of caution, ain't nuthin' out there free, so if you think this Vanessa doesn't have something up her sleeve, you're the one that's really trippin'. Now I need you to tell me that there is absolutely, positively nothing going on between you and her."

Looking Rich dead in his eyes I'll be able to detect if he is being truthful or not. If he blinks twice while answering or fidgets I'll know he is lying, and if he does both . . . I am in deep trouble.

Instead, Rich raises his head to look directly at me and presses his soft sumptuous lips against mine and we share the most sensuous kiss I have ever experienced. My body tingles, my nipples become erect, and my pussy begins to pulsate. I want Rich all over again. His thickness rests in my hand and I begin to caress it back to life and am about to devour him with my mouth. However, he pulls away, turns to the nightstand, and reaches for an envelope that's on top.

I hadn't noticed the envelope before, but Rich passes it to me and waits for me to open it. I stare at the envelope for a few seconds as if whatever is inside will reveal itself without my having to undo it.

"Val, open it already. What you think . . . it's laced or something?"

"No, I was just curious," I answer, finally ripping the side seam of the paper.

Inside are two plane tickets to Cancún in my name and Rich's along with a reservation sheet indicating the hotel where we will be staying and the list of amenities. My heart comes to a full stop and misses a beat. I can't believe this man. Rich and I have never ventured outside of the country, so this comes as a big surprise. We have been to Miami, the Poconos, Atlantic City, Atlanta, and Chicago on a business trip, but never outside of the USA.

"Cancún. Rich, you got us tickets for Cancún, Mexico?"

"That's right. We're about to be international up in this piece, but look at the date."

"Oh snap. That's our anniversary weekend. Rich, I can't believe you remembered. You're really going all out for us this year?"

"Val, I never forget our anniversary, but this year I want to do things right. You feel me?"

"Yeah, I feel you," I say, returning to my position in his arms as he runs his fingers through my hair. We made it to ten years. Even with all the haters, we are still together and we'll always be together.

I am starting to feel all emotional and tears are promising to roll out of my eyes. Before they can fall, I hug Rich tighter than ever and he embraces me with the same intensity. The love is all around and I want us to feel like *this* all the time.

Damn, just when I thought I was gonna have to put my foot up his ass, he goes and does a complete one-eighty on me. How in the world could I ever doubt his love? Maybe this trip is our little retreat and we can set a wedding date that will actually take place before the year ends. I guess all hope is not lost and that Vanessa trick can kiss my everlasting backside, because this chick ain't going no-damn-where!

12

❧

Bon Voyage... NOT!

"What's this I hear about you requesting a week off?" Vanessa's voice was stern and a bit annoyed. She didn't want to display too much emotion for it truly wasn't her style, yet the thought of the two of them venturing off to some secluded place for whatever reason bothered her to no end. "And don't act like I haven't noticed you skipping out early this past week. What the hell, Richard?" Vanessa paced back and forth around her office.

"Listen Richard, I don't know what you're trying to pull here going on vacation or what have you, but we have a lot of work to do before the month's end. Not to mention the little matter of us. Your cake is about to be cut off, so the thought of you having it and eating it too is over."

Vanessa hung up the phone disgusted. She hated Richard's attempt to entertain two women; she was far too much of a woman to share one man. Things hadn't gotten that bad out there that she needed to waste her time with a man who had the baggage of another woman. She was better than that. A woman of her caliber demanded to be a man's one and only and this Val character was definitely cramping her style. Vanessa had played the game of cat and mouse for months now, primarily because the bigger picture was the VP position, yet she wasn't about to continue to compromise her standards. Especially if it meant she would knowingly be the other woman.

Vanessa twirled around in her office chair. She had to think of something to stop this trip from happening. She knew that this trip could potentially be catastrophic if it were to transpire fully. They couldn't share precious moments together at her expense.

"Cynthia."

"Yes, Ms. Knight!"

"Get Mr. McDougal on the line."

"Should they ask what this is regarding—" Cynthia couldn't finish her sentence before Vanessa interrupted.

"Inform him that I've just come up with a strategy that will allow the merging of McDougal Magazines and QT Clothing. Leave the rest up to me."

"Yes, ma'am."

Vanessa plugged through her computer in search of the QT Clothing file. She knew that it was a project that was dear to her heart and had millions written all over it. She also knew McDougal Magazines was looking for an exclusive endorsement of a project and mentioned a few months back in *Women's Wear Daily* that they had a strong interest in becoming investors for a new line. Even though this was her pet project, one she vowed only to use when it was absolutely necessary, she knew it was just the thing that would lure Richard back from his so-called vacation.

"Ms. Knight, Richard is on line two for you."

Vanessa thumbed her desk for a moment then responded, "Tell him I'm on another call and will have to call him back. Oh and

Cynthia, just FYI, I'm going to be unavailable to him for the en-tire day. If necessary, I'm out of the office, okay?"

"Are you going to be out of the office today, Ms. Knight?"

"Only to Richard . . . that will be all Cynthia."

Vanessa smiled. She didn't have time to get into an argument with Richard this morning. She was going to be far too busy draft-ing the proposal and plotting the way to spoil his trip. She thought to herself again . . . then picked up her phone.

"Company travel, please. Hi Louise, I'm wondering if you have any trips booked for Richard Washington for next week. I was told he had booked a trip and wanted to surprise him with a pos-sible upgrade on something if it's not too late."

"One moment please." There was a short silence while Louise looked for a reservation. "Aah yes, I have a reservation for a Mr. Richard Washington right here traveling to Cancún, Mexico. Ms. Knight, you can definitely upgrade his accommoda-tions since Mr. Washington's reservation for two is the standard package."

Vanessa smiled and thought to herself, she was the only first-class woman in his life . . . and trip or no trip, she planned on being the last.

"I'd like to request a bottle of your best champagne to be placed in their room when they arrive. Please make sure the card reads, 'Always Here, Vanessa'."

"Aah, that's nice. Would you like to add any other amenities?"

"No, that would be all for now. However, if it's possible to send me a copy of the itinerary so should I desire to send any more gifts, I will know how to proceed."

"Will do, Ms. Knight."

"Thank you so much. I will be calling you soon to plan my

annual trip to Aspen. I'm not sure if my parents will be joining me this year. I may have another traveling companion."

"Sounds like someone may be in love."

Vanessa chuckled aloud. "No honey, I don't do love, I just do whatever is necessary to take me to the next level."

"Well you go, girl."

"On that note, I'm going to go. Thanks again."

Vanessa shifted her eyes back to her computer screen and began typing away at the McDougal proposal. She was on the brink of getting everything she'd ever wanted. Although she contemplated whether or not to share her top-secret file with Richard, drastic times called for drastic measures, and this by far was pretty damn drastic.

"Ms. Knight, Stephen Douglas is on line two for you."

Vanessa pursed her lips together, sighed aloud, and then exhaled. Why should Richard be the only one having his cake and eating it too? She was slipping on her A game and it was time to rebound and turn the table back around. The nerve of Richard to plan a trip with that holiday girl was too much. If nothing else Stephen would give her just the edge required for immediate gratification after Richard's little vacation stunt. Two could play at this game . . . and with Vanessa, she always played to win.

"Stephen, honey. How are you?"

"The better question is how are you? I've been in trial all week, but still managed to call you every free moment I had."

"I know, babe, but I've just been so busy. I want to make it up to you though."

"Really, how?"

"Meet me at my apartment around nine tonight. Let's just say I'll let my actions speak louder than my words."

"You'll get no arguments from me," he teased.

"Good. So, tonight at nine," she confirmed.

"I'll be there. I love you."

Vanessa hated when Stephen said that to her primarily because it reminded her of what she had had with Dexter. Since his death, Vanessa made sure she kept herself guarded from any semblance of love. With every step Stephen took in moving their relationship forward, Vanessa made sure to throw herself into her work or some other project, making herself completely unavailable and pushing their relationship several steps back. Richard was the perfect distraction. As long as Richard was in her life, she didn't have to focus on loving Stephen. Vanessa knew that until her heart healed, there was no room for love, not from Stephen, Richard, or anyone.

"Listen Stephen, I've got to run . . . work, work, work . . . I'll see you tonight."

Vanessa hung up the phone, eyes still on the prize. She refused to buy into the whole love thing. Love was for losers, and if there was anything Vanessa didn't do, it was lose.

13

Not About You, All About Me!

Stephen made his way into Vanessa's bedroom. His blue jeans and dark gray sweater covered his six-two frame perfectly. He stood in the doorway with a little light blue box in his hand and smiled as he looked at Vanessa.

"Well, I thought we were having dinner," Stephen said as he blushed profusely.

"I thought I'd spoil your appetite by giving you dessert first."

Vanessa could tell that Stephen was impressed with what she'd done. The aroma of dinner drifted through the house, but the scent of vanilla masked the smell, as Stephen got closer to Vanessa.

"I brought you something." Stephen extended his hand. The small box had a Tiffany's label on it.

"Oh, Stephen, you shouldn't have." Vanessa smiled.

"Allow me." He slowly opened the box exposing the delicate silver and diamond necklace. The shiny silver glistened against the turquoise velvet lining of the box.

Stephen softly clasped the necklace around her neck. The diamond key charm necklace brushed against her skin.

"Now, Ms. Knight, you have my attention, as well as the key to my heart."

Vanessa tried hard to hold back her annoyance. Stephen was pathetically sweet, and she needed only to do him. No emotion and definitely none of this tear-jerking drama. She pulled Stephen down on the bed, placing his chest against her bosom, and began kissing him. In between kisses, she whispered, "Thank you for the necklace, but baby, let's not talk." She straddled him, and lifted him toward her as she removed his sweater. She forced the position of his kisses from her lips to breast, then to her stomach, then thighs. Once she had him where she wanted him, she opened her legs wide, allowing him full access to her body.

As Stephen began kissing Vanessa's vagina he made sure not to miss a spot. Her mind wandered as he kissed then licked her clit. Vanessa moaned with anticipation, as Stephen fondled her with his touch and tongue. Then slowly and softly he blew between her legs. Vanessa moaned intensely as Stephen gave her the ultimate oral pleasure. After a few minutes, Vanessa's body fell limp. She watched as Stephen placed her legs gently down from behind his shoulders. His smile assured Vanessa that he knew he had accomplished his mission with her. Vanessa turned onto her side, and watched Stephen as he went into the bathroom. As he began to freshen up, the aroma from the kitchen wandered up the stairs.

"Umm, something sure smells good," Stephen proclaimed as he continued to freshen up. "After you, I'm not sure I have much of an appetite left," he teased as he reached for the mouthwash and poured a small cup.

"You were great. I definitely needed to relax," Vanessa responded, halfway paying attention to his compliments of both her and the food that was heating. "Dinner is in the oven. You do want to eat, don't you?"

Vanessa focused on Stephen as he gargled. She noticed Stephen's expression as he swished from one cheek to the other. His eyes displayed confusion as if he wasn't sure if he wanted more from her or was cool with what he had just gotten.

Vanessa plopped back on the bed with her eyes toward the ceiling. With one big spit, she heard Stephen rinse out his mouth and waltz back into the bedroom.

"Dinner can wait, I want some more of you," he said flirtatiously as he spread her legs preparing himself for round two.

Vanessa's stomach turned as she lay in the bed staring at Stephen while he slept. She felt nauseous as the words *I love you* echoed in her mind. Although she never verbally said those words to him, she knew if anyone deserved to hear them from her it was him. This thing with Richard had gotten completely out of hand, making this little love triangle even more difficult for Vanessa to handle. She wasn't raised to sleep around and she made it a rule to never entertain more than one lover at a time. When Richard was promoted to co-director, Vanessa felt it necessary to open her bag of tricks and do whatever it took to gain full access to Richard's every thought—both personal and professional. How the manipulation of sex had turned into the potential of something more was beyond her imagination. And at the moment, she felt as though she was completely losing control.

As a child Vanessa had been bred to meet and marry well. She learned firsthand, from her mother, how to manipulate men—or anyone, for that matter—in order to get what she wanted. Even though her mother had everything, more was always all that mattered.

"It's necessary to learn, dear," Vanessa reminisced back to her mother's birds and bees conversation with her at sixteen, *"the value of being a woman. For what lies between your thighs is power. You never know when you'll need to use your power to put you into position, but it's very important to remember the purpose of your power is to gain and maintain control. People in control never lose control. Allowing yourself to fall in love lessens your ability to maintain control. Only when you know for sure he's truly worth it . . . do you let yourself fall . . ."*

Vanessa stroked her hands against his cheek and turned her body in the opposite direction. Lying still, her mother's words echoed in her mind. As she closed her eyes trying to force herself to sleep, she felt empty. Her eyes opened as she positioned herself on the bed looking up at the ceiling. Tears formed in Vanessa's eyes as she thought about all the love lost in her life. Not due to breakups—she never was one to have a lot of relationships—but from her need to be in control. Because of her mother. Vanessa thought more of the loves she had rejected out of fear. As she brushed the tears from her face she realized that her tears weren't totally about her mother. They were really about what she lost when the one man she loved died. In a flash, her sadness turned to anger.

"You promised to never leave me. You told me you would love me forever. I trusted you, and you lied to me. I needed you and you abandoned me." She whispered under her breath with hopes of not waking Stephen.

She turned and hugged Stephen tightly. Stephen wasn't Richard, and Richard surely wasn't Dexter, but for the moment Stephen made her feel safe and not alone. She felt his hand touch hers. His body was still and his breath was soft against her skin. Vanessa pressed her body close to his, wrapping her free arm around his waist. She closed her eyes again, hoping that the comfort she felt with Stephen would allow her to temporarily forget the pain she felt for Dexter. It was hard because Stephen reminded her so much of Dexter. Stephen was smart, came from a good family, and was a successful attorney. Vanessa couldn't fathom the thought of actually allowing herself to fall for Stephen and then having something happen to him like it did with Dexter. The thought of losing in love again was unbearable and something she couldn't risk happening. What if Stephen decided to leave, or that she wasn't enough woman for him? Vanessa let out a big sigh. Those were crazy thoughts. She knew she was more than enough for any man. But the thought of becoming vulnerable again scared her.

Vanessa tried like hell to avoid her conscience; she'd mastered it for many years since Dexter passed away. When it came to her thoughts of him, her tough exterior was all a façade for her scarred interior. Enough! The hell with it. Life was what it was. And if it took Richard or Stephen to fill the void of Dexter, she'd vowed to regain control by any and every means necessary.

14

The Last Straw

This week has been one of the happiest weeks of my life. No one and nothing could possibly bring me down from my high. My Richard is back. He came home at a reasonable hour every day this week and even took me to the Lobster Box on City Island after work one day. He also called me every day at work just to say hello, which is something he hasn't done in a while and today he dropped by to take me to lunch. I guess it's safe to say Rich realizes the grass gets just as brown on the other side too!

I can't believe that Rich and I are finally taking a vacation outside of the country. Now this here is the stuff that I've been talking about. I don't know why I've been stressing so hard lately allowing that deranged bitch to blur my vision. Rich has and will always be mine, and no one could blame me for overreacting, because even a night owl could see in broad daylight that Rich is a great catch.

Things couldn't be better between Rich and me. I mean ever since he showed me those tickets to Mexico, we haven't been able to keep our hands off of each other. We've been busier than rabbits. Hell, he even caught me off guard a time or two, but a sistah is always prepared for her *grande papi*. There is no possible way he could find the energy to bone some other broad. Not the way he's behaving. It appears he is definitely making up for lost time, because the week before we were definitely experiencing a drought. The land was arid and feeling neglected, but now it's receiving plenty of fertilizer and love.

The day after Rich told me about our vacation, I decided to go on a little shopping spree and my man surprised me again by giving me a wad of cash to splurge. Shortly after Rich rose up off the cash, I called Gina and all I had to say was "Woodbury Commons" and my girl responded, "I'll be ready in an hour."

An hour later I'm in front of Gina's house blowing the horn. Two minutes later Oscar opens the door for his queen and waves hello to me and I do the same. As Gina is about to exit, Oscar draws her back in and gives her one of the juiciest kisses I have ever seen. My beautiful goddaughter comes in between them and pushs her little head out to wave and say hello. Any other time I would get out of the car to give her a big hug, but I don't want to intrude on the lovebirds who are still tonguing down like teenagers in the back stairwell of a school.

I roll down the window. "Get a room," I yell and laugh.

They finally part lips and Gina stoops down to give Ashley a kiss on her forehead and saunters down her porch steps like she is walking on cloud nine. As she walks, Oscar's eyes remain glued to Gina's ass, while he smacks his lips like she was the last supper. That right there is what I call true love in rare form. It's different from my relationship with Rich, and there is no doubt that he loves me—but our love isn't what most would consider traditional. Our love is much more complicated and dramatic.

I quickly unlock the door for Gina's grand entrance.

"Damn, girl," I say when she sits down and straps herself in. "Do y'all ever take your minds out the gutter? I mean damn, you gonna turn my goddaughter into a freak if y'all don't learn to control yourselves in front of her or you gonna end up with ten more little Ashleys."

We both laugh.

"Val, don't hate. My daughter will be raised to know what love and affection is. We teach her right from wrong and she'll grow up with the knowledge that sex is okay when it's with your husband or the one you love."

"If you say so, cuz as long as y'all allow her to watch the sin box they call television and let her attend public school, society will surely tell her otherwise. But I ain't gonna lie, if more parents took the initiative that you and Oscar take to raise their children, half of them wouldn't be locked up or living the grimy type of lifestyle they out there living today. You feel me?"

"True indeed," Gina says, nodding her head to me and the radio. "So what's this about you and Rich going to Mexico?"

"Gina, don't look so surprised. It ain't like me and Rich haven't traveled together in the past."

"That's not what I'm saying. This is just so sudden and that's not like Rich. He's not spontaneous, but I'm happy you're finally going somewhere other than the freaking Essence Music Festival. That ain't no real vacation. That's like going to Atlanta for Freaknik—damn old-ass people trying to recapture their youth."

I can't help but bust out laughing. Gina is so right.

"Don't get me wrong, Essence use to be the bomb back in the nineties, but ever since those teenyboppers and barely twenty-one-year-olds started attending it ain't been the same."

We chat the rest of the way and I fill Gina in on the stuff that has been happening with me and Rich, including cutting up Rich's suits and him stepping in at all times of the morning. She plays the role of supportive friend, but I can read her face and though she doesn't want to step on my happiness, I know she wishs I'd leave Rich the heck alone.

Traffic sails smoothly for the majority of the trip and within an hour and a half we are pulling up in the Woodbury Commons parking lot. Three hours later our hands are filled to capacity with bags from Dolce & Gabbana, BCBG, DKNY, Juicy Couture, bebe, and Guess. I don't plan on bringing any of my regular clothes with me to Mexico, only my new purchases. My wardrobe is going to be hooked up and before the weekend ends I plan on getting my hair weaved so I can go swimming without messing up my 'do. And right before we leave, I'll get a manicure, pedicure, and a bikini wax. Hell, I may just trim the entire pussy. This way Rich can get a better view while he licks my plate clean.

By the time I get home, I'm exhausted. It was my hope that Rich would be home so I can model my new gear for him, but he is nowhere to be found. I need to rest up anyway, because knowing him, as soon as he comes home, he'll want some of my goodies.

The week couldn't go by fast enough. Things remained good between me and Rich all week. He came home every night at a reasonable time and I made sure to get home early enough to have dinner prepared. This is something I used to do every night when we first moved in together, but eventually our schedules got hectic and we started eating out regularly. Home-cooked meals were a thing of the past, but this week I wanted Rich to know that he was and would always be my king. Most women know that the way to a man's heart is via his stomach and some good pussy.

Our flight was scheduled to depart at 8:32 P.M. Friday night. We left work a little early in order to get our luggage and catch a cab to the airport. We decided it would be less hectic to take a taxi instead of driving around searching for parking in those big lots. We had packed days before, so when we got home from work all we had to do was retrieve our bags and say *adiós* to the Big Apple.

Since we had all of the correct paperwork, check-in at the airport went smoothly, though I didn't enjoy having to remove my shoes or my jacket. I didn't have on any socks and had to walk on that disgusting plastic runner and since we're going to Mexico, I wore a skimpy lace top, which was quite revealing. Aside from that, it was all good.

Once we are seated on the plane, I hold Rich's hand tightly. It isn't that I'm afraid of flying. It's the takeoff that bothers me. My stomach always flutters and my ears pop, but once we are in the air I learn to love the friendly skies.

The flight is only half full and Rich and I are fortunate enough to have a row to ourselves. My head is comfortably resting on my man's shoulder and I have the biggest grin on my face. This is the vacation I have always dreamt about. Just me and my man, spending some quality time alone without any interruptions or the hiccups of everyday life. Neither of us will have work on the brain or anything else. Just sex, sex, and more sex.

Rich has made me the happiest woman alive. Just when things were starting to get crazy between us he saves the day and possibly our relationship. It's little things like this that show me how much he really does love and value our relationship. I never thought I'd utter these words, but I was starting to fear the worst for us.

My thoughts are interrupted as Rich begins to guide my hand

to his man-handle. Surprisingly it is already erect. We have only been in the air for about thirty minutes and the seat belt sign is off. I proceed to lift the armrest so I can massage his penis without any interference. His dick begins to get harder and I slip my hand inside of his pants. My nipples begin to pucker as I deftly remove my thong and guide his hand to my love spot. I have always dreamed of getting kinky while flying the friendly skies. When Rich feels my slick center, he whispers, "Baby, can I taste you, right here, right now?" My lips gently part for a low moan. We look down the aisles in both directions to ensure the coast is clear. When we see that the flight attendants are busy at their stations, I hurriedly put the flimsy blanket they provided us over Rich's face as he lays his head in my lap.

Rich traces feathery kisses down my stomach as he makes his way down. While his hands gently caress my hips and ass, his lips and tongue work on my thighs, moving slowly toward my inner lips. The warmth of his breath entices me before his tongue. Finally, his tongue opens me, and he begins to lick me. Rich's tongue works all around, up and down and I know he wants to penetrate me deeper. I spread my legs as far as the seat will allow, offering my entire pussy to his mouth. He focuses his attention to my clit and takes it between his tongue and upper lip, holding it tightly while his tongue delves inside. He tongue laps my clit as if he was taste testing Baskin-Robbins' 31 Flavors.

My breathing becomes labored and my body gets tense. It's difficult to contain myself from bawling in pleasure as I feel the climax building. Rich reads my body language and knows that within seconds I'll be down for the count. My legs begin to tremble and my temples begin to pulsate as my body releases and gushes with pleasure. I use my neck rest to muffle my moans as much as possible.

"Did you like that?" he asks with a huge grin.

"Mmh, what do you think?" I reply, slowly coming down from my high.

The room is breathtaking and I fall in love with it the moment the bellman opens the door for us. Our junior suite at the Omni features a comfortable area with modern/casual furniture, a king-size bed, and is nicely decorated for a pleasant stay. We don't have a deluxe ocean view, but any view from this hotel is beautiful. Most people don't concern themselves with the room, but it's important to me since I plan on spending at least five of our seven-day trip in the room making love to Rich.

Moving forward, I promise myself that Rich and I are going to spend all of our anniversaries in style, living it up on some island or country. Once we tipped the attendant, we both decide to take a nice long shower to finish up what we started in the air. I was unable to return the favor to Rich while on the plane. After Rich took care of me, the flight attendant kept roaming the aisles like she was looking for something and when she got to our row, she stopped. By that time, Rich was just laying in my lap pretending to be asleep. However, she glanced at us suspiciously, which pissed me off, because she was really messing up my groove. I was so horny from Rich's earlier feast that I wanted more. She stood there for what felt like forever, but it was only a few seconds. Finally she asked if we would like a few extra pillows to which we declined.

When we get out of the shower, I notice a nice bottle of champagne chilling on the table. Still naked with beads of water dripping down the center of my back, I saunter over to the place where the bottle sits.

"Rich, look," I say, pointing to the bottle. "Did you order champagne?"

"Nah, but that's probably just some courtesy stuff from the hotel or travel agency. You know I booked this trip through the company agency, so they probably hooked it up."

"Oh. That's nice." I remove the bottle from the bucket to inspect the brand of champagne. I'm not a wine connoisseur, but I know a little something. "Damn, baby, this is Bollinger Blanc de Noirs Vieilles Vignes Francaises, 1997." I probably mispronounced half the words, but I've seen this label on restaurant menus enough to know the price. "This here is more expensive than a bottle of Dom and even rarer. I think I saw this brand on the Food Network and they said something about only importing a few hundred bottles of this stuff to the States a year."

"Word," Rich says while putting on his boxers.

He is looking sexy as ever and pampering his skin when I notice a gift card leaning on the side of the bucket. Just as I was about to bring it to Rich's attention he struts into the bathroom with his shaving kit, which means he will be a while. Jubilantly, I decide to open the card. At first, I don't understand the meaning of *Always here.* Then I read who the card is from. Vanessa!

It's without a doubt that Vanessa is sadistic and I can't understand why Rich can't see right through her schemes. My head throbs as my mind refuses to accept the information I just read and there isn't any medication that can relieve the pain that courses through my body.

My first thought is to march into the bathroom and ask Rich why this woman is harassing us, but he will probably say something lame like she is just being nice. Second, this is our first night in Cancún and the last thing I want is for her to spoil our anniversary, which is tomorrow. Third, I'm starting to feel sorry for her, because obviously if Rich is here with me, he doesn't want her fake ass.

When Rich returns to the bedroom, a serene look covers my face along with a forced smile. My stomach churns and is doing somersaults. My head is ringing, because I want to scream aloud, but I have to quell the urge.

"You all right?" Rich asks. "You look like you just seen a ghost or something." He chuckles. *If you only freaking knew,* I think to myself.

Unable to laugh with him, I maintain the phony smile, but it takes every muscle to look natural. "I'm okay," I say, still clutching the card from Vanessa tightly in my hand. "But I think something I ate on the plane didn't agree with me."

"Yeah, that stuff was kinda nasty," he says, rubbing his stomach. "But a brotha was hungry. Come over here, girl. Let me take care of you." He beckons.

On my way over to him, I chuck the card in the wastebasket and fall into his arms. Vanessa really doesn't know who she is messing with. If she continues her little charade, she'll be receiving a card collection of her own. Namely cards that say *Get Well Soon* or *Our Deepest Regrets.*

Saturday morning in Cancún is truly magnificent. As I lay in Rich's arms, I can see the sun making its debut, and the sound of crashing waves serenades my ears.

It is still early and Rich is sound asleep, snoring lightly. If it wasn't for the excitement I'd be fast asleep too, but I still can't get over where we are. When we got in last night, I couldn't see much of the island, but we'll have more than enough time to check out the area. However, it's not going to be today. Rich and I already said we wanted to laze around for the first two or three days and then we'll go sightseeing, horseback riding, and shopping. Today, the only thing we are going to do is lay our asses on the beach, down some fruity drinks, soak up the sun, and sneak off wherever we can for some outdoor sex.

By ten-thirty, Rich and I have showered and are headed down to the hotel restaurant to have breakfast. Thereafter, Rich is going to rub me down with some suntan lotion so I can get a nice tan and I plan to do the same for him. I wear the sexiest little two-piece bathing suit and on the way out of the room, I have to fight Rich off. He behaves as if we weren't fucking up a storm only one hour earlier. He can't seem to get enough.

When the spread we ordered arrives, we don't waste any time digging in. People walking by probably think we are having a food competition to see who can finish their plate first. In the middle of our meal, a server comes and asks for Rich by name.

"Are you Señor Richard Washington?" the man asks, bathing Rich's name with his Spanish accent.

"Yes. Why?" Rich asks. A concerned look covers his face.

"No, no, sir. You no need to worry. *El teléfono* for you. I bring it here. You sit."

"Okay," Rich says as he nods his head and wipes the corners of his mouth with the napkin. "For a minute, I thought these jokers were gonna tell me some mess like my credit card was declined or they don't have us registered for the whole week."

"For real, right," I answer, enjoying my meal. Since it's only a phone call and nobody died, I continue to eat. No need in letting the food get cold and go to waste.

The man returns with the phone. "Señor, here you go. Just

press that button," he says, pointing to one of the keys. Then he disappears.

"Hello," Richard answers.

"Oh, wassup?" An uncomfortable look sweeps over his face. "Nah, I'm here with Val."

Pause.

"I had to take a vacation, because I was going to lose my time."

Pause.

"Who is it?" I ask, getting annoyed at the caller for intruding on our personal time and asking so many asinine questions, but Richard looks straight past me and pretends not to hear me.

"Nah, I can't do that. Can't you just go ahead and handle that without me?"

Pause.

"Listen, I don't get back until next Friday. Why don't you reschedule for the following week?"

Pause.

I watch as Rich angrily stabs his food with the fork. It's obvious the call is work related, but I'm only able to hear one side of the conversation. I quickly lose interest in my food and try to study the different expressions on Rich's face.

"Why would you do that? You knew I was going to be away," Rich states.

Pause.

"No, I don't want to miss out on that and there's no need to go there either. It would be my biggest account and I don't want anyone else dealing with them."

Pause.

"Yeah, I'll be back. I don't have a choice, do I?" Richard was agitated. "No problem. Don't worry about all that, I always come prepared. Bye."

Rich replaces the receiver onto the base and stares out into space.

"Honey, are you okay?" I ask, trying to console him.

"I'm a'ight," he answers and scratches his head.

"What happened?" I know I need to tread lightly, but I am hella curious.

"It was Vanessa," he answers solemnly.

"What the heck did she want and how in the hell did she know where we're staying?" I ask, not even bothering to hide the contempt in my voice. I am sick and tired of this crazy woman.

"I must've mentioned it in passing," he answers quickly, rushing to get off the subject. "Anyway, apparently the senior vice president of operations and the director of planning and merchandising from Saks is coming to Jorge Jacobs on Monday."

"What?" I bark loudly causing other patrons to stare. "So what does that mean?"

"It means that I have to be back in New York by Monday to show them our new fall line and discuss our plans with them for moving forward."

"Rich, you can't be serious. Why can't they postpone it until you get back?" I already know the answer to that. This is that heifer's way of trying to come between us and spoil our vacation.

"Baby, there's a lot at stake here. If I don't show, I run the risk of being overlooked for the VP position. Baby, trust me, I ain't happy about this either, but at least we get to celebrate for another day and a half," Rich pleads as he reaches for my hand and tries to console me, but I am heated. "Val, I'd rather be here spending quality time with you. Trust me." I want to trust him, but I don't trust Vanessa's motives especially after this stunt and the note. I just want to pull away, because if he hadn't been doing her in the first place, she wouldn't be trying to control his every move like this. I know Vanessa is doing this on purpose. The thought of Rich and me going on vacation is killing her softly, so she had to devise some great plan to get him back.

This only adds more fuel to my fire and Vanessa is about to be toast.

15

Daye Meets Knight

The only thing saving Vanessa from me putting my fist down her throat or my foot up her ass is Jorge Jacobs. Any other chick that tried to disrespect me like Vanessa has been doing for way too long now would've already felt my wrath. Instead of having the time of my life and celebrating ten years together we found ourselves taking part in a puppet show, with Vanessa's hand way up Rich's ass. I can't believe how Rich allowed this woman to manipulate him yet again. The cancellation of the cruise is one thing, but Rich already had approved vacation time and surely this so-called emergency could've waited until his return. Instead he succumbed to the pressure and he allowed Vanessa to interrupt our anniversary.

Rich and I end up flying back on a late flight on Sunday. Pissed off is not exactly how I would describe my feelings. I can't understand the power this witch has over my man's life at Jorge Jacobs.

I know this isn't Rich's fault, so I'm not placing the blame on him. The blame rests squarely on Vanessa's shoulders. Her jealousy is causing her to behave irrationally, I think during our flight back.

Briefly, I thought about staying in Cancún for the remainder of the trip. It was already paid for, so why not? Then a real ugly picture of Vanessa spending late nights with Rich entered my thoughts and I quickly repacked my suitcase. My staying would've given her a golden opportunity to sink her fangs even further into Rich. However, upon my return, I chose to just chill instead of going back to work for the rest of the week. I definitely had no plans to return to the office, because I would've looked stupid coming back so early. Hell naw. I was due a vacation anyway.

Coincidentally, Gina has a doctor's appointment and has taken Tuesday off to go for her annual checkup. Her appointment is in the morning and she'll be done by lunchtime. We immediately decide to have a girls' day in the city.

As we stand in the Blue Water Grill waiting to be seated, I spot Rich at a table laughing it up with Vanessa. Every bit of anger that I've been suppressing over the past few months is about to explode. I can hear her cackling from way across the room. This is my second time seeing her in person, but we have never been properly introduced and I figure it's due time. I calmly make my way over to their table. Gina, who was sitting down, jumped up to follow me, thinking the hostess is ready to seat us.

"Ma'am," the hostess bellows.

I continue to walk toward my target.

"Ma'am, the restroom is downstairs. Your table is not ready yet." She spoke loud enough for all the patrons in the front of the restaurant to hear, but I don't give a damn about some table.

Just as I arrive at their table, it looks like Vanessa is brushing something off Rich's lap. Her hands appear to be a little too familiar with that region of his body.

"Rich!" I snap.

He looks at me, surprised. Vanessa turns as if she were expecting me and smiles. At that moment I could've smacked the smirk right off her face, but I hold back.

"What in the hell is going on here? Why is this bitch's hand in your damn lap?"

Gina, who is now standing at my side, doesn't know what is going on, and it takes her a minute to figure out what is happening. I hear her mumble, "Oh shit" under her breath.

Rich gives me a dumbfounded look, like he got caught with his pants down, but he never answers my questions.

Vanessa looks at me, her smile disappearing. She is starting to look uncomfortable, but I don't give a damn. Seconds later, she stands up and brushes imaginary lint from her barely there fuchsia-colored skirt. She announces that she is going to the restroom, but before leaving the table, she proceeds to give him a quick peck on the cheek. That's when I lose it and when she spins around to walk past me, her face meets my fist. My reflex is so quick and forceful that her head snaps back.

By this time, a small crowd has gathered around us, including a few restaurant staff members. Suddenly a nondescript-looking man, short by my standards, appears and looks me over as if I have done something wrong.

"Vanessa, are you all right?" he asks, consoling her and snapping at the waitstaff to get her some ice for the welt that is forming beneath her eye. Fortunately for her, I'm not the same person I used to be back when I lived in the projects. Otherwise, I would've shanked her ass with a box cutter and that pretty little face would be scarred for life.

Rich also goes to Vanessa's aid, but not before he gives me the nastiest look I've ever seen.

"Ma'am, we have to ask you to leave," the same hostess that harassed me earlier says timidly. She keeps her distance, figuring I am probably some angry black woman, but the only person I'm angry with is Vanessa. Everyone is tripping and sidling up to that tramp, and no one with the exception of my girl Gina knows what is really going on. Hell, I'm in pain too!

"Val, let's go," Gina says, lightly pulling on the sleeve of my blouse. I snatch my arm away from her.

"Yes, Val. I think you should leave too," Rich seconds.

Although I see Rich's lips move and I hear the words come out of his mouth, my brain can not register what he has just said. I am stunned and can't recall the faces of the two people who forcefully escorted me out of the restaurant. Everything feels surreal. However, I do remember the smug look of satisfaction on Vanessa's face.

16

Check and Mate!

I can't believe that bitch just hit me! Vanessa thought to herself as she reacted to the sting that penetrated her face. Even though the shock of the blow was intense, Valentine had played right into her preplanned hand and reacted accordingly. The simple gesture of whispering into Richard's ear before preparing to leave the table was just the cue that was necessary to send the wrong message to a woman named "Valentine," causing her to react just as any typical ghetto girl would—with violence.

"Security!" Vanessa barked. She peered over at Valentine as if her world was just about to end.

Richard, who was now standing at Vanessa's side, ordered Val to leave, which was just the response Vanessa was looking for. Although her face hurt like hell, she had Richard just where she wanted him.

"I want her arrested," Vanessa persisted as she witnessed Valentine being thrown out of the restaurant.

"Ms. Knight, are you okay?" Mr. McDougal inquired with concern. "Who was that person and what's going on?"

Vanessa flipped her long mane, trying to regroup from the blow to the face and regain her composure. Just as she tried to explain, Richard interrupted.

"My sincerest apologies to you both." Richard's words were confident yet sincere. "I'm going through a very difficult separation, and unfortunately that woman was my ex-fiancée. I can't believe she did that." A look of sheer embarrassment crossed Richard's face. "Vanessa," his voice was low, "I'm so sorry."

Vanessa couldn't contain the smile that crossed her face. All she needed to hear was the word *ex*, plus the look on Richard's face and she knew she'd won.

"She isn't taking things well, and I'm so sorry my personal issues have spilled over into my professional life." Richard was mortified.

Both Vanessa and Mr. McDougal empathized with the situation.

"It's good things have ended. I've heard of situations like this becoming violent, but I've never witnessed such a situation firsthand."

"Let's not allow this ordeal to ruin the rest of our afternoon. We should be celebrating." Vanessa motioned for the waiter then requested a bottle of their best champagne. "Gentlemen, if you'd excuse me, obviously I need to freshen up a bit. When I return we'll toast to the deal."

Vanessa reached for her bag, trying to ignore the throbbing of the left side of her face. She prided herself on being pretty, and hoped that whatever traces of today's affair didn't cause much damage. Before entering the ladies' room, Vanessa reached for her cell phone and dialed 911.

"Detective Bridges, please?"

Vanessa dabbed her eye while waiting on a response.

"This is Detective Bridges."

"Dan, hi. It's Vanessa."

"Well, well, Ms. Knight. To what do I owe the pleasure?"

"I wish I could say this was a pleasure-based call, but I need to file a report."

"Is everything okay?"

"No, Dan, that's why I called. I can't have something like this surface to my family. I'll need you to handle this one for me personally and using extreme discretion."

"I got it, but what happened?"

"I was assaulted by a coworker's ex-girlfriend at Blue Water Grill. We were at a business lunch, and I guess she mistook that for something more. Nevertheless, she hit me, and although restaurant security threw her out, I need justice to be served."

"What's her name?"

"Valentine Daye."

"Are you serious?"

"I know, right? She's a complete ghetto basket case."

"Are you soft on him?"

Vanessa changed her tone. "You should know me better than that, Dan. Nothing with me is personal, it's always business . . . Besides, that's not the point. The point is Richard and I have been working on this project for months and that crazy psycho bitch could've jeopardized everything with that little stunt."

"Some things never change."

"And they never will." Vanessa walked into the bathroom and assessed her face. Slight swelling to the eye. Her honey-colored complexion needed a little blush. Nothing an extra coat of Chanel foundation couldn't cover, but other than that she was fine. "Tell me you can handle it."

"Any bruises?"

"Yes, but they'll still be there tomorrow. I'll come in personally and do a formal report and take photos. I want her picked up tonight though."

"I'll check her for priors and see what comes up. Do you happen to know anything else about this Ms. Valentine?"

"Like where she resides, perhaps?"

"Exactly."

"She lives at Two seventy-five Clinton Avenue in Brooklyn."

"How do you know this?"

"Again, Richard and I work together. I know everything there is to know about him."

"And this is business, right?"

"Look Dan, what the hell are you implying? It's not like you to act all juvenile and jealous. We haven't been together since college. Get over it. We had a good time, you were a great lay, and I still like you a lot but you're a cop, so there's no future for us."

"It's always about image with you."

"Image is everything. Speaking of which, I have one to protect. I have to get back to my party. You've got this, right?"

"I do."

"Thank you, love. I'll be in first thing in the morning."

"No problem. See you then."

Vanessa hung up the phone, ran her duster across her face, and shifted her hair back into place. She sighed with slight relief, knowing that her plan had just been fulfilled. She gathered her purse and headed back out the restroom door. As a child Vanessa had mastered the game of chess, having full knowledge that in every move, the queen was to be protected. Just as she had as a little girl, Vanessa thought out every move with precise calculation.

Bishop move left, take the king. With Valentine on her way to jail, Richard was up for grabs.

Vanessa laughed, seeing victory with each blink of her eyes. She peered past the swelling that bubbled the bottom lid, and saw Richard sitting restlessly at the table just left of Mr. McDougal. She knew her plan had worked. Even the most loyal man couldn't withstand this kind of humiliation. Valentine had crossed the line and exposed her queen.

Vanessa swayed back to the table. She defined grace even with a blackening eye. Upon eye contact with Richard, she released a small smile.

"Are you sure you're okay?" Richard rushed up to pull out her chair.

"Of course," she said, taking her seat next to Mr. McDougal. "Forgive me for taking so long."

"It's perfectly understandable," Mr. McDougal said. "How's your eye? It appears to be a little swollen."

Vanessa tried to make light of the situation. "Well, she did take a mean swing. What we won't do for love, right?"

"I'm so sorry about all of this," Richard said, not making eye contact.

"Nothing to be sorry about." Vanessa aided his embarrassment. "If your love ethics are half as wonderful as your work ethics, I would definitely suggest you're a man worth fighting for."

"Here, here," Mr. McDougal concurred.

"I'll drink to that." Vanessa lifted her glass, using her other hand to squeeze Richard's knee.

As he lifted his head as well as his glass, Vanessa could sense his relief. It was her job to make every situation work in her favor. And she knew this afternoon was no exception. As the three of them toasted to the sealing of their new deal, and the continuation of a wonderful evening, Vanessa felt good about her move. With Richard now completely by her side, and Valentine one foot out the door and hopefully the other one on her way to a jail cell, Vanessa had mastered the game once again. Check and mate!

17

❧

I Can Love You Better
Than She Can!

"What the heck just happened in there?" Gina asks after we leave
the restaurant premises.

I'm still in a freaking daze as we walk through Union Square
Park to get to the train station. My hands are tightly balled into
fists as I try to restrain myself from going back into the restaurant
and finishing what I have started. My mind races in a hundred
different directions, but the one thing that stands out most is
Rich's reaction. How could he betray me like that? What have I
done as a girlfriend to deserve or warrant such treatment? My
whole freaking world revolves around Rich. I live, eat, and breathe
Rich. Outside of his mother, nobody and I mean nobody loves
Rich more than me. Not even his sister. Doesn't he know that I
would *lie for ya, die for ya?*

"Val, talk to me, girl. I hate to see you like this. What the hell is
going on? Are you all right? Why was that woman all up in Rich's

face? Did you know he was going to be at that restaurant? Is that the trick that you've been talking about from his job?"

Gina wants to play twenty questions and I'm not in the mood and who can blame me? I just saw the woman who has been threatening my relationship for the past couple of months grop-ing *my man's crotch* and then kiss him right in front of me as if she were me. Then she attempts to walk past me as if this was some everyday occurrence and her behavior was acceptable. I don't think so. I'm Rich's fiancée, not her. Somebody needs to school her and she better recognize or next time it may not be a friendly tap to the face.

While Gina continues to walk and talk to herself, I stop to retrieve my cell phone from my bag. I have a trick up my sleeve for this chick.

"Hello, Aunt Z."

"Who dis?" my aunt Zenobia answers.

"It's Val."

"Oh, wassup, girl? You know I'm at work. Why you ain't call me on the office phone? I can't stand it when my cell rings in the office."

Then turn the ringer off, I think, but don't dare say aloud. "Be-cause I need a favor from you and I know they record the calls that come into your office, right?" Gina finally realizes my ass isn't walking beside her and backtracks to where I stand.

"Sometimes, but it's done randomly. Anyway, what you need?"

"Can you find out where a person lives and the type of car they drive and stuff like that if I give you a first and last name?"

"Yeah, but I may need more than that, like a Social Security number or former address or something more tangible, because there are tons of duplicate names in this system. You should know.

Just take a look in the white pages, so if the person's name is real common it'll be hard to narrow down the search."

"Okay, I know where they work and I have a first and last name."

"Val, you in some type of trouble? What you need this stuff for? Cuz you know I could get fired for giving out confidential information," she states matter-of-factly. Damn, all I need is one little favor, but my aunt never makes things easy for me. I can tell she has left her desk and is probably outside of her office building puffing on a cigarette now.

"Auntie, I'm not in trouble, but you remember that woman who came to church a while back?"

"Yeah. What about her?"

"I need you to do some detective work for me."

"Val, don't be having me caught up in no mess, cuz I ain't trying to lose this here job. I been here too long and worked my way up. Sheeiiit! I can retire in another ten years."

"Auntie, truthfully, if I just follow her on my own, I can get half of the information I'm asking you to get. But I don't wanna turn into a stalker."

"All right now, but only because you my niece. What's her name?"

After I gave my aunt the little bit of information I do know, I feel a hell of a lot better. I don't exactly intend on showing up at Miss Lady's house, but I do want to keep her information handy. I'm more than sure she knows all of our information, so why not vice versa?

"Val, you are going to stop ignoring me and tell me what the hell is going on."

After I flip my phone shut and replace it in my bag, I turn to Gina with an insane smile on my face.

"The chick in the restaurant is who I've been telling you about, Vanessa from Rich's job."

"Well, I figured that much out already, but why do you have that insidious smile on your face?"

"I'm just thinking about payback for ole girl. You know they say it's a bitch! Anyway, never mind me. You saw how she was all up in his face and couldn't keep her hands or lips off of him."

"Well, I didn't see her hands on him, but I did see her all up in his grille. The way she was behaving, you would have thought she was his woman."

"Exactly," I agree. "And that ain't cute. It's downright disrespectful, which is why I cuffed her in the face."

"Val, I wouldn't want to be in your shoes right now."

"Gina, this has gone too far. There is no way Vanessa could known I was going to show up at the Blue Water Grill, but she used the opportunity as prime time to show her ass!"

"I was taken aback and I thought my eyes were deceiving me," Gina says, looking just as perplexed as I feel. "But he was certainly playing along. Maybe they got more going on than meets the eye. This may not be like those other fly-by-night chicks."

"Gina, you had to pull me down from my high, right? Rich loves me and he's not going anywhere. She's just trying to get beneath my skin."

"And apparently she did."

We laugh, but the reality is that this is not a laughing matter. Trying to steal my man is not a joke and the fact that Rich is entertaining Vanessa and now siding with this twit is a serious problem. Still, I don't want Gina to know the seriousness of the situation. Gina doesn't know why we came home from our vacation early. I didn't tell her about the card that Vanessa left in our room either. Even though Gina is my best friend and I can tell her anything, this is not the time for her to play critic.

There is so much on my mind and I've been bottling up all

this anxiety for the past few weeks. No one has ever caused Rich to disrespect or dismiss me the way he did at the restaurant. But it seems that I've underestimated Vanessa and it's time to fight fire with fire.

During the majority of the train ride, we ride in silence. However, Gina is about to get off the A train to transfer for the number 2 train at Fulton Street. She must've been reading my mind, because before she gets up she turns to me. "You gonna be all right?" she asks.

"Yeah. I'm cool."

"How long have we known each other? Your ass is not cool. Why don't you come over to my house instead of going home alone to sulk? I'm still hungry, so let's go get something from one of the Jamaican restaurants around my way and just chill for a while. Oscar won't be home for a minute and Ashley is still in school."

The train doors are about to open, so I don't really have time to think. But Gina is right. I don't want to go home and wallow in self-pity and I don't feel like hearing anything from Rich right about now either. Without much thought, I jump out of my seat and follow Gina off the train.

When we arrive at her house, we sit down and eat our food in silence. The food is good, but I'm not enjoying it much. Instead, I was starting to feel sick.

"Gina, I'll be right back. I need to use your bathroom. I don't feel so well."

Gina barely takes the time to raise her head up from her tray of food. She merely nods and grunts something inaudible.

By the time I enter the bathroom, all the food I've just eaten comes rushing back out of my mouth. A wave of nausea hits me and I collapse holding on to the rim of the toilet seat. My stomach feels queasy and I begin to feel light-headed. I try to regain my balance, and just as I am about to stand I start vomiting again. The force of the vomit causes my eyes to tear. When I think nothing more can possibly come up, I begin to gag and cough to clear my lungs.

"Val." Gina begins pounding on the door. "Are you all right? What's wrong?" she asks, sounding concerned.

I want to let her in, but I am too weak and the door is locked. I try to get up again, but it feels like someone has knocked the wind out of me, so I remain on the floor hugging the toilet for dear life.

"Val. Honey, let me in. Let me help you," Gina pleads.

"Gina, I'm okay. Just give me a few minutes."

"Are you sure? I'm gonna stay right here until you open the door in case you need me. Okay?"

"Okay," I answer.

Two minutes later I am able to pull myself up and flush the toilet. The putrid smell of vomit is overpowering and makes me want to throw up again. After washing my face and rinsing my mouth with the Listerine in the cabinet, I make my way out of the bathroom. Gina is sitting on the floor facing the bathroom door. She quickly stands up to escort me back into the dining room.

"Girl, you had me worried. I was sitting here enjoying my food and I hear you in there choking to death. What happened? The food didn't agree with you?"

"Gina, I don't know what the hell happened. One minute I was feeling fine and then my chest started feeling constricted and I thought I was experiencing indigestion. All I wanted to do was relieve myself, but I didn't expect it to come out of my mouth." I laugh.

"How are you feeling now?" Gina asks as she walks to the

kitchen and retrieves a bottle of water. "You're pale as a ghost. Here, drink this," she says, handing me the bottle. "You're probably dehydrated now."

"Yeah, I feel weak as hell. Damn, I never knew throwing up could take so much energy away from you."

"Go lay on the couch for a while." Gina leads me to the large plush sofa. "Girl, try being pregnant and getting morning sickness. That mess ain't no joke." Gina laughs then she looks at me seriously. "You're not pregnant, are you?" she asks seriously.

"No. Hell, no!" I quickly respond. "The pill is my friend, okay. It's just . . . today was a stressful day and from the moment we left the restaurant I started feeling sick. I think a lot of this stuff is really starting to take a toll on me."

"Well, you have the rest of the week off, so you need to relax. I know it's gonna be hard, but try not to let this get to you like that. The bottom line though, is that you need to talk to your man and figure this whole thing out. For years I've been wondering why you put up with Rich's mess. Don't get me wrong, he's cool as hell, has a good job and is definitely eye candy, but look at how sick this is getting you. All of this on account of a man? Girl, you're like a sister to me. I love you and I don't wanna see no man do you like this."

"I know, Gina. I'm so confused. I love Rich so much though. I just love him sooo much," I say as tears fill my eyes. "Why can't he see that? I would do anything for him. I've been in his corner from jump street and even when he did me wrong I stayed. When he needed money to help his mother with her hip surgery, I worked overtime to help lighten his burden. Remember when he got in trouble for possession a few years back? It was me and Pastor McCash who helped him get off with a slap on the wrist. He could've done up to four years. We've been through thick and thin and we're like blood and he's letting some prissy skank come between us? She doesn't want him. She wants what he's about to get and all of this is just a game to her. I can spot her type a mile away. What pisses me off is that Rich is so blind he's letting Vanessa reel him in hook, line, and sinker."

"Coochie can be blinding," Gina interjects. "You just lucky Rich ain't get sloppy and forget to bag it up from time to time. He could've gotten some chick pregnant or even worse, brought home a disease."

"I thank God for always having my back." I chuckle.

"The only thing I will say is that you can't spaz out over Rich like that. You attack these women and that's just as wrong."

"I know, Gina. I just love him so much and it hurts to see stuff like that. Besides, for once I was right. Vanessa was kissing all up on him and then touching his lap. Really! I don't think so."

"Either way, it's obvious that he's been allowing her to behave this way. He's just not worth it. And more importantly, you've got to love yourself more."

By the time I leave Gina's house I feel ten times better. I end up telling her about all the things that have been happening between Rich and me and for once, Gina isn't judgmental as she listens intensely. She's consoling and it's just what I need.

During the cab ride home, I decide not to argue with Rich and just talk. I will do my best to remain civilized through the entire conversation, because the last thing I want is to cause more friction between us. As it stands, Vanessa is coming off looking like the victim and it's the other way around. I'm the one being stripped naked as she fucks me over to take my man.

The thing is I've been going about this all wrong. After talking to Gina, I can see things a bit clearer and how my actions may have caused Rich some grief today. My attacking Vanessa today only makes me look crazy and I may be a lot of things, but being mental isn't one of them.

The cab driver thinks he is slick by driving slowly and taking the scenic route to my house, but I don't argue. The long ride simply gives me time to clear my head, come to my senses, and see how far off track our relationship is getting. I realize that Rich is the center of my universe and I'll do everything in my power to stay with him, even if that means taking Vanessa out. Literally! Maybe she'll meet an unfortunate fate, which would cause her to have second thoughts about trying to steal my man. It wouldn't take much to devise a plan and I know a few people who would gladly do all the dirty work for me too.

"What is the house number again?" the driver asks.

"Two seventy-five. It's the first large building on the right-hand side." I look at the meter and pull out a twenty for the driver. "You can pull up next to the police car right there." I hand the driver the money, open the door, and hop out.

"Here's your change, miss," he says, handing me back three dollars.

"It's okay. You can keep the change."

It's good to be home. I enter my building and though it's balmy outside, the lobby is pleasantly cool. "Hi Roger," I greet our doorman as I walk in. He is reading a newspaper and puts it down when he hears my voice.

"Good evening, Miss Daye. How are you this evening?"

"Feeling a little bit better," I reply.

"Good for you. Well, my day just started. I'll be here when you leave for work in the morning."

"I have plans to sleep in late tomorrow. This is my vacation week, so you won't see me again until tomorrow night, because I'm calling it a day."

"I hear ya. Well, have a good one." Roger waves as I enter the elevator and push the button for my floor.

My purse is a complete mess and I spend the entire elevator ride rustling through my bag in search of my keys. Just as the door opens, the keys magically appear.

As I exit the elevator and walk toward my apartment door, I see two men standing near my doorway. My first inclination is to get back on the elevator and inform Roger that two strange men are on my floor hovering around my apartment. These men could try to rape or rob me. I don't even know how they could've gotten in since building protocol is to call all residents whenever guests arrive. Then my neighbors, Kenneth and Ellie, step out of their apartment and I become a little more at ease. Certainly they won't try to do me harm in front of witnesses.

My neighbors are real do-gooders and always manage to crack me up. They moved into the building about two years ago. Kenneth is a legal aide for a charitable organization that assists underprivileged individuals who are unable to afford an attorney, but prefer not to be represented by shiftless public defenders; Ellie is an executive director at the New Life Starts Here Homeless Shelter. Both of them are out to save the world one person at a time.

"Hey, Kenneth and Ellie. Where are you two headed?"

"Hi, Valentine," they say in unison. "We're going to ride our bikes and grab a bite to eat. It's a nice enough evening. They said it was going to rain, but the weather's holding up pretty well," Ellie replies. "Then we'll probably feed the birds in the park."

"Oh, well have fun."

They pause to stare at the men standing near my doorway. "Is everything okay?" Kenneth asks as he scrutinizes the men with an impaling stare.

"Are you Ms. Valentine Daye?" one of the men asks as he steps forward.

"Who wants to know?" I ask defiantly.

"I'm Detective Odom and this is Detective Sedinsky." They flash their badges and I read them for confirmation.

Right away, it dawns on me that these men were probably here to deliver bad news of some sort. Why else would they be at my door? *Oh my goodness, is Rich all right? Is my cousin CJ okay?* My heart races with fear.

"Are you Ms. Valentine Daye?" Officer Sedinsky asks again.

"Yes. Yes, I'm Ms. Valentine Daye. Is my fiancé, Rich, okay? Has he been in an accident or my cousin CJ? What happened?" I ask, panicking.

Please don't let anything happen to Rich, I pray silently. *The man gets on my nerves, but he's all I got and want.*

Upon hearing me ask about Rich, Kenneth and Ellie come to my side for support. Ellie takes my hand and squeezes it softly.

"Ms. Valentine Daye, you are under arrest for assault and battery."

"What?" I ask in disbelief. "Assault and battery?" *Oh, hells no!* I think.

"Yes. Charges have been brought against you by a Ms. Vanessa Knight. You have the right to remain silent. If you give up that right, anything you say can and will be used against you in a court of law . . ."

"Oh my goodness," Ellie remarks, her jaw dropping. Her mouth remains open as the officer read me my rights.

Kenneth and Ellie are shocked at the accusations the cops threw at me. My neighbors know me as a law-abiding citizen, who goes to work every day and lives with her fiancé. They aren't privvy to the things that occur behind our doors and it's supposed to stay that way. I don't bother to deny the charges or resist arrest. I don't need anyone else poking their head out because they heard a ruckus. This is embarrassing enough without creating a scene in front of Kenneth and Ellie.

"Valentine, you'll be okay. If you need my services, let me know," Kenneth offers.

"Thanks Kenneth," I say as they haul me off. "I'll be okay, this is just a big misunderstanding. If you see Rich, please tell him what happened and where I am."

"We will."

I really don't know if I'm going to be okay, because this isn't my first offense. However, the other mishaps occurred years before and were misdemeanors. This is the biggest blow yet, but it ain't over 'til the fat lady sings. Vanessa wants to play dirty, well now she is in for one hell of a ride and if I have it my way she will pay with her life.

18

❧

A Little Something
on the Side!

"Vanessa, again, I don't know what to say. I always knew she was
a loose cannon but tonight Val went too far."

Her eye throbbed at the sound of his words. She brushed her
hand against her eye. "I don't want to talk about it."

"Are you sure you don't want me to come home with you tonight?" Richard asked as Vanessa got into her BMW.

"I'm positive," Vanessa said regretfully. She knew Stephen
would be at her place, based on earlier events, and she couldn't
bear taking any chances with Richard when she was so close to
having him all to herself. "Are you going home?"

"No, I'll get a room or something. I can't deal with that or her
anymore tonight."

Vanessa was careful with her words. She knew what to say, how
much to say, and when to say it. "Get some rest. I know it's been
a long day for you. I'll give you a call tomorrow." She batted her

eyes as she rolled down her window and closed the car door. "You did a wonderful job today."

"I want to be with you tonight," Richard pleaded.

"You will soon enough." Vanessa smiled sinfully.

"Why not now?"

"You rest, and plan your next move." Vanessa smiled, and then added, "You can stay a couple of days, until you know what you're going to do. But I won't have you move from one situation to the next without your plans in order. She wore your ring, remember . . . and I don't shack. I don't expect a proposal, but I sure as hell won't tolerate seconds."

"What the hell do you mean, seconds?"

"All I'm saying is that we need to create our own situation. Listen Richard, now isn't the time to talk about this. Get some rest. Come over tomorrow and we'll take it from there, okay?"

"Yeah, a'ight."

Vanessa motioned him close to her and kissed him softly on the lips. "Good night, love."

Vanessa placed her car in gear and drove away. She hated not having Richard come home with her, but she also knew that that's how it had to be for tonight. How the hell she was going to explain her eye to Stephen was beyond her. She really didn't know how she was going to explain it to her parents, who would be at the charity event tomorrow night.

She knew she had to cancel, and send Stephen back home. The only reason he was staying with her was because it was convenient for him to not have to travel from Jersey the day of and Vanessa knew that if he were to escort her to the charity event, he'd need to be easily accessible to her.

She pulled up to the door of her building and got out of the car. She left it running for her valet Rodney to take down to the parking garage.

She entered the glass revolving door of the building almost dreading the welcome that awaited her. Vanessa knew she shouldn't have continued to lead Stephen on but didn't quite know how not to. Stephen was her insurance just in case things went wrong with Richard.

No, she didn't love him, but she could tolerate him enough to do what she needed to with him. As she entered the elevator, she knew what awaited her on the other side.

19

In Jail Without the Bail

"No this home wrecker didn't," I say aloud as I laugh to myself. Officers Odom and Sedinsky are busy shooting the breeze and guffawing as if my ass weren't cuffed up in the backseat and headed to jail. Things couldn't get any worse and I couldn't sink any lower. I still can't believe what is happening to me. Jail? This has to be some kind of sick joke. I bet if Rich knew what his little sneaky-ass princess did now, he'd leave her alone.

There was a time when nothing or no one came between me and Rich, not even those tired-ass broads who couldn't find their own man, but these past few months have been a living hell and the temperature just keeps rising.

Once we arrive at the police precinct they don't waste any time placing me in a ten-by-ten holding cell with three other people who for whatever reason are cuffed to the wall. I must admit, for a hot second, I was scared of what type of crimes they may have committed, but then I realize they are chained to a wall and can't mess with me. However, if these people are considered some kind of threat, they shouldn't place me in here with them. It isn't as if I was a flight risk or a menace to society. Besides, this assault charge is only a misdemeanor. I'll be in and out of this hellhole in less than two hours, because they have no real reason to keep me here. Ms. Priss Bitch has proven her point, and I sure as hell have a point to prove as well. However, moving forward I have to be smarter about my attack.

After the fingerprints and mug shots were completed they placed my ass back in the holding cell. Fortunately, the three who were in there earlier are now gone and I am alone and have plenty of time to devise a plan for Vanessa's demise.

"Guard, guard!" My fingers are tightly wrapped around the cell bars. Two minutes after yelling at the top of my lungs someone finally decides to come to my aid.

"Is all of this noise really necessary? What the hell is wrong with you back here?" a petite but stocky female officer asks, mustering up an attitude. "Ya need to calm the hell down. Now what is your problem?"

"I've been in here for over two hours and I haven't been allowed to make a phone call, go to the bathroom, nothing! What's taking them so long?" I ask, trying my best to suppress my anxiety and anger. The last thing I need to do is piss her or any of these asshole police officers off.

"Listen, you have to go before the judge and you already missed your opportunity for night court. I'll try to get you your phone call, but that's it."

"What do you mean, I have to go before a judge and I missed my opportunity? Why? Assault is only a misdemeanor charge."

"While you were getting your fingerprints and mug shots taken they came to pick up the other riffraff that was here earlier and took them down to the court. Now, I'm not going into a debate with you, but I'll arrange for you to get your call."

"So how long do I have to stay here?" I ask, exasperated. This revelation hit me like a ton of bricks. *Why is this happening?*

"Oh, your ass will be here at least 'til morning."

"Hell, no. Y'all can't keep me in here until the morning. I should be able to be released on my own recognizance," I say, raising my voice.

"We can and we will. Wait here . . . oh my bad." She stops to laugh at her own joke. "You ain't got nowhere else to go," she says as she laughs and walks out of sight.

Bitch is just mad that she looks like a man, I say to myself as I watch her walk away. Hopefully Kenneth and Ellie have been able to see or make contact with Rich either in person or on his cell phone to let him know my current predicament. Once he finds out where I am he will go ballistic on Vanessa and it'll serve her right. Now Rich will see the type of conniving, twisted, and deranged woman he's dealing with. All I did was give her a little love tap and she's pressing charges? Please, she's lucky I'm not the same person I was ten years ago, because it could've been worse.

The sound of footsteps and laughter are headed toward my cell, so I take a deep breath to prepare myself for whatever bull they decide to toss at me. I realize that to these officers, this is all a game to them. They could care less about the lives of the people inside of the holding cells. To them, we are all guilty until proven innocent and not the other way around.

"Ms. Daye, we are going to open the cell and place these handcuffs on you to take you to an office to allow you your phone call. Okay?" asks the male officer, who resembles a young Michael Jordan. The female officer only sneers at me as she pops her gum and applies her hands to her hips as if that was supposed to intimidate me. We are the same height and on the streets, I could easily take her fat ass.

"No problem," I reply demurely.

When we arrive at the room, which is basically empty sparing a desk, a chair, and a phone, they remove the cuff from one hand and lock it to the chair. They leave me alone as I make my call.

Please be home, I think to myself as the line rings.

"Domino's Pizza. May I take your order? But before I take your order, let me tell you today's house specials."

"What the . . . CJ, stop playing. It's your cousin, Val. Is Aunt Z home?" I ask. My cousin is obviously in a playful mood, but I don't have the time or patience to be a participant in his game tonight.

"What up, cuz. I ain't seen your ass in a while. What's good?"

"Listen, CJ. I really need Aunt Z. I'm in a bit of trouble and I need to talk to her now."

"Damn, is that how you treat a bruh? You could still speak to me. You ain't got to be rude, rushing me and shit. You always were a conceited little bitch. Think your ass too good to conversate with ya cuz? Whatever!"

"CJ, put your mother on the got-damn phone. Any other time I would talk to you, but I'm locked up right now, so forgive me if I don't sound pleasant. Okay?"

"Oh, shit. Word! You got locked up. I thought you had a good job at WFAT? What you got knocked for? Boosting? Oh snap!" CJ drops the phone and I can hear him wailing with laughter in the background.

"Yo, Ma. Ma, pick up the phone. Ma, where you at? Val is on the phone. She got locked up for boosting."

I look at the clock that's directly in front of me, and almost two minutes has passed since I've been on the phone with my genius cousin, CJ, and I only have three more to spare.

"Hello," Aunt Zenobia answers groggily.

"Hey, Aunt Z. I'm sorry if I woke you up, but I'm in a little bit of trouble."

"What kind of trouble? Did you kill that hoochie? Or is that mess CJ's in here hollering about true?" she asks, sounding more alert with each question.

"Listen, I didn't kill anyone, but I wish I had. I need you to call an attorney for me. My girl Gina knows a good lawyer. You still got her number?"

"First off, tell me what the hell you're in for."

"I punched that whore Vanessa in her face."

"Well, if yo ass would've answered my call earlier I could've told you about this shit earlier. If this Vanessa is one and the same, I got some news that will fuck your head up. That woman Vanessa Knight, who works at Jorge Jacobs with your man, is the heiress to Soul Shine. She lives at Seven-forty Park Avenue in a muthafuckin' penthouse."

"Did you just say Soul-fucking-Shine?" My mouth hung open. That can't be right. Vanessa is the heiress to Soul Shine? Soul Shine nearly took Afro Sheen out of business back in the day when they introduced the first no-lye perm to the market and they're still one of the most popular hair care companies in the business. Heck, they even have two magazines, *Soul Tresses* and *EliteWear*. Soul Shine makes barrels of money. They're responsible for holding at least ten trade shows across the country annually under the guise of hair care and Soul Shine is one of WFAT's largest advertisers. Dang, if I were her, I wouldn't even be working. At the same time her parents probably cut her sorry ass off and now she has to work to earn her keep.

My aunt continues with her breaking news story. "Vanessa's father is Justice William Montgomery Knight, the Supreme Court Judge and her mother is Cornelia Elaine Mitchell-Knight, heiress to the Soul Shine Corporation. Girl, if the chick farts you will be left with smogs of money. If she so much as sneezes—*Achoo!* That ain't snot coming out of her nose. That's money. She's rich, bitch!"

"So why doesn't she just buy a man? Why is she so hungry for Rich? He's not even her speed. Shouldn't she be parading around with some high-society prick?" This doesn't make any sense, especially since someone of her status can have anyone, but then again, every lady likes a thug. But this lady better back off!

"Anyway, it looks like I'm gonna be here for the night. They claim that I missed night court, but I'll stand in front of the judge in the morning. Please get me somebody who can get me off. I don't even understand why they're keeping me. Since when did assault become a felony?"

"How many assault charges have you been brought up on over the years? And it depends on the grievance that was filed against you. That broad probably told the cops she fears for her life and is filing an order of protection against you right now. And if she told her father, he can tie you up in the legal system for a minute. Even if the charges are trumped up."

"Your time is up," the female officer reminds me.

"Aunt Z, I gotta get off the phone, but if you can, please get me representation, because this situation could get ugly. I was told I'll be in front of the judge as early as 7 A.M."

"No problem. We love you, girl. Don't let nobody take advantage of you while you're in there." My aunt laughs in an attempt to lift my spirits.

"I'll be all right," I say, trying to convince myself. I'm only in a holding cell. This is a far cry from Rikers Island and I'm alone in the cell. What could possibly go wrong?

My night was messed up. How do they expect people to sleep on these nasty, thin-ass cots? They offered no pillows and probably never changed the sheets. The amenities they offered were disgusting. I found myself sitting cross-legged with my back pressed against the wall and fully alert. I couldn't rest. I had already seen at least two large cockroaches crawl by and when I tried to throw something at them they flew around taunting me until they got tired and flew away. The space was damp, moldy, and cramped. The size of the box reminded me of my walk-in closet at home, and I would have given anything to be on the floor of my wardrobe right now in exchange for this piss pot. My mind was exhausted, but my body wasn't and rest was for the weary. Instead of counting sheep, the night found me counting the bricks, the names written on the wall, phone numbers of people I could call if I wanted a good lay, tons of gum stuck to the floor and the cot, the bars surrounding the cell, the paint peeling from the walls and ceiling, and the lint balls on the blanket. Anything to keep me distracted from the here and now.

A voice lulls me out of my trancelike state. "Ms. Daye," the chocolate officer from earlier calls to me. "Listen, we don't normally do this, because it's after hours, but you have a visitor."

It has to be close to ten o'clock, but it's hard to tell since there are no windows in the cell and no clock on the wall.

"I'm going to bring you to the interrogation room, where your guest is waiting."

Guest? I question. He has to be kidding. This is not my home and I didn't invite anyone to come over. But I merely shake my head, grateful for the reprieve from the smelly box they have me canned in. It's probably Rich coming to apologize and to let me know that he has everything under control. But truth be told, none of this would've even happened if he hadn't started messing with Jezebel.

When he opens the door to the room I can't believe my eyes. Of all the people to come visit me the last person I had in mind was her. Wasn't it bad enough that she got me locked up in the first place, now she had to pour the alcohol in the wound too? She actually wants to see me wallow in pain.

Mr. Goodbar tells me that I am allotted ten minutes. Just as I am about to object and let him know that this is an unwanted visitor he closes the door and leaves.

It takes every bit of restraint to suppress my anger and gain control of my hands, since they generally have a mind of their own. The vision of them tightly wrapped around her throat and watching her gag for air is soothing.

I dare not sit near her for fear that the contention within me would win the battle and when the officer returned he'd find Vanessa mangled or dead. In either scenario, she'd be leaving on a stretcher.

"Did I disturb your beauty sleep?"

I am already onto her game. She had reeled me in once, but she wouldn't be so fortunate the second time around.

"What's wrong? Cat got your tongue, Valentine Daye? By the way, what were your parents thinking when they named you? Was that some kind of joke? That's just as bad as naming your child Alizé or Cristal. I guess you project chicks don't know any better, humph?" Vanessa chuckles, but she is the only one laughing. "It's quite amusing actually. The whole 'ghetto mentality.' It's like you all have your own little rat race to keep each other down."

During her entire put-down speech I say a little prayer, because only He can pull me through these next couple of minutes. She disrespected my name, called my parents a joke, and basically discredited people who live below her standards. Yet it's people like us who keep her pockets phat.

"Since you're not in a talkative mood, I just wanted to thank you for your display earlier today. You fed right into the palm of my hand. You nearly took out my eye because I whispered in Richard's ear. Tsk-tsk. You actually did me a favor and now your man, excuse me, my man, Richard has seen you for exactly who you are, an out-of-control animal, and I found out you've been down this road before. When will you learn? Your behavior was completely irrational, but I don't expect better from some little 'hood rat from the projects. You've been holding Richard back, and I've been showing him the light. He's been in the dark far too long and deserves better. I don't know what he ever saw in someone like you, but I'm here to show him the good life.

"Valentine, I should also commend you on your good behavior tonight. I know I've said some things that you might find upsetting, but after your earlier stunt, you know better than to screw with me again. I know people and the next time you even think of laying a hand on me, your head will spin so fast, you won't know what hit you. Only I don't need to use my hands to get results. You could learn from me, little one.

"Well, my time is up. I can't stand to be in this joint another minute, but you try to have a good night's rest while I take care of Richard. Ta-ta!"

I watch as Vanessa saunters over to the door and knocks a few times. She looks back at me with a sinister grin while she waits for someone to open the door. When no one comes immediately,

I can sense her panic and just as she starts banging furiously some-one opens the door and she jets.

After Vanessa leaves and I am escorted back to my coffin, Vanessa's words leave me scarred and scared. I end up puking up the remains of the food that I had earlier at Gina's in the corner. I didn't think it was possible to throw up any more, but it was. And for the rest of night, I am left with the putrid odor of my vomit and a bad taste in my mouth.

20

A Lot of Nerve!

"Bitch!" Vanessa swung her lengthy hair to and fro as she fastened her coat and climbed into her car. "The nerve of her sitting across that table looking all smug. Obviously she doesn't know who she's dealing with."

It was always amusing to Vanessa when she talked to herself, or in this case fussed at herself. "And to think, that little witch actually thought a stunt like that was going to fly with a woman of my caliber. I don't know what Richard ever saw in Valentine. I mean, she is a cute little thing. I'll give her that, but her name alone should've had him running in the other direction."

Vanessa put her seat belt on, started the car, and entered her Park Avenue address into the navigational system. "The sooner I get out this hellhole of a neighborhood the better. Five minutes in that place will take me at least a week's worth of scrubbing to get rid of the stench."

Vanessa could still feel the sting of her eye. Valentine was definitely going to pay for making her miss the opportunity to attend the society ball. Not even starred makeup artist Bobbi Brown herself could camouflage that shiner from her oh-so-nosey mother. This would be just the ammunition needed to send either Richard or her trust fund flying. Her mother was always looking for a reason to cut Vanessa or her brother off financially. And after the debacle her brother suffered when he fell in love with an ex-stripper gone straight two years ago, Vanessa knew not even her father would come to her aid—especially if they got wind of Richard's past.

Even though Richard was now successful, and so was her brother's ex-girlfriend, Rachel.

Vanessa smiled at the thought of Rachel's story. Similar to Richard, her story was a classic. Rachel had been a hardworking, lower-class stripper, who worked her way through med school, became a doctor, and had a flourishing practice when she met Vincent. Vanessa's mother Cornelia went to great lengths to learn everything about Rachel that she possibly could the minute their relationship turned serious. From what Cornelia was able to gather, little Ms. Rachel Worthy didn't live up to her name, in terms of being worthy enough to date her son.

Once Mrs. Mitchell-Knight hired a private investigator and received a full background check on Rachel, it was over. She went straight to the source, and demanded Rachel break things off with Vincent or else. Feeling empowered, and under the notion that their love was strong enough to survive the threat of his mother, Rachel decided to battle Mrs. Mitchell-Knight and nearly lost it all. Not only did Vanessa's mother discredit Rachel's good name at the facility where she practiced, she threatened the hospital board by threatening to withdraw their annual donation if Rachel wasn't

dealt with. Mrs. Mitchell-Knight forced Rachel to choose between
her career or Vincent. Feeling defeated, Rachel vowed to leave
Vincent alone. Unfortunately, Vincent didn't put up much of a
fight. He knew what he stood to lose and didn't want to ruffle any
feathers.

Mother always was a tough cookie, she thought as she swerved
onto the expressway.

Vanessa knew she had inherited her mother's shrewdness, and
since she was her mother's mirror image, she was somewhat left
alone when it came to love. She also knew not to push her luck,
and opted not to attend the ball. However, she would eventually have to tread a similar path, but she had a few tricks up her
sleeve when and if she finally decided to introduce Richard to
her parents.

Vanessa looked at the dashboard for the time. Prior to her
trip to the police station, she'd called Stephen and made up an
excuse for him not to come over. She made sure to call Richard
and invite him to come by, saying she had changed her mind
and wanted to see him. Richard would be waiting for her when
she got home and would wonder where she'd been, especially
given the hour. She wanted to tell him yet feared that Richard
would just find a way to defend Valentine's actions. It disgusted
her that he still felt anything for Valentine, but not for reasons
that one would think. Vanessa knew that it would be difficult
to fall out of love with someone if there was any significant
amount of time involved in the dating process. Richard and Valentine had been together forever, so she knew their bond was
tight. Hell, although she felt no compassion for Richard and
Valentine, she did realize that erasing a part of your existence
especially where love was concerned was virtually impossible.

Something that where she and Dexter were concerned, she herself couldn't do.

For almost five years Vanessa had shared her life and love with her first real boyfriend, Dexter Windell. Although their relationship was arranged, it was a perfect union. They dated in college. His father was the founder and CEO of Windell, Clarington, and Stokes, one of New York's most prestigious African-American law firms. Dexter was his father's most prominent protégé. Everything about Dexter screamed perfection. He was cultured, well traveled, fluent in three languages, and commonly grounded. He loved his family, wanted children, and loved the idea of having a family of his own.

Dexter and Vanessa were compatible in every way. They enjoyed the same food, marveled over the same art, and they both secretly loved to lounge and watch television, but boasted about Broadway plays they never actually got a chance to see. They would spend hours in each other's arms, doing absolutely nothing, yet everything in the same moment. She loved him, and knew that no matter what she felt for anyone else, her love for Dexter would never die.

Tears began to form in Vanessa's eyes as she thought about her last conversation with Dexter. Although it had been well after midnight and she was exhausted from a long day of finals, she remembered how short she was with him on the phone.

"Baby, please talk to me for a little longer until I get home. I'm almost there," he asked.

"Dex, I'm so tired. I had three exams today. It's late and I have one more test in the morning. You know I don't do well without at least eight hours of sleep and I'm already minus two. I'm hanging up," Vanessa whined.

"Vanessa! I need you. I'm so sleepy I swear I think I gonna fall asleep at the wheel if you don't talk to me."

"Stop it! Nothing is going to happen to you! I love you, but seriously I'm hanging up. I'll call you tomorrow, honey."

Vanessa pulled her car over and began to cry. Questions bombarded her again. If only she had stayed on the phone with him, maybe the accident would never have happened. The coroner stated in the report that the death was sudden. He died instantly upon impact with the pole. Was it her fault, she questioned again and again. He had begged her to talk to him.

From that moment on Vanessa knew a part of her heart had been permanently cut off. A piece of who she was died the night Dexter fell asleep at the wheel. And no matter who she fell in love with, no love would ever take the place of her love for Dexter.

Because of that, Vanessa was determined to pull Richard away from Valentine. Her behavior was based on deep-rooted jealousy. She hated the fact that they had such a strong history. In her heart, Vanessa knew none of this was truly Valentine's fault; she was determined to live with the notion of misery loving company.

"Little bitch, should've just left well enough alone, but she didn't. Instead she had to try and fight me on this."

Vanessa rubbed the tears from her eyes, and proceeded back onto the street. "Now she's gonna have to pay."

Unfortunately though, Valentine had no clue what she was paying for exactly. To Vanessa everything dealing with love was war. And her fights were battles that buried her heart. The true fight was the one within herself that she clearly hadn't overcome. Dexter was gone, and because of that she was miserable. Anyone crossing Vanessa was either for her or against her. If someone dared to go against her getting what she wanted when she wanted it, they would experience the penalty of death. She would kill off some portion of their lives, be it their careers, or their happiness in love.

To Vanessa, Valentine now had the ultimate death sentence— one she intended to execute to the fullest.

21

❧

The Ultimate Betrayal

I know you wanna leave me, but I refuse to let you go. If I have to beg and plead for your sympathy . . . That's the tune that played in my head all night. Sleep never bothered to visit me in the cell from hell.

Morning couldn't have arrived quickly enough. I managed to doze off for an hour at best, but even without a mirror, I know I look like a hot mess. They won't even allow me time to go to the bathroom to wash my face or brush my teeth. So not only do I look like a hot mess, I smell like one too!

When we arrive at the courthouse, the court officer takes pity on me and is kind enough to escort me to the bathroom. With what little conveniences I am offered, I do the best I can to clean up my appearance in order to look presentable while facing the judge.

As soon as we enter the courtroom, my eyes scan the people scattered about the room. Sure enough, my aunt Zenobia and my cousin Shaquetta are there to support me. I put a smile on my face and nod my head at them since my hands are in cuffs. Still, my heart sinks when I don't see Rich. At the very least I expected him to be here to support me, but more importantly to prove Vanessa wrong, because he loves me and not her.

My heart is hurting and it's a pain I have never experienced before. It feels as if someone has a sharp knife and is carving into the muscle slowly and twisting the blade in circles. The pain is undeniable and excruciating. Sadly, I don't understand what I've done to deserve this treatment.

"All rise," the court officer announces.

I force myself to stand and stare straight ahead to watch the judge take her seat. My mind races, because having a female preside over my case might be in my favor. I feel like my fortune is about to change. At least my prayer is that my luck will change. I can't bare another sleepless night in that small, stinky, filthy, bug-infested cell.

My do-good neighbor Kenneth Graff stands up as my attorney. Apparently he and Ellie never bothered to go out. Instead Kenneth decided to do a little legwork and followed up on my case. He informs me that he never did see Richard, but he left several messages on our voice mail and he slid a note beneath the door in case they missed each other. I'm extremely disappointed, but happy that Kenneth volunteered to represent me. I don't know if he is any good, but anything is better than a court-appointed attorney.

While we wait for my case to come up, Kenneth advises me of the possible outcomes, which I already know. The worst-case scenario is a few months in jail, but Kenneth feels that they'll probably place me on probation. Unless Vanessa wants to be vindictive and plead fear for her life. That wouldn't shock me. But from where I'm sitting, she already got what she wants, Rich. If Kenneth couldn't get ahold of Rich last night, he is probably laying up with her right now.

Forty-five minutes later my case is called and to my surprise the charges are dropped. I'm free to go!

"That's what I'm talking 'bout," I hear my ghetto-ass cousin yell.

I wrap my arms tightly around Kenneth even though he doesn't have much to do with my release. Still, he cared enough to represent me and show his support—none of which he had to do. Apparently, Vanessa had a change of heart and dropped the charges.

Aunt Zenobia and Shaquetta run over to hug me and are screaming for joy like I am the next contestant on *The Price Is Right*. The judge slams her gavel down and orders us to be quiet and leave the courtroom or else. I knew what the "or else" meant, so I grab them by the hand and lead them out of the room.

When we get into the entrance hall, I start screaming with my family. That was too close for comfort. I love Rich, but I had had enough of jail for one day. Still, if trouble comes looking for me, trouble is going to get what the fuck it came for, because Valentine is not the one. Ya heard!

"Valentine."

I turn around and am face-to-face with the love of my life.

"Rich," I say as if I were starstruck. My tongue suddenly felt like it was stuck to the roof of my mouth. "How are you?" I ask, even though he should be asking me that very question.

"I'm good," he says, looking antsy. "Can I talk to you for a minute?" he asks, looking from me to my aunt Zenobia and Shaquetta.

"What the hell you gotta say, negro?" My aunt Zenobia steps up to him. "Matter of fact, where have you been?"

"That's right, punk!" Shaquetta adds. "We should beat yo black ass right now. You sorry ass . . ."

I step between Rich and my family. This is my battle to fight and I have to give my man the courtesy to hear what he has to say. *I* need to hear what he has to say. In truth, Rich deserves a good beat down, but if that's going to happen it will come directly from me and nobody else.

"Y'all chill out," I exclaim. "Give us a moment."

"Well, we right here if you need us. We ain't going no-fucking-where!" Aunt Zenobia yells as she pokes Rich in his chest, emphasizing each word.

Rich takes my hand and we walk through the corridor. We finally end up standing beside a vacant telephone booth near the restroom that I visited earlier.

"How are you?" Rich finally asks.

"I've been better."

There is a long pause as we both stare through the picture window, watching the frenzy of people entering and leaving the court building.

"Rich, talk to me. What's up?"

"Val, I don't know where to begin," Rich says, still looking out the window. Guilt is etched all over his face, and he refuses to look at me.

"Well, start with being honest for once. I know I deserve that much. What is going on between you and that high siddity, Vanessa?"

"This is not about Vanessa. This is about me and you."

"Rich, cut the BS. This is all about Vanessa, because prior to her stepping into the picture things were right between us. But now, what? You think you're too good for me? You think that Vanessa loves you? That chick will not ride or die for you, Rich. I would. I've been there for you since day one. I've been in your corner more times than you can even count, so don't tell me this is not about Vanessa."

"Val, the mess you pulled yesterday could've cost me my got-damn job. If it wasn't for Vanessa smoothing things over with our client, I would be pounding the pavement right now. I can't let you and your petty jealousies jeopardize my future."

"Vanessa? Jeopardize your future! Pleez! Let me tell you some-thing . . . you wouldn't even have a damn future if it wasn't for me. Yeah, you had a dream to be something other than a stunta slinging rocks on the corner, but I helped you make all this shit happen. Jeopardize your future! You've got some nerve. Man, don't you ever come to me with no weak-ass game like that again."

"See, this is what I'm talking about. I can't even have a con-versation with you and when I try to you always bringing up the past. You stuck in the past. Then you're always ready to jump down my throat. All of that is tiring. Have you ever thought of letting me explain myself? Or pausing for a second? Just pause. Take a breather. Damn."

My mouth wants to respond, because I'm seething from his insults and hurt by Rich's rationale. Instead, I choose to sit quietly on the ledge and listen to what I know will be more crap. Since Rich wants the floor to speak, I'm going to give it to him.

The palms of my hands are sweaty, my forehead is moist with sweat, and my legs are trembling. Nonetheless, I want to prove to Rich that I can remain calm and that I can listen without inter-rupting. I want most to show him that I don't have to always raise my hands to prove my point.

"Val, I'm not discrediting anything that you've ever done for me. I love your little ass. It's just that I feel like I need some space right now to get my head straight. You feel me? I'm tired of us going at it like this. I'm trying to get my paper right and make moves at my job and when you go on tirades and cut up my suits, threaten people, and punch my colleague in the face during important meetings that only sets me back. I don't even know what I want no more. The only thing I'm sure of is I'm out there to get what's mine. I've got an opportunity of a lifetime and I'm going for it.

"The meeting that you busted up yesterday was about the possibility of getting RichWear off the ground and a bunch of other stuff. Now, Vanessa believes in me enough to introduce me to the right people so we can make things happen. She's been nothing but good to me, and Val as much as I love you . . . I gotta give us a rest right now."

Although my ears are perked up and I'm a decent lip reader, I know this man did not say what I think he just said.

"What? Rich, exactly what are you trying to say?"

"For now, Val, I think we need to part ways."

"Part ways! I don't understand. Rich, you're my world and all that I've ever wanted. And I can change. I can learn to control my temper. Don't you know that I love you, baby? I want and need you, Rich. We can work this out. We've always gotten through rough patches." A huge lump is in my throat and my eyes begin to sting with tears. This can't be happening.

"Val, this is more than a patch. This is more like a few acres. I need to be in an environment where I can think clearly. A place where I'm not constantly on edge and worrying about you endangering my career. I realize that I have to put my priorities first for a change."

"Your priorities? I've always placed *your* priorities above all else. I make it my priority to love you unconditionally, which means working out our differences no matter what. Rich, I make sure that you don't have a want or desire in our home by catering to your needs. I cook, I keep a clean house, and though you pay the majority of the bills, I make sure they're paid on time. The only thing missing is I'm not barefoot and pregnant and if you say jump, I ask how high."

"Here we go, Val. Always with a flare for the dramatics. But it doesn't matter, because I'm leaving."

"So now you're leaving me for that bitch? I thought there wasn't nothing going on between you two? I thought it was all business? Are you moving in with Vanessa?"

"That's not important right now."

"Yes, the hell it is. It's real important and I don't hear you denying anything either."

"What you should know is that the reason Vanessa dropped the charges is because I convinced her that we wouldn't have any more trouble with you. You should be grateful that she's not going to pursue this any further."

I know he didn't just say "we" and I should be grateful, I think to myself. I wouldn't have to be thankful for jack if Vanessa hadn't snuck her ass into our fortress in the first place. This relationship only has room for two people, me and Rich. They both have another thing coming if they think they can just push me to the side like some unwanted trash. He was my man first and he's going to stay my man!

"Guess what? Promises are meant to be broken," I say, standing tall, hands planted on my hips and lips perched in the air.

"Val, don't be ignorant. I suggest you let this go, because you really don't want to go there this time."

"Why not? You think just because she's the heiress to Soul-fucking-Shine and her daddy is a judge that she scares me?" Rich's face is covered with surprise. "Yeah, I know who she is. I knew even before she paid me that little visit last night in jail. I could've beat her ass again right there in the visiting room and who could blame me. I was already locked up and she came to taunt me. But you know what? I'm not as stupid as you pegged me, but your bitch is stupid. I'm sure her family don't know nothing about you and I'm guessing if they did you wouldn't be able to step foot near her again. Man, you from the projects. The G-H-E-T-T-O—the ghetto! So, Rich, keep fooling yourself; because they don't give a damn about how much money you make or how much status you obtain. Old money don't like new money. They don't know you or care about you like I do. But you're willing to give all of this up?" I say, waving my hands across my body. "For that uppity trick, Vanessa?"

"Val, you said your piece and I know you're upset, so I'll let everything you just said slide. On everything I love, you know you will always have my heart. I will always take care of you and if you ever need anything, I got you. As a matter of fact, I'ma pay the mortgage and the maintenance for the rest of the year on the condo. When I get my next bonus I'll pay off the remainder of your debt as well. I'll make sure you're financially set."

"Don't try to buy me off. I don't need your money. I got a job. You must have me confused with someone else, 'cause I ain't no gold-digging ho!"

"I never said that you were a gold-digger or a ho, Val. I just wanna take care of you and make sure you're all right."

"What I want is for you to man the fuck up! I want you to be true to me and keep your promise and get married. Or was the ring just to shut me up?" I scream and my voice cracks from exhaustion. "Did you propose to make me happy or to stop me from looking at other prospects?"

"What other prospects?"

"Yeah, that got your attention, right? Rich, you are my only prospect, so stop tripping. But I guess I was never prospect enough for you, huh?"

"Valentine, right now there's just too much bad blood between us. I need to wipe the slate clean."

The dam breaks and a stream of tears bathes my cheeks. Earlier when Rich said he wanted to talk, I didn't think he'd have the heart or audacity to break up with me. Rich reaches over to console me, but I fight him. I beat him worse than any one of his chicks I confronted on the streets. I punch him wherever he didn't cover, kick wherever my foot fell, bit his hands, arms, and neck, and jab him in the ribs. I want to inflict pain on him so he can feel how much he hurt me. Rich doesn't raise a hand back at me and when I'm tired of beating on him I fall to the floor and cry until I can't cry anymore.

22

❧

It's Going Down

I'm going to kill that bitch, I sob to myself. Rich is long gone and I remain in the same place, right where we argued earlier. My body won't allow me to get up. I'm too weak and want to die, but not before I take Vanessa out with me.

"Val. Val? Where are you?" My aunt Zenobia shouts through the halls. Her voice grows stronger as she continues to call my name, and I know they are getting closer.

Give me the strength to get up and hide, I quickly pray. The last thing I want them to see is me looking like a shipwreck washed ashore.

"She's probably in the bathroom," Shaquetta announces.

"Where's the bathroom?"

"The sign says it's over there."

Within moments their shadows hover over my small frame. My aunt rocks back on her heels, astonished by my appearance.

"Oh my goodness, what did he do to you?" Shaquetta asks, observing my disheveled look.

"Stop standing there and let's help her up," Aunt Zenobia says anxiously. "We're going to take you into the bathroom, okay, honey?" she says, handling me as if I were a three-year-old.

When we go into the bathroom, Shaquetta quickly pulls a handful of towels from the dispenser and moistens them with water. Aunt Zenobia takes a comb from her purse and begins combing my hair and straightening out my clothes. She hands me a capful of mouthwash and tells me to rinse. While cleaning me up, they talk about me as if I wasn't present or as if I am deaf.

"I told her that negro wasn't shit."

"Yeah, but I didn't know he was grimy like that, Ma. He didn't strike me as the type to dog her out like that."

"What made you think he was any different from all these other mutts out there? If he got a dick, he's gonna mark as much territory as he can."

"For real! Dang, if the good ones are messed up, what chance do I have?" Shaquetta questions.

"He wasn't no good from the git-go. Rich has always been a snake and he's lucky my niece is nice and let his slimy ass slither by all this time."

"What about your man, J-Boogie?"

"My man ain't the subject here, but to answer your smart-ass question, J-Boogie is a man, ain't he? I puts my trust in no one but God."

"Mmh. Oh well."

After they made me look presentable enough to leave the building they ask me if I'm hungry. Actually I'm starving, but the only thing I want to do is take a long hot bath and crawl into my own bed and cry.

"Listen, we gonna stop by your place so you can wash your

nasty ass, because you was probably mingling with them other prisoners and whatnot. You gonna pack a bag and spend a few days with us," Aunt Zenobia instructs.

The last thing I want to do is leave my nice two-bedroom condo to spend time in the projects. Now, I'm not putting down their lifestyle, because it is what it is. However, my aunt could've moved out of that apartment years ago. She makes just as much money as I do, but is content with the project life. I worked too hard for everything that I have only to end back up where I started.

When we arrive at my apartment I head for the bathroom and lock the door. I set the tub and put some Epsom salts and bubble bath in the water. Then I run the sink and sit on the toilet and wail. I cry and I cry until my body grows weary. I bawl as I strip naked and allow my body to disappear beneath the water. My tears gently mix in with the soapy suds. It feels like hours passed, but it couldn't have been more than a half hour when my aunt knocks on the door to check on me. I mumble something loud and inaudible to assure her that I'm fine and she leaves.

After my aunt leaves me to myself, I decide to really give myself a thorough cleansing with the loofah scrub. I drain the water in the Jacuzzi, turn on the shower, and then proceed to wash my hair. When I finally emerge from the bathroom, my aunt and cousin have an entire spread of food on the table. I didn't notice any dirty pots and pans, so they must've ordered takeout. They have already begun eating and invite me to sit down at the table to join them.

"Let me blow dry my hair and throw on some clothes."

When I enter my room, everything still looks the same. The

pictures of me and Rich on various vacations sit on the dresser. His cologne and jewelry adorn the high chest and his cell phone charger is plugged into the wall. However, when I enter our walk-in closet, I realize that his garment bag, duffel bag, and suitcase are missing. I quickly peel through his clothing and see that the only gear left are the outfits he hardly wears.

What the fuck? Rich was dead serious when he said he needed some space, I think. I figured when he came home and attempted to leave that I'd be able to sweet-talk him into staying, but he is already one step ahead of me. Rich must've come home in the middle of the night or early this morning, packed his gear, and bounced. Then he decided to fill me in on a decision that he probably made long before I even popped that bitch in the face. He was probably only looking for an excuse. Rich wasn't the spontaneous type, so this was something he must've been contemplating for a while and finally found his way out.

Reality strikes the mess out of me and I scream. I begin throwing stuff around the bedroom. One of the bottles I throw hits the mirror on the wall and it crashes onto the floor and shatters. Glass covers the floor and sparkles like diamonds embedded in the carpet.

Shaquetta makes it into the bedroom before Aunt Zenobia. She dives to the floor as I continue to hurl objects in every direction.

"Stop this madness, Val. Cut this out right now. I know you're not tearing up your nice furniture and your room over that sorry-ass man? You got better sense than that," my aunt warns.

But I don't listen. I tune her out and before I know what is happening she tackles me to the floor.

"Valentine, I know you're hurting, but I need you to stop. On account of this negro you are about to lose your mind. You've already been to jail. What, you want to end up in the crazy house next? Pull yourself together," she says, still pinning me to the ground.

"Now I'm going to get up. Are you gonna flip out again?" she asks calmly.

I roll my eyes and take a huge breath as I turn my head away. Her eyes are burning a hole in my head.

"You better answer me, Val."

"Yes, I'm good," I say, trying to calm down. Fortunately she is my aunt, because had that been anyone else, I would've flipped them off me and stomped them out.

"Good. Shaquetta and I will wait in the dining room for you. I got something to tell you that I think you'll want to hear, so dry your hair and get dressed."

Tears threaten to fall from my eyes again, but this time I'm angry. Angry at my aunt for not allowing me to grieve; angry at Rich for leaving me; angry at myself for allowing myself to be in this situation; angry at the world!

"Come get something to eat," my aunt says. She is sitting at the table waiting for me while Shaquetta sits in the adjoining room watching the Wendy Williams show.

"Girl, that man done turned you out and got you plum stupid."

"Aunt Z, you act like you ain't never been in love before. What the hell do you expect? I've been with Rich for nine years. You expect me to just act like our relationship was some drive-by shit?"

"I've had my share of heartbreaks, but not once did I fight over a man like I see you always doing and I damn sure ain't gonna hurt myself in the process."

The food on my plate is getting cold as I toy with it. I can't seem to lift the fork to my mouth even though the greens and macaroni and cheese look and smell good as hell.

"I'm not hurting myself, but I know who I wanna hurt though."

"What you need to do is let them be. If Rich wants to lie in that bitch's bed, let him. One day he'll realize what he's lost. Give him time and some rope to hang himself."

"I need to see them both suffer. I want her dead and I want him to reap what he's sowed. If he were here right now, I'd cut him."

My aunt has a contemplative look on her face. I know she's trying to choose her words carefully, which is hard for her. Aunt Zenobia is used to shooting straight from the hip, but seeing how fragile I am she wants to play it safe.

"You know how I've always said Rich wasn't shit?"

"Yeah," I answer.

"Do you know why?"

"Yes, because he's always dogging me out."

"That's only part of the reason. Your ex-man is a snake."

"Auntie, that's nothing new. Everybody knows that he creeps."

"Listen, chile. I said he is a damn snake of the lowest denominator and the reason Colombo is dead."

"What? What the hell are you talking about? You're not making any sense. Colombo is dead because of the game. He got caught up and almost took me with him."

"No, you're wrong. Who do you think got him caught up? Don't look at me like you confused. It was your man, Rich."

"Aunt Z, I don't believe you. Do you have any proof? Who told you this nonsense?"

"Val, don't worry about who told me. My sources are reliable."

"Rich wasn't even there that day everything went down."

"And you never wondered why? Who else from Colombo's crew is still alive?"

My heart almost leaps through my chest and my head starts spinning as I digest what my aunt is insinuating. None of what she is saying could possibly be true. Rich isn't that type of person. He would never purposely set someone up to get hurt. Rich isn't underhanded and he definitely isn't a killer or the type to be an accomplice to the things my aunt is spitting. Rich has a conscience and something of this magnitude would've been riding him like crazy. It's impossible to believe that he'd keep something like this from me. My aunt has to be mistaken. She has her facts mixed up, because my Rich isn't capable of these grimy accusations.

"Don't look so baffled. The only other people still out there are Law and Crisp, and both of them are down with your boy. All them other cats is dead: Chief, Took, Butter, June Bug, G-Money, Iron, Whiz, and Pop. Word is Rich helped to set up that whole thing and I believe it. Law is a follower, not a leader and Crisp is as dumb as they come."

"None of this makes any sense. Why would Rich set up Colombo if he didn't have any intentions of taking over his business?"

"From what I understand he had some personal beef to settle with Colombo, he wanted to get with you, and he wanted out of the game. That's enough reason to get somebody got."

"I don't believe anything that just came out of your mouth, because if he wanted out of the game, he could've walked away. You busy listening to them tricks in the projects who are always up in other people's business. Those bitches will say anything, because the majority of them are jealous and want to get with Rich."

"Riddle me this—who you know to ever walk away from the game alive and still around? And I ain't talking about them dudes that got shot up and rolling around in wheelchairs either."

I can't think of anyone off the top of my head and don't reply. The dumbfounded expression on my face answers for me.

"Oh, I thought so. You can believe what you want, but I'm speaking the truth. I'm done shielding your ass. I've known about this for years now, but I kept my mouth shut. You were happy; life was treating you good, so I never bothered to interfere."

"Whatever. You never had a kind word for Rich, so spare me."

"Well, I tried my best. Now I wasn't too keen on Colombo, but as far as I knew he ain't never cheated on you. He was loyal to yo ass."

"Yeah, and he used to kick my ass loyally too! Or did you forget about that part?"

"Well, I don't know what's the lesser of the two evils."

"The lesser is someone who can be loyal to me and love me without feeling threatened and the need to control me with his fist."

"All I'm saying is that I know you wanna kill Vanessa and hang Rich by the nuts, but I think you should let them be."

"Aunt Z, all I'm asking you to do is let me handle my business the way I see fit. I have to deal with things my way. Otherwise, I wouldn't be who I am. Do you have the information I asked you for the other day?"

"You gonna jeopardize your freedom for some silly bitch and some chump?"

"Do you have the information or not?" I say, repeating my question.

"Yeah, I got it. It's in my purse."

"Good, because this ain't over until I say it's over. They wanna play me like a clown? That bitch gonna come to the jail threatening me while stealing my man? Oh hell-to-the-no. Let the mutha-freakin' games begin, because it's going down!"

23

❧

Enough!

"This was a bad idea. You've got to go!" Vanessa stormed through the doors of her apartment, waving her hand in the air, not wanting to hear anything Richard had to say to her.

"What are you talking about? What's going on?"

Vanessa turned to him, her eyes full of disbelief. "What's going on? What's going on? How can you even ask me that? You know full well what's going on!" Vanessa stopped short with Richard right at her heels.

"No, I really don't. One minute we're fine and the next you're kicking me out?"

"I can't believe I let you talk me into dropping the charges on Valentine." She was ranting. "And what's worse is like a fool I actually did it."

"Vanessa, we both agreed it was the best thing for everyone. So, why are you trippin' all of a sudden? You're acting like a crazy lady."

"So now I'm the crazy one. I don't know why I've put up with this crap this long. First, you lie to me about being with someone, only to find out not only are you involved but you're also engaged. Second, you beg me to allow you time to get it together, convincing me that I'm the best thing that's ever happened to you, only to have to deal with a slew of juvenile confrontations from that ghetto rat you call a fiancée. And if that wasn't reason enough, look at my dang face . . . that skank attacked me in a restaurant, which inevitably resulted in my parents' being furious with me for not being able to attend the one function that reigns as a tradition in my family."

Vanessa took off her coat and tossed it on the chaise lounge nearby. She went straight to her minibar and prepared a cocktail. As Richard approached her she flipped up her hand, shunning him away.

"Not now. I'm mad!"

"I hear you baby, but what I don't understand is how you think this is all my fault!"

"If it's not your fault then whose is it, Richard? 'Cause it sure as hell isn't mine."

"You haven't been exactly forthright yourself, you know. What about ole boy? And what about your family, you haven't exactly welcomed me into your life. I told you it was over with Val. I left her and I'm here. What more do you want?"

Vanessa was pissed. How dare he try and flip this on her. She knew she was wrong though, this wasn't just about Richard or even Valentine. It was a combination of everything lately. Richard was just the closest person to lash out at. Something she wouldn't have to do if Dexter were still alive. Her frustrations were fueled by her missing Dexter. She sighed, trying to figure out what she was going to do about the here and now. This whole thing with Richard was making her sick. Valentine had definitely tried her patience and she'd just about had it with the entire situation. Part of her felt as though she really cared for Richard, but with her recent thoughts of Dexter, she wasn't sure if she actually loved him.

At twenty-nine, Vanessa was feeling the pressure of being involved. Although she had options, in her heart she was beginning to feel as though she didn't have many choices left. She knew she was growing soft on Richard, and loved what he could potentially represent if he were to become vice president of Jorge Jacobs. But as he stood in front of her, glistening from having just gotten out of the shower, fine as ever, she wondered if it was even still worth it now.

"Damn it, Richard!" she screamed as she came from behind the bar, placing the half empty glass of scotch down. She plunged toward him, removing the towel from around his waist, exposing his penis, and began kissing him. As she tugged the back of his neck with one hand, and fumbled with the other to tear away her stockings, she shoved his penis inside her, moving her hips wildly back and forth. She moaned loudly, begging him to pound her harder.

"You bastard . . ." she screamed. "You damn bastard."

"You like it, don't you?"

"Yes!"

She stopped him then leaned her body against the nearby stool.

"From behind!" she demanded as she positioned herself against the stool. "I don't want to look at you."

"Oh, you just want me to fuck you?" Richard stated as he stroked his manhood.

Vanessa didn't say a word; she only waited for him to enter her again. Sex was always the one distraction for her that took her to a place where she didn't have to face the things that truly both-ered her. She knew Richard had his faults but he also had good qualities and the potential to be someone great.

"You know you don't want me to leave?"

"Shut up!"

"You know you love me."

"Shut the hell up!" Vanessa screamed in between moans of pleasure.

"Tell me."

"Harder . . . harder!"

"Tell me you love me."

"I . . . I . . ." She bit her lip, moaning louder as Richard stroked his massive manhood in and out of her glistening walls.

He pumped vigorously and Vanessa wildly responded, moving her body to the rhythm he created. She clutched the edge of the bar, hoping to feel every inch of him inside her as she prepared to climax.

"Enough . . ." she whispered.

His body moved faster, indicating that he was almost to his sexual peak.

"Enough . . ." she repeated, only this time in anger and much louder than before.

"I'm almost there . . ." Richard said, clutching her hips tighter, concentrating on a big finish.

"Get off me," Vanessa yelled, releasing her grasp from the bar and pushing her body away from his. "Now!"

"What the hell is wrong with you, Vanessa?"

She scooted away from him and reached for her drink. "You're what's wrong with me. This is what's wrong!" Her free arm flailed in surrender as she gulped the rest of her scotch down. "All we have is sex."

"That's not true," Richard said, releasing himself of the fluids that hadn't the opportunity to come out during sex. "I love you, Vanessa."

"Is that how you show it, by cumming on my plush carpet?" She reached for the towel that rested near the sink of the minibar.

"You didn't let me finish." Richard smiled, took the towel, and began cleaning up.

Vanessa watched him as he cleaned the specks of his love juices up. She couldn't figure out what was wrong with her. She knew Richard loved her, and had sacrificed so much to be with her but . . .

"I just don't think I can do this anymore. I know it sounds crazy and that's what this entire relationship's been, crazy. But this isn't me. The lying. The back and forth, me feeling like I'm sharing you and now this . . ." Vanessa pointed to her eye.

Richard looked up at her, forcing Vanessa to see the scratches and bruises that covered his face. Vanessa gasped, realizing that in her flurry of fits, she hadn't stopped long enough to actually hear Richard let alone pay attention to him.

"What happened to you?" She rushed from behind the minibar to Richard's side.

"Valentine!"

"When? What . . ."

"I told her that I didn't want to have anything else to do with her today at court. She lost it and I let her. I just wanted it to be over. All of it and it is."

Vanessa took his face in her hand. The wounds were as noticeable on Richard as the shiner that covered Vanessa's eye. "I can't believe she did this to you."

"I did this for us."

Vanessa lowered her eyes, avoiding contact with his. "Why?"

"Because her losing me would be like me losing you, and I needed her to just get all of that hurt out."

"So you let her beat on you? How is that for us?"

"Because, by me not reacting to her, she knows that I'm not coming back. I want you, Vanessa."

Sincerity covered his face as Vanessa peered into Richard's eyes. She smiled as she examined the wounds a little closer. "Guess we do have something in common." She kissed his face then traced her eye with the backside of her hand.

Vanessa unbuttoned her blouse and extended her hand toward Richard.

He rose and leaned in close. She kissed his lips.

"What are you doing?" Richard mumbled.

"Letting you finish," Vanessa concluded.

Vanessa knew that having Richard there wasn't the best idea no matter how good he made her feel. In Vanessa's mind it was just a matter of time before this temporary living situation became a permanent problem.

24

&

Damn, Let It Go Already!

Vanessa shuffled around her office flipping through files and making notes along the way.

"Syco Industries has to come down on their wholesale price in order for the company to see the profits they need for the next quarter. Worthington is ready with their fall collection, and Kennedy is about to launch their—"

"Excuse me, Ms. Knight. Mr. Washington is here to see you."

Vanessa turned toward the intercom system. *What now?* she thought to herself. Within a matter of five days Richard had managed to completely smother her. She had been in such pursuit of getting Richard that she never really thought about what that would actually mean when she got him. Every second they weren't together, he either called or sent her something stating he was thinking about her. Although she liked being pursued, this was getting ridiculous.

"Send him in."

Vanessa walked around her desk and plopped in her seat. Intensely she started thumbing through her files with hopes of giving Richard the hint that she in fact was busy.

"Hey babe, I was wondering . . ." Richard made it from the door to her desk in seconds. Just as he leaned down to kiss her on the cheek, she stopped him.

"Richard, I'm busy. And what's with all this 'babe' stuff at work? You know I don't like that. It's unprofessional and immature. Neither of which is going to get us anywhere." Vanessa stood from her chair, leaving it as a permanent gap between them.

"What's wrong with you?"

"Syco Industries!" Vanessa placed the file down, looking Richard square in the eye.

"Why didn't you just tell me this was stressing you out? I just closed the Jacobson file, locking down that deal. Do you want me to lend you a hand with this?"

"What? You don't think I can handle my workload?"

"I'm not saying that. Vanessa, again, what's the problem? I've never let you down on anything before with work. My business is always together, so what's with all the panic in your voice now? I didn't come in here for this. I came to see you to get a little—"

"That's the problem, Richard. You've taken our personal life a bit too seriously. We're both up for partner. And I've worked too hard to just throw it all away."

"I thought we were a team. When did the 'we' become an 'I'? So now, you gunning for the VP position?"

"I've never not been, Richard. That's what I mean. If you haven't noticed, I'm the only woman on the executive floor. You think I don't know what people think of me . . . just some spoiled little rich girl, who doesn't need a promotion. I don't mind being with you, but until we know what's what, there cannot be any conflicts of interest. So flouncing yourself in here to have your way with me every chance you get is just not acceptable."

"Who said anything about having my way?" Richard chuckled. "But now that you mentioned it, I could use a little sumptin' sumptin'."

Vanessa didn't crack a smile. "I have work to do." She shifted from the desk to the bookshelf in her office.

"You've been a real bitch lately, considering all I've given up for you. I thought we were what you wanted."

Vanessa spun her head around as if she were demon possessed. "I've worked my ass off to help you these past few months. If we are ever going to exist, we have to be a power couple. I come from a long line of power, and if you plan on sticking around, then you need to get with the program."

"How in the hell am I supposed to know where you come from? You have yet to introduce me to your family. You keep talking about this damn plan, but frankly it seems that no matter what I do, I'm not fitting into this plan."

Vanessa huffed. "What do you want, Richard?"

"I know your parents are planning to attend the gala launching the new clothing line. I overheard you telling your parents that no one was escorting you. So what the hell, I'm no one now? Do they even know I've moved in?"

Vanessa's cinnamon complexion quickly paled. For a moment, she was speechless.

Vanessa lowered her head, and turned toward Richard. "I know how this may seem, but it's not like that."

"How is it, Vanessa? From the look of things, you're embarrassed by me."

Richard sat down in Vanessa's chair. "You don't want anyone

here to know we're in a relationship, as if that's such a bad thing. But I'll roll with that because I know business shouldn't be mixed with pleasure. Yet, this shit with your folks is on a whole other level, 'cause it lets me know that you're not serious about us."

Vanessa opened her mouth to speak but nothing came out.

"And regarding the promotion, I've wanted this for myself before you even stepped foot in my life, so really it doesn't have anything to do with you. I was driven a little bit more because I felt like by getting this promotion, we both grow together as a unit, but whether you're here or not, I was going to make this happen. But know this, you're either down with me for real, or you're not."

"Richard." Vanessa walked over to the chair and stood in front of him. "I'm not ashamed of you. No, my parents don't know you live with me. Mainly, because I wasn't raised to shack up. My family believes in going the length, building a family, doing things the proper way. And you staying in the home that my parents own is unacceptable, and like I said earlier, not permanent. Secondly, this is for your protection, because if I told them that we're living together, I'd be inclined to tell them why we made the decision to do that. I don't make it a habit to tell untruths to my parents. I may omit some things, but I don't blatantly lie. Besides, our history is shaky and not newsworthy . . . yet. I know my parents. They know of you. But what would you have me tell them that would make you look good in their eyes?"

Vanessa continued. "You come from the projects, you've worked your way up—which is impressive and would be highly noted. Yet less than a week ago, you had a fiancée with whom you were living with. A crazy woman who just attacked me while we were at a work-related meeting. For months now, we've been carrying on an affair behind her back, until you managed to get up the nerve to leave her. You have nowhere to live, and several loose ends to tie up before we can officially say we're anything. But you want me to present that to my parents, because you feel, what, insecure? Why do you think I invited my parents to the gala? It wasn't because they don't have other important functions to attend."

Vanessa sighed, "I felt the gala would be the perfect place for them to get a chance to know you as a person." Vanessa turned away then walked toward the door. "Don't be melodramatic with me, Richard . . . and don't you dare ever accuse me of being ashamed of anything. When I make a presentation, I have one thing on my mind and that's winning! Our situation is sloppy right now . . . so this isn't the best time to introduce you to anyone."

Vanessa opened the door to her office. "I know what I'm doing. Now, if you'd excuse me, I have work to do," Vanessa completed as she proffered the door to Richard.

Vanessa watched as Richard walked toward her. "I'm sorry," he said. When he disappeared from her office, she closed the door releasing a sigh of relief. The truth was she wasn't sure about Richard or the direction of their relationship anymore. She'd been so insecure about getting the promotion to vice president of business affairs herself, that she'd actually stopped competing for it. And if Richard didn't get the position, she wasn't sure how far things could go anyway. Her agenda going into their relationship was clear but now everything had changed: her heart, her mind, and her motives. Love was never factored into the equation, and as of late, the roller coaster of emotions she was feeling had her spinning more and more out of control.

25

Kick Me While I'm Down

A lot of foulness has been running through my mind in slow motion. Scenes of me running up on Rich and Vanessa and snuffing them both out. The look on their faces would be full of shock as they cuddled up in her penthouse for the last time. I'm mainly interested in making Vanessa pay for stealing my man. She deserves to suffer a slow and painful exit. I ain't even gon' lie, if this was ten years back when I didn't give a damn about nuthin' but myself, the only thing Vanessa would've been fit for was a body bag.

My mind is playing tricks on me and the rest of the week goes by in a blur. I can't get my head straight for obvious reasons and a barrage of questions keep ringing in my head: what did I ever do to deserve this ill treatment from Rich? Why would Rich bounce on me like that? Does he still love me? Was he really ever happy with me? What does that bitch have that I don't, besides money? Does he think he is too good for me? Did Vanessa turn him against me? How long had he been planning to leave me? Did Vanessa have some dirt on him to make him leave so suddenly? Was that stuff Aunt Z mentioned about getting Co-lombo got true? Would Rich really set one of his boys up? Was there a dark side to Rich that I just never knew about? Did he really do that for me? If so, why would he take such great lengths to get me and then leave me? What was the other motive Aunt Z mentioned? The more questions that came to my mind, the more I realized that I really didn't even know Rich. All these years and I hadn't a clue that this man could possibly be a murderer just like that bastard Colombo. Only Colombo was man enough about his dalliances and didn't run and hide like a punk. Rich on the other hand created himself a new identity and was acting real brand new.

When the following week rolls around, I don't even want to return to work. I'm depressed and in a deep funk. Anyone and anything will cause me to snap.

Throughout our nine years, we had never been through a breakup of any kind. In the past, Rich may have spent a night out and claimed to be at one of his boy's or even his mother's, but this is different. This is for real and I'm losing it.

Gina came to my apartment to visit the day after I was re-leased from jail. After sobbing the story of what had happened after I left her house, she practically flew over to see me. When I open the door to let her in, I can tell she has been crying. Gina is definitely my girl. Some people need a clique of friends to feel whole, but as far as I'm concerned, I only need Gina. She is the real thing. Through thick and thin, she's truly my girl for life!

The following Monday when I return to work, I'm in a zombie-like trance and do my best to keep to myself. It isn't my intention to throw up any red flags, so I try to avoid intimate conversations. However, my area is similar to a water-cooler area. People enjoy coming around my desk to gossip and make idle conversation. I'm not in the idle conversation–type mood. To make matters worse, everyone wants to hear full details of my week away in the sun. I would never reveal that the sun was merely a black abyss in a gloomy sky—my man left me for a whore while I nearly rotted in jail. My anticipated vacation had been nothing but torment. Thankfully, my desk is covered in the work that had accumulated during my absence and I'm able to bury myself beneath my workload for the first two days.

When Wednesday rolls around the pile has dwindled down to a small stack and coworkers begin flooding my area again. I'm able to keep them away, because the radio ratings came in. WFAT ranked number three overall, which isn't good since there were only four urban stations in the city. However, we are number one during the midday drive. Those numbers are decent, but we have lost our number two position and the general manager and corporate management are up in arms. The office is in a frenzy and since I'm good at brainstorming, I volunteer to help build a strategy to retain and further grow our audience. Though we have a marketing and research department to craft this idea, I thought it would be good to prove my worth in other areas. I have other aspirations and in order to make more money, it would be in my best interest to make myself useful and show off my marketing skills.

Although I took on other projects and found myself extremely busy, I couldn't get Rich off my mind. For years, he was my nourishment and kept me full. He filled my heart with joy through good times and bad, because no matter how bad things may have gotten between us, I knew he would always be there. He was my life partner and best friend. We laughed together, made passionate love (and the sex was still crazy), shared private moments, cried, fought, and worshipped together. I want this to all go away and just be a nightmare that would disappear when I wake up. But it isn't.

Reality hits when I try calling his office and his assistant answers the phone. I never bother leaving a message, because I'm sure he will never get it. As long as the wicked Vanessa of the West is there, I'm sure of this fact. The only thing stopping me from going to his job and waiting for him outside is the possibility of another confrontation with Vanessa. I know if I saw them step outside all giddy and gay, I won't hesitate to pounce on her and this time it won't be a little shiner. She'll have a full-blown head injury and cracked ribs after I mercilessly stomp her into the concrete. However, it would be fine with me if I never saw the inside of a jail cell again.

For the entire week I am sick. I can barely keep anything down and reduce my diet to dry cereal and green tea in the morning. Ginger ale, crackers, and an apple for lunch and lettuce, spinach, grated carrots, and cucumbers for dinner. I must be losing weight in the process. Ron doesn't waste any time commenting on that fact either as I walk by his office on Thursday while heading to the marketing department.

"Damn, baby," he says. "I like my women with meat on their bones, so don't go losing no more weight up in here."

My only response is the look of death my eyes shoot his way and he immediately backs off. At least I think he's left me alone, until I return to my area and find him sitting in the guest chair in my semiprivate office.

I saunter to my desk and sit down. I pretend he isn't even there, which is nearly impossible but I don't want to be bothered.

"Val. I know you see me sitting here."

"I didn't invite you to invade my space and I'm very busy, so what do you want?" I snap.

"Just checking in on you. Ever since you returned from vacation you've been in a mindless stupor and if you think people haven't noticed you're wrong. I thought that vacations were for relaxation. It looks like you went to visit hell, had a brush with the devil, and came back instead of chilling on some tropical island."

If only Ron knew how close to the truth he is, because the devil did pay me a visit. The devil disrupted my life as I once knew it.

Trying to maintain my breathing pattern, I look at Ron as if he is the one with the problem. Ron is the last person I'd ever confide in. He's only interested in getting some ass, and mine isn't up for grabs.

"Why are you acting so nasty to me, Val? What have I ever done to you?"

"Ron, why is my behavior of any concern to you? And you've hit on me so many times, it's a wonder I haven't filed a complaint against yo' ass! You know I have a man, and if I told him how you've been trying to push up on me you'd be laid out on the floor. Now to answer your question, I get tired of you pestering me. I wish you'd find yourself a woman who will give you the time of day so you can leave me alone."

"Pardon me for paying you a compliment every now and again. I didn't realize you were so bothered by me singing your praises. I was only trying to be friendly and I do find you attractive. You always seem so serious. Now if trying to put a smile on your face from time to time is a problem, I'll leave you alone. You don't have to worry about me invading your space, pushing up on you, or being concerned about you anymore either. If folks wanna speculate and talk behind your back, guess what, that's their business. I'm out."

Ron stand up from the chair and walks out of my office without so much as a backward glance. I'm glad, because if he had turned around he would've seen the lone tear roll down my cheek.

When I get home that evening I'm sick to my stomach and I'm all cried out. The only thing crying proves to do is make me weak and I'm far from being a weakling.

An entire week has gone by and not a peep from Rich. To make matters worse, he changed his cell phone number and I know this isn't Rich's doing. He's incapable and too lazy to do anything like this on his own. For years we had shared a joint cellular account. It was my responsibility to make the monthly payments, because Rich and I agreed I would handle all the household bills. But with the change of his number, it's definitely time for some action.

26

❧

Page Six

"Where in the hell are my black pearl earrings?" Vanessa barked. "The limo is out there waiting and I can't be late."

"You had them on the dresser. Chill out!"

Vanessa rolled her eyes at Richard, unsure of whether or not he was telling the truth or just way too involved in her business to know where she kept everything. She looked at him, not being able to resist the smile that donned his face. He looked amazing. *Damn!* Vanessa thought to herself. Richard had on a midnight black tux, with platinum accents including platinum shirt, tie, and cuff links. He did clean up well, Vanessa thought, but still there was a sense of dissatisfaction.

Richard neared Vanessa with his hand extended. "Here you are my love, and might I say how beautiful you look tonight."

Vanessa forced a smile. She had decided on an elegant black Marchesa beaded halter gown with complementing Prada strapped sandals. The two made a fine couple, yet that didn't detour Vanessa from her obvious strange attitude. She had been bitchy for days with regard to Richard, perhaps because of him moving in and them officially becoming a couple. The meaner she was to Richard, the easier it was for her to deny her true feelings.

On so many levels she wanted to love him, but knew the battles she would have to fight as a result of that. First, there would be Valentine. Although Vanessa felt secure that physically Val would never do anything else to her, or Richard for that matter, a ghetto 'hood rat of her sorts would definitely create emotional drama for months to come. There was no way Valentine was going to just let what took her years to perfect go without more of a fight. And although Vanessa knew she could hold her own, Valentine would be a major factor in the stability of their relationship.

Second was her job. After receiving her master's degree, Vanessa knew that the number one rule in business was to never make business personal on any level.

Her final reason, which brought her the most grief, was her family. Although it was her father's job as a judge to be objective, once Lady Cornelia got wind of things getting serious with Vanessa and Richard, the shit would certainly hit the fan.

Vanessa had to be smart.

"I arranged for a separate limo to pick you up and take you to the event. I'll catch up with you there, okay?" Vanessa said in passing as she reached for her wrap and made her way to the door.

"My limo? What are you talking about? Aren't we riding together?"

"I'm picking up my parents who are staying at the Waldorf Astoria. I told you they were attending the event."

"What's that got to do with us taking separate cars?" Richard demanded.

"Richard, we've been over this a million times. Business and pleasure don't mix well with my family. There is a time and a place to tell my family about us, and this isn't the time. Well, not to parade our relationship in front of them anyway. This is work."

"They do know about us though, right?"

Vanessa tried to gloss over the question with a quick kiss on Richard's cheek. "You look incredibly handsome, sweetheart. I'll see you a little later, okay?"

She darted out of the door, quickly pressing the button on the elevator before Richard followed. She hadn't time for any further explanation nor could she give anything more than what she already had.

Luck was not on her side. Within minutes Richard swung the door open and raced after her.

"Vanessa wait!" He shouted without realizing she was still in the hallway. "This is ridiculous. What the hell is going on?" His voice lowered as he gently closed the door behind him.

Vanessa pursed her lips together. "Nothing, Richard! Why are you acting so paranoid? It is what it is. Please don't ruin a perfectly great evening over riding together to our work event. If we rode together, my mother would drill you to pieces with questions. I can't have them know you are living with me temporarily. You've got to trust me."

Vanessa searched Richard's face, looking for some sign that he'd bought what she was selling. Her head began to throb. At this rate tonight was going to be a long one.

That was the hesitation. Vanessa finally figured it out. Ever since Richard had completely broken things off with Val, his confidence seemed to escape him. He had become clingy and a bit needy and Vanessa didn't like that. Richard had always been take charge, doing what he had to in order to hold her down, but now, he was just . . .

"Cool!" Richard responded dryly.

The elevator door opened, and Richard extended his hand, allowing Vanessa to enter first.

"If this is what you want, Vanessa, really I'm good."

"Really?" *Damn*, she thought. He was starting to appear sexy again.

"Yeah, I don't want to fight. We've been doing too much of that lately. I'ma just chill, a'ight?"

"I'm glad to hear that! We're going to be fine. We'll have a great time tonight at the gala, and then when we get home . . ." She leaned in to kiss him, but with a subtle step back, he paused.

"Don't mess up your makeup, wouldn't want you to be flawed tonight."

Her brow rose and she cut her eyes, trying to read his face, but she couldn't. She didn't know if she truly desired to know the true meaning behind his words.

"You're right. I need to be flawless tonight."

The two made their way out of the elevator and into the lobby of the building.

"Your cars are waiting," the bellman announced as Vanessa walked past him.

"So I'll see you there shortly."

Richard nodded but kept his silence.

The driver opened the door to her limo; she slipped in blowing a kiss good-bye to Richard. He remained there, waiting until she was safely inside.

Once he was no longer in sight, Vanessa leaned against the cold leather seat, wrapping her shawl securely around her shoulders, and sighed. What had happened to get her to where she was? And further, did she have what it took to stand up to her family? She felt that the distance toward Richard was wearing thin. He had

sacrificed so much for her that her appreciation beyond sexual gratification would have to become more obvious.

Now would be the best time to establish a true relationship
between the two of them professionally anyway. At least if she
did it now while they were on the same level, once Richard was
promoted, there would be no questions as to why they were dating. To the blind eye, it could be true love and nothing more.

"Where to Ms. Knight?"

"The Waldorf Astoria. I didn't realize how cold it was going to
be tonight." Vanessa tried to rethink her prior arrangements with
her parents. Instead of meeting them for drinks at the bar, she
decided that perhaps it would be a better idea to just have them
come directly out to the car and head to the event. She didn't
want Richard to be by himself for long at the event, especially
with how she'd just left things. She knew there would need to be
some type of reinforcement of her feelings for him before it was
too late.

"Jerome, I've opted not to do drinks with my parents. Once we
pick them up, I'll need you to get us to the event as quickly as possible."

"Will your parents know the new plans?"

"I'll phone my father now. Thank you, Jerome. Just be mindful
of the urgency in which I'll want to arrive at the event."

"Yes, ma'am. I'll get you there in ample time."

Vanessa reached for her cell phone to call her father. Although
she could already hear the protest coming from her mother, she
didn't care. Tonight was going to be all about her and Richard. At
that moment, nothing else mattered.

✣

"I still don't understand why you are in such a hurry, Vanessa, really. Whatever it is, can't it wait? You have this driver driving like he's in NASCAR!"

"Mother, please!" Vanessa touched up her makeup. "I told you this is a very big night for me and Richard. All of the partners and investors are going to be there. I don't want Richard doing a thing without me. With the consideration for promotion weighing heavily on this event, I need for everyone to know just how serious I am."

"I think your determination is remarkable dear," Justice Knight doted.

"Thank you, Daddy." Vanessa smiled, hoping that would cool her mother's engines a bit.

Cornelia frowned. "I'm not buying that one bit."

Vanessa kept her compact opened, with hopes of avoiding her mother's glare.

"Vanessa is a shoo-in for this promotion. Why wouldn't she get it? She's worked hard, and is a genius when it comes to her work. This is about that man, William. And it's shamefully obvious to me that that is what this is truly about."

"Now dear!"

"There will be none of that. I'm surprised at you, William, for not picking up on your daughter's entire demeanor." Cornelia placed her hand on her husband's knee. "Your daughter's in love."

"Love, that's absurd!"

Vanessa firmly shut her compact, her eyes now fixed on her mother's face.

"Is it, Vanessa? What's absurd to me is how you could possibly allow yourself to fall in love with some common street thug."

"Do we know he's from the street?" William quizzed.

"Cornelia always knows, dear." Vanessa's mother answered him sarcastically.

"I am not having this conversation with you, Mother, not tonight."

"Cornelia, can't this wait until later?" Justice Knight chimed in. "This is a very important night for Vanessa. Let's not ruin it by slinging around accusations."

"I wish I could say that it was an accusation, honey, yet Vanessa knows that it's not."

Vanessa sighed. "You know what, Mother? I don't understand why you continuously do this. Why do you always think that someone is hiding or keeping secrets from you?"

"Because, dear, they usually are!"

Vanessa reached for a glass and poured herself some water. "I have nothing to hide," she said, taking a small sip.

Cornelia rolled her eyes. "Then when were you going to tell me and your father that you were attacked by Richard's ex-fiancée a few weeks ago? Is that why you didn't attend the party, because you were battered by some ghetto bimbo? Darling, really, what has gotten into you? And then you sit there and deny your feelings for this man. I don't understand!"

"You wouldn't, and frankly I don't have the energy to explain it."

The timing of the limo stopping couldn't have been more perfect, as Jerome opened the door, saving Vanessa from any further conversation. As she exited the car, she was greeted by a flash of photographers and a familiar hand offering assistance.

"I was waiting for you." Richard smiled as he helped Vanessa out of the car.

His smile was dashing and his sentiment sincere. "I'm glad

you're here . . ." was all Vanessa could say as she held on tightly to Richard's hand, drawing his body near to hers.

"You're shaking. Are you all right?" he whispered.

Vanessa looked into his eyes then back toward her parents, who had made their way out of the car. "Yes." Her voice was faint.

"Ms. Knight . . . Mr. Washington, can you tell us a little something about the new line?"

"Will you pose for a picture?"

"Do you think this new division will help bring Jorge Jacobs to the next level?"

Vanessa clenched Richard's hand tightly. This was their night and she didn't care what that meant in terms of her mother. To Vanessa, Richard may have a shady past, but he made her feel special in the right now. And with their future hanging in the balance of what already appeared to be a successful evening, Vanessa knew that the best was yet to come.

"Mr. Washington . . . Ms. Knight! Can we get a photograph for Page Six?"

Vanessa smiled, leaning closely into Richard's arm. "It would be my pleasure!" she said, responding for the both of them.

27

❧

Bred and Mother!

Applause surrounded the parade of people waiting to speak to Vanessa and Richard, who had officially just launched the new line for Jorge Jacobs. With the partners whisking Vanessa away, Richard was able to have a moment to himself. Tonight had marked the beginning of everything he had ever wanted. Thoughts of Valentine quickly came and went as Richard stood in the Crystal Serenity reception area. As a server carrying champagne passed by, Richard reached for a glass.

"Wow! Things have certainly changed," he said to what he thought was himself.

"Big leap from the projects, isn't it, Richard?" Cornelia whispered.

"Excuse me?" Richard turned to face Vanessa's mother. "Mrs. Knight, I didn't know you were standing there. I'm sorry, what did you say?"

"Oh, I think you heard me, dear." Cornelia reached for a glass of champagne, took a sip, then shooed the server away. "It's impressive to me how you've managed to accomplish so much coming from so little. You should be proud."

Richard wasn't sure if Mrs. Knight's words were complimentary or insulting.

"I am very proud," he replied.

"Interesting enough, Vanessa tells me you two have become more than just colleagues. That's a concern."

Richard smiled. He guessed Vanessa had finally broken it to her family that they were a couple.

"I'm glad Vanessa finally told you about us. We've been together for a while now, but wanted to wait for the right time to go public with our relationship. If you're worried about the timing with the promotion at stake, don't be. I love Vanessa and I'm not concerned about what people think or how we got here. As long as I know she loves me in return, we're cool."

"Darling . . ." Cornelia sighed. "Do you really think Vanessa loves you?"

"Yeah, I do. What Vanessa and I have is real. We have so much in common."

Cornelia laughed, bringing an immediate frown to Richard's face. "Now that's funny. What could you two possible have in common? Vanessa's a socialite, having been bred from one of the finest African-American families on the East Coast. She is the heir to an estate that's worth over one billion dollars, with a father who is ready to run for political office." Cornelia pulled in a bit closer. "What you two have in 'common' is costing our family potential future damage. I heard about the little run-in with your ex-fiancée."

Richard took a deep breath and two steps back from Cornelia. "That was an unfortunate situation for everyone involved."

"No, my dear, it was just unfortunate for us."

Not knowing where this was going and becoming a bit frustrated, Richard spoke. "Mrs. Knight, what is it that I can do for you?"

"I want to tell you a story, Richard. Please indulge me for a moment, and then I'll leave you alone."

Richard nodded his consent and Mrs. Knight continued.

"When I was a little girl, I asked my father for a pony and without hesitation he said no. I knew we had enough money and couldn't understand why he was being so cruel. I looked up in astonishment, and asked why. And he said to me, 'Cece, the only thing a pony is good for is a cute little ride. If you want a horse, I'll buy you a thoroughbred.'

"Now, I'd seen my fair share of ponies, and horses for that matter, but couldn't tell you truly what a thoroughbred was. So, I studied everything I could about this animal. Learning about their backgrounds, their bloodlines, understanding their performance and finally why they cost so much. And I discovered that it's because their bloodlines can be traced back to three generations of winners. No exceptions. Their blood is not soiled by anything impure with a somewhat shady past. They've been bred with the likes of their own, regardless of another horse's appearance."

Cornelia regained her close position to Richard. "You see, Richard, a thoroughbred gives the illusion of just another racehorse when you look at it on the outside. But what makes a thoroughbred distinctly different from that other horse is what is on the inside, making any true breeder protective not to mix the stock.

"This ex-fiancée of yours . . . it's safe to say you come from the same stock. Two eagerly ambitious people from the projects who climbed their way up the corporate ladder and became something of themselves! Admirable at best."

Richard's face burned with anger, yet he kept his composure as Cornelia continued.

"Now, Valentine—I take it that is her correct name . . ."

Richard nodded, anxious to get to the point.

"There is your something in common." Cornelia peered in a little closer, dusting a piece of lint from Richard's tuxedo. "As the breeder of my Vanessa, you have to know, that regardless of where you think you are going in life, it's where you come from that won't allow this relationship to last. The justice and I are very particular about our investments. They must date back to three generations of success."

Cornelia patted Richard on the back. "You're a fine young man. Very similar to that pony I wanted as a child."

Richard firmly bit his bottom lip. He struggled to preserve his poise. He knew that there was a time and a place for everything and this was neither the time nor the place for such a confrontation.

"But Daddy was right; it would have been only good for a cute ride. Enjoy your evening, Mr. Washington."

"Mrs. Knight," he managed to mutter.

As she waltzed away, Richard seethed with anger. Had this not been a civilized event, he would have set her tired ass straight for even attempting to belittle him.

She was right, he came from the gutter. His father was a hustler, and his grandfather was as well. And even though he didn't know either of them, he knew enough about himself to want to slap the champagne out of Mrs. Knight's couture bourgeois ass.

His first thought was to get gangsta on her by having one of his chicks give her a good beat down, but that would be too obvious, especially after the stunt Val pulled on Vanessa. Yet an even better way to burst Mrs. Horse Bitch's bubble would be to knock up her prized possession and breed a little Richard Washington II, just to shut her up.

"Hey you . . ." Vanessa said, sneaking up behind Richard and placing her arms around his waist. "I've been looking for you everywhere. What are you doing over here by yourself?"

Richard turned to Vanessa, who wore bright eyes and a perfect smile on her face.

"Just thinking," he replied, masking his true feelings by returning her a joyful expression.

"Hopefully you were thinking about us." Vanessa leaned in close to his chest. "I love you."

Richard's heart warmed at the sound of those words, yet quickly faded with the remembrance of her mother's words just moments ago. "I've waited a long time to not only hear you say that but to know you mean it."

"I do mean it, Richard. You truly make me happy." Vanessa stared into Richard's dark brown eyes. "Either that, or I've had way too much champagne," she joked.

Richard pulled her close, giving her a big hug. With Vanessa by his side, it really didn't matter about his background, together they were winners. He wasn't anybody's cute pony, and the bond with Vanessa would definitely be for the long haul and not a temporary ride.

28

❧

Apples Don't Fall Far

"Yo, your mom was bugging the other night," Richard said, smiling as he rolled off Vanessa. The glow from their lovemaking brightened the room as her pearly whites sparkled against the sunlit room.

Distracted by her pounding heart she wasn't sure what Richard had just said. She kissed him gently on the brow, making her way across his face to his lips.

"I love you," she whispered, rubbing his chest. "Now what were you saying about my mother?"

Richard returned the kiss, only this time it was longer and more intense than the one he'd just been given. With his next breath, he repeated his statement.

"My mom? When did you two speak?"

Vanessa's heart pounded. She wondered what her mother was up to now and what new plan she had to sabotage their relationship.

"She pulled me to the side the other night at the party and

straight went off on me, saying stuff like I'm not good enough for you."

Vanessa pulled away. She'd gotten to him. "I'm sorry. That's just her way."

Vanessa could feel the heat that had just been between them instantly fade as her body became cold.

"Her way?" Richard's voice was sharp. "Oh so it's just her way to make people feel like shit while she talks about how high her horse is?"

"Richard, my mother may never approve of this relationship, I told you that. That's why I was in no hurry to introduce you to my family. But I did, so that should tell you something."

"What does it tell me, Vanessa? That being with you means I have to constantly prove myself to your bourgeois family?"

Vanessa sat up, pulling the blankets close to her body to cover her bare skin. She leaned over and placed her long tresses in a ponytail.

"That's not fair, Richard, and you know it. My mom is from a different breed."

He sighed. "Oh she told me all about her breeding."

"Please let me finish," Vanessa interrupted. "Richard, my mom comes from the old school. If she had it her way she would arrange both my brother's and my marriages. When you come from a family that has generations of success and money, people become territorial. That's all."

"That's no excuse to be rude. And your mom's bitchy behavior was foul."

Vanessa nodded her head in agreement.

"How are you going to love me and spend your life with someone your family hates so much?"

"Did she say she hated you?" Vanessa teased. "Oh, the last

boyfriend she hated, well, let's just say I don't exactly know whatever happened to him."

"That shit ain't funny." He snickered.

"It's so ridiculous, it actually is. Richard, I'm an adult. My father isn't like that. Although he'll have his concerns about the seriousness of this relationship, he won't be a snob about it."

"If you had a daughter and she wanted to date a man like me would you approve?"

Without hesitation Vanessa answered, "No!"

"What the . . ."

"Baby," she said, pulling him close. "You've got to understand I'm an heiress. I don't talk about the kind of money we have, but look around, sweetie, this isn't lotto winnings! My net worth is a pretty penny. My parents are concerned because my decisions affect everything they've worked so hard to build. And technically they have a right to their opinions and to protect their assets from future or potential liabilities. My family thinks about things far beyond the now. Are there outside children involved? What will be your family's needs? We have an image to protect so what will their image bring to our family? Those kinds of issues are the sort of things my mother is getting at."

Vanessa's eyes met Richard's. "The fact that I lost my virginity before I was married was a major thing to my family. I was raised better than that. It didn't matter that I was engaged to the man that took my virginity. The fact that I had soiled the relationship by having sex before marriage could've cost me my inheritance."

"Are you serious? Yo, your family be tripping over some dumb shit. They uptight as hell. When did you lose your virginity? Yo, better yet, when did you get engaged?"

"My relationship before you. He was an attorney in my father's firm. We went to college together and then we were engaged after graduate school. He . . ." Tears formed in Vanessa's eyes.

"What happened to him?"

"He died in a car accident."

"Whoa. Baby, I had no idea. I'm sorry to hear that, Nessa."

Vanessa rolled onto her side, pushing herself up from the bed. "I realized tonight that I think I'm finally ready to leave the past in the past." She smiled. "Whatever my mother said to you is unacceptable. I apologize for her behavior and assure you it won't happen again."

The champagne-colored silk robe gloved Vanessa's body as she slipped into it, walking away from the bed. Barely making eye contact with Richard, she turned. "You just have big shoes to fill, is all. My ex was everything to a lot of people. You're what comes next."

"So no matter what I do, I'll always be second best."

"The night he died, I died. The me that's with you is a totally different creation." Her voice was shaky. "Richard, you're not second best. Our entire relationship is a first. It's all in your perspective."

As the words tumbled out of her mouth, Vanessa knew she was lying. Even though she had rebelled for years after Dexter's death, she knew it was just a matter of time before she'd have to face her demons and deal with the emotions that were causing her to act out. Richard meant the world to her, and for that she was grateful. However, like her mother, she wondered just how far this was going to go. And with Vanessa's feelings moving from like to love for Richard, she knew that it wouldn't be long before the bad apple that was her mother would spoil the whole bunch.

29

❧

Trouble on My Mind

The stress over losing Rich causes my body to writhe with pain. My stomach feels like it's doing somersaults and no amount of pain relievers will reduce the pain. I feel like a black cloud is looming over my head and the only way to remove it is to deal with the problem.

Earlier, as I was leaving the office, something caught my attention and I felt like a deer caught in headlights. Strewn across the table in the reception area I caught a glimpse of the society section of the *New York Post*'s Page Six. There was a picture of our infamous shock jock, Noches Star, aka Nosezianno, looking a hot mess in "hooker gear." She wore a leather bustier dress that looked painted on and barely covered her ass, a mink stole (it's early summer), fishnet stockings, six-inch stilettos, and more bling than Busta Rhymes and the Flipmode Squad combined. Noches's getup was a complete disaster. Still, what was even more shocking was who she was cozying up with. Accompanying her was Logo Benton, the most recent number one NBA draft pick, and according to the media, "The Gift." Noches could be a looker if she removed a few layers of the plaster she decorated her face with. Aside from that Noches had to be a good ten to twelve years older than Logo. I picked up the paper to see if they mentioned how involved Noches and Logo were, the type of event they attended, and if the radio station was involved. As I scrolled down farther, something even more disturbing caught my eye. On the opposite page in black and white was a huge photo of Rich and Vanessa, looking a bit too fancy, free, and happy for my liking. The byline read: "Vanessa Knight, Jorge Jacobs's director of business and heiress to Soul Shine, accompanied by Richard Washington, also of Jorge Jacobs, announced the launch of a new clothing line under Jorge Jacobs. Logo Benton has signed an endorsement deal to promote the clothier."

Now they were flaunting their relationship for the world to see. They weren't all over each other like Noches and Logo, but they held hands, which came across loud and clear.

After staring at the picture for at least five minutes I'm shook. My face becomes rose red and I feel a stabbing pain in my eye. For once, I'm able to hold back on the tears, but I'm heated and can feel the heat emitting from my head.

"Val, are you all right?" Kristina, the receptionist, asks.

"What?" I say, irritated.

"I asked if everything was all right. You've been standing there mumbling under your breath for a minute."

I try to regain my composure, because I can't afford to lose my cool in the office.

"Yeah, I'm good," I say, closing the paper and returning it to the table.

"You saw the picture, huh?"

"What?" I ask. I'm in no mood to chitchat and discuss my personal business with our busybody receptionist.

"The picture on Page Six?"

"What about it?" I say, agitated.

Kristina jumps back like I've just bit her with venom and cast her eyes downward, but I can care less. She is always in business that has nothing to do with her own.

"Well, can you believe they were out in public? I mean, there were rumors that they were an item."

"What rumors? How long have you known?" I'm seething with anger.

"I've known for a while. A few of us knew they had been kicking it for a couple of months, but I didn't know they were gonna make it official."

At that moment, I want to slap that stupid grin off Kristina's face. I can't believe she was throwing this up in my face like it's a game. Even I'm not that insensitive. And who are the others that know? Were they laughing behind my back?

"But that just goes to show you that all the money in the world can't buy you taste. Did you see all that jewelry and those shoes? She looked like a straight hooker going on a ho stroll on Forty-second Street." Kristina begins laughing and a wave of relief causes me to join in on the laughter.

Kristina is referring to Noches Star and there I am thinking she's referring to Rich and Vanessa. My heart rate returns to normal.

After the laughter dies down between us she continues. "Girl, I saw your boo looking all good on the opposite page. Why you ain't up in the picture with Rich?"

In a flash the expression on my face goes from humor to re-

vulsion. Kristina, though we chatted from time to time, is an out-
sider, and I wasn't about to let her into my world. My private life.
My relationship with Rich is truly the envy of the office. Nearly
every woman at WFAT comments on how good of a man I have.
How fine Rich is. How smart Rich is. How Rich holds me down.
How sweet and considerate Rich is. How lucky I am to have a man
who has a job with benefits and I never disputed their claims,
because everything they said was true. Rich is all of those things
and then some, but he is human and with that comes flaws. I'd
never admit any of his shortcomings to associates, work colleagues,
or passersby. I'm not one of those women who joke about how unsatisfied they are with their man. If anything, I sang Rich's praises
and allowed those around me to do the same. The last thing I
want is Kristina, who is switchboard central, to be gossiping my
business to everyone in the office. I can't let on that things are
presently unstable between Rich and me. Instead, I have to front
like life was all good.

"Photographers use the pictures that they like best. Anyway, it
wasn't about me and Rich, it's about Jorge Jacobs and the new
venture with Logo," I say, plastering a fake grin on my face.

"True, but it would've been nice to have seen you on Page Six,
instead of that stiff-looking broad in the picture with him."

Kristina's words are my exact sentiments. Without responding, I bid her good night and make my exit.

It is a few minutes to twelve on a Thursday night. I need someone
to talk to. Someone to help me through my agony.

The first person that comes to mind was Gina, who I know hit
the comfort of her sheets at ten o'clock sharp. That is unless she
and Oscar decided to get busy. I decide to take the chance and call.

After three rings someone picked up the phone.

"Mmh . . . hullo . . ."

"Gina? You asleep?"

I can hear her situating herself to sit upright. She knows if I'm calling at this hellified hour something must be wrong.

"Yeah, gurrrl. I fell asleep not too long ago though. Are you okay?" she asks, coming to her senses.

"Yes and no."

"Hold up. Let me go into the bathroom. I don't wanna disturb Oscar." Oscar must've felt her leaving the bed, because I can hear his groggy voice in the background and Gina soothing him back to sleep.

Now that's the type of relationship that I want right there! A man that feels my presence when I step out of the room. A man who wants *me* and only *me*. A man who makes *me* feel wanted.

Gina will forever be my best friend, but as I listen to them all cozy in the background, I feel envy do a nasty strut across my soul. The enormity of the feeling blazes a fire deep down in my chest and at that moment, I don't want to reveal my feelings to Gina. I realize that Gina, though she sympathizes with me, will never understand what I'm going through. How can she? She's living the good life with her husband. She has the perfect life. They are the perfect family and the most pain that Gina ever had to endure was when she gave birth to Ashley.

Gina's voice interrupts my thoughts.

"Girl, what's wrong? Did that no-good man come back?"

"No. Rich didn't come back. He's still chilling over there with the tramp."

"So what's wrong? When I asked if you were okay, you said yes and no."

"It's just that my body has been feeling so tired lately and things are kind of crazy at work," I say, trying to avoid the real reason for my call.

"Well, you've been through a lot lately, so of course your body is going to feel tired. You're lucky that's all your body is doing. You probably need to take a personal day or call in sick to get yourself together."

I listen, but my mind is elsewhere.

"Yeah, you're right."

"So what's going on at the job?"

"The job?"

"Yeah, you said something about things being crazy at work?"

"Oh, yeah." I hesitate, trying to remember the happenings at the job without bringing up the upsetting photo of Rich and Vanessa in the *New York Post*. "Well, the ratings came in and WFAT is next to last in the market. Management is tripping, so I volunteered to help out . . . but I think I've bitten off more than I can chew right now."

"Well, don't overdo it. Your job isn't to improve the ratings."

"I know. I did it to take my mind off of Rich, but the loss is devastating. It's like losing someone to death. He's still here, but I can't even see him."

"Girl, I hate that you're hurting like this. If I could see him right now, I'd spit in his damn face, but he didn't deserve you. He wasn't nothing but a dirty dog and you needed to cut his ass off a long time ago. I'm upset that he decided to leave you and not the other way around."

I've gone there without meaning to with Gina and already know the words that are going to come out of her mouth before they even form in her head. This is the tune she has been singing for the past five or six years. After the second incident of me find-ing out about Rich cheating, Gina has been chanting these words like a voodoo woman. These are the last words that I want to hear. I need words of encouragement or angry words that say she understands my pain. Not Gina's same tired, "hewasn'tnothing-butadirtydogandyouneedtocuthisassoff" mantra.

The purpose of me calling Gina isn't to turn my frustrations toward her, and my blood is boiling with anger. Mean words not really meant for Gina race through my head, so I decide to end the call short.

"Listen, I'm gonna try to get some rest for work tomorrow."

"You are starting to feel sleepy?"

"Yeah," I lie. "My eyes are finally starting to feel a little heavy."

"Okay, good. Well, give me a call when you have some down-time at work. And don't overwhelm yourself by overloading yourself. Take it easy. Okay?"

"Yeah. I hear ya."

"Love you, sis."

"You too."

It's at times like now that I actually wish I had a sister. I know Gina doesn't mean me any harm, but that phone call leaves me unsatisfied. I find myself more upset than when we first got on the phone and I know that until I do something I'll continue to feel this way.

Before I know what I'm doing I'm in my ride heading over to my aunt's house. Even though she has a job, I know there's a strong possibility that she'll still be up chilling and smoking a blunt with J-Boogie. If she isn't up Shaquetta will be around.

After parking the car one block away, I head to my aunt's

building and the block is live. People are everywhere as if it was six or seven o'clock in the evening. Guys are chilling out front, playing dice, smoking blunts, talking yang, kicking it with the young girls who are fast and have been around the block one time too many in their young lives, selling dime bags and hustling other goods, while someone blares the latest mixed hip hop CD from their souped-up SUV with spinning rims. As I go by there are a couple of heads that recognize me and say hi, and a few knuckleheads try to spit game my way. I choose to ignore them.

Before I get to the elevator someone calls my name. I turn around in time to see my cousin CJ heading my way and I'm glad to see a familiar face. Though I speak to him on the phone from time to time, we rarely see each other.

"What up, cuz?" he says while stooping down to embrace me. "I see you made it outta the clinker."

He's laughing hysterically at his joke, but I know he's higher than a rocket after takeoff. I smelled the weed on him when he hugged me along with a little something else sweet on his breath.

"I'm glad you find it funny. Is Aunt Zenobia asleep yet?" I ask.

"She ain't even home," he states flatly as he pulls a joint from behind his ear to light up again.

"Not home? Where the heck is she at one in the morning? Don't she got work in the morning?"

"Yeah, but she probably chilling at J-Boogie's. Anyway, I ain't my mother's keeper, shawty. So what you up to this time of night?"

"Nothing much. I couldn't sleep and decided to come talk to Aunt Z about something."

"Well, ya ass shoulda called first, but since you here, you can always talk to me. I'm a good listener." The biggest Cheshire cat smile appears on CJ's face while he absently nods his head. I think about leaving, but I'm not in a rush to go back to my place, which no longer feels like home without Rich. Before I know it, we are sitting on the bench across from his building and I've told CJ everything that's in my heart. I tell him about the information Aunt Z had shared with me about Rich and Colombo, Vanessa and Rich's relationship, her visit to our church, the ruined vacation and the note, the incident at the restaurant, my night in jail and Vanessa's visit, and end it with the fact that Rich packed his belongings and straight up left me for her. CJ listen intently and I'm glad that I decided to open up to him.

"So what you wanna do, ma? You wanna get his bitch-ass back or what?" CJ says, standing up.

"What?" I ask, surprised, but I don't know if he's serious or running game.

"If you wanna get some payback, I'm with you. You my little cuz and a good woman. I ain't got no real love for dude, so it ain't no skin off my back if we bust a cap up his ass."

I must've taken one too many puffs from CJ's blunt or I'm just fed up. Either way, he is speaking my language and feeding my rage. It really doesn't matter, because at this point I'm miserable and payback is waiting for that witch, Vanessa.

"I'm a little messed up, so you should drive," CJ insists.

"No problem," I say as I lead the way to my vehicle on the next block.

"Yo, this here is a nice li'l whip you pushing, ma," CJ says, admiring my ride. "You should let yo' cuz hold it sometimes. Nah mean."

I know exactly what he means and I have no intentions of

allowing CJ access to my property without my presence. I never bother to respond and I'm grateful that he doesn't push the issue.

Once we are settled in my ride, CJ connects his iPod to my CD player and begins bumping a new Jay-Z joint. I roll down my window and let the warm breeze caress my face as we cruise down the lively streets of Brooklyn at two o'clock in the morning.

"This is my joint, right here. My man Jay-Z got the industry on lock. I'm 'bout to amp up my game like that playa. For real, though. I been stashing my cash and whatnot, been in the studio, and I'm about to leave the game alone. You feel me," CJ says as he puffs on another L.

I nod, happy to have him distract me from what we're about to do, even though it saddens me to know that by year's end CJ will probably be doing another stint at Rikers, and his dream for a better life is farther away than him trying to travel to China by foot. My only hope is that it won't be because of tonight's incident.

My head begins feeling light as the weed begins to really affect me. I don't normally smoke, however, on this particular occasion I feel like I need something to give me a jolt to go through with taking Vanessa and Rich out. My heart races as I turn the corner to head onto the Brooklyn Bridge. Once we cross the bridge, it'll be only a matter of minutes before we pull up in front of Vanessa's crib. This is real and there is no turning back.

CJ can be coldhearted when he wants to and I know what he's capable of as I glance at the shiny metal piece that he laid atop the CD storage space that separates us. Though tonight is atypical for me, it's just another day living in the 'hood for CJ. He doesn't like or dislike Rich, but our present circumstances cause him to hate Rich now. In the past they spoke out of respect for me, but that was the extent of their relationship. However, CJ knows that I'm hurting, and that I've gotten locked up for busting a chick in the face over Rich. I'm family and he's gonna do whatever it takes to remove me from my state of misery.

"You real quiet over there. You a'ight?"

"I'm cool," I say as I take a deep breath, trying to reassure myself more than CJ. I want to get there before I lose my nerve, but the vision of Rich and Vanessa cuddled up on Page Six causes fury to build in my heart and tears to well up in my eyes. We are less than two miles away as I begin to speed up First Avenue in an attempt to catch the traffic lights.

"You sure?" he inquires again while trying to smoke the remains of his blunt and not burn the tips of his fingers.

The hot tears scorch my face, temporarily blurring my vision. I use the heel of my hand to wipe my face and try to regain my composure.

"Yeah, I'm good. We're almost there." I glance out my window to avoid looking at CJ and to see our exact location. The car is moving so fast that the signs seem to be going by in a blur.

"Cool. Don't worry; it'll be all over soon. That punk will be a distant memory real soon."

A *distant memory*. Is that what I want to happen to Rich? I could care less about Vanessa, but I'm sure about never seeing the love of my life again. I'd walk on burning coals and jump through a ring of fire for Rich. However, if Vanessa were out of the picture permanently, Rich and I could be a couple again. After taking out his mistress, he'd know the lengths that I'd go to in order to keep him. He'd have to know how much I love him then and I'd truly only be returning the favor since he took Colombo out for me. Once I explain it to him that way, he'll definitely understand.

A smile creeps across my face and I place my focus back on the road as I wipe the last tear from my eye.

"Oh, shit! Val, look out," CJ blurts as his hand covers mine over the steering wheel.

30

❧

Vengeance Is Mine

The apartment is silent as we creep about looking for signs of life that will soon be snuffed out. Even though darkness descends on us as we attempt to silently make our way through the entrance foyer, the smell of wealth engulfs our senses. CJ stops momentarily to peer at his surroundings and is as mesmerized as I am by the space and its treasures. However, we aren't on a shopping excursion and this isn't Macy's window and I nudge him to continue our mission.

Votive candles flicker in the foyer, which leads to a massive room that resembles a museum. Large oil paintings cover the walls and I know without question that each piece is authentic artwork signed by the artists themselves. From the gorgeous Persian area rugs to the large crystal chandeliers that hover beneath the gilded ceiling, I truly begin to understand the power of money and its obvious influence.

Farther back are additional rooms, but to the left stands a spiral staircase which CJ and I spot at the same time. We navigate the place as if we've been there before and we have no doubt that the bedrooms are upstairs.

When we get to the top of the landing there are several rooms to select from. The majority of the doors are ajar. The longer it takes us to arrive at our destination, the more time it gives me to hate Vanessa. My only salvation is the fact that vengeance will soon be mine as we travel the long opulent corridor. The mere thought that I'll never see this much money no matter how hard I work in my lifetime causes me to seethe, building an inferno even the devil couldn't rival. The gold banister, which I don't doubt was is gold or gold plated, amounts to more than my last eight years' salary.

The artwork strategically masking the walls along with the unusual floor-to-ceiling curtains probably costs more than my entire department's annual earnings. Suddenly my hate turns to envy, but hate decides to challenge envy and wins the battle. It's the stronger of the two feelings. Then for the life of me, I can't understand why. Why does Vanessa find it necessary to take what rightfully belongs to me? Was Rich a game to her? A sport? It's obvious Vanessa can have anything money could afford, so why? Or is Rich one of her latest acquisitions, purchased lock, stock, and barrel, as well? The questions swarm me like a hive of bees buzzing for honey.

Rich and I don't belong in this world. This is a world reserved for people like Vanessa and her kind.

A pair of mahogany-paneled eyebrow-arch doors loom ahead and I know this is our final destination. Gingerly we walk along the glistening hardwood floors toward the entryway. I hesitate and CJ slides the gun from his waist and removes the safety. The sound jars me.

"CJ, hold up," I whisper.

"Wassup? You wanna handle this solo?" he asks.

"It's just that I'm not so sure about us doing Rich. I just want her out of the picture."

"Yo, for real, we can't leave no witnesses." CJ's arms are crossed.

"This mofo can turn on you and if we gonna do this, we gotta go all the way."

"Rich would never turn on me like that," I say, defending his honor as a lump forms in my throat.

"For real, then why is he up in the next chick's crib? Stop making excuses and let's do this."

It's then that I realize it's now or never. There is no such thing as a half stepping gangster. Maybe I'm in over my head, but I want to get rid of my misery and both Rich and Vanessa are the sources of my pain. She caused him to leave me. If she had never stepped into the picture, we'd still be together, but Rich got so caught up and brainwashed that he let a good thing go. The bottom line is that if I can't have him, no one can. He was my man first and will be my man until the day he dies!

CJ looks at me one last time and I give him my nod of confidence that I'm ready to go. He turns the knob on the bedroom door and it swings open.

The door opens to reveal the most palatial bedroom ever seen between the pages of Southern Living or Architectural Digest. The carpet is so plush that my feet sink in as if I'm walking on sand at the beach. The L-shaped room is sparsely decorated and for a moment we think we've entered the wrong room. We hear faint sounds and I boldly walk toward the noise. The closer I draw the more pronounced the noise.

The moonlight shines through the large picture window and their bodies glow from the light. His dick is pummeling in and out of Vanessa as she lays suspended beneath him, moaning and gasping with pleasure. Her utterances fill the air and the sight of their bodies intertwined is staggering. Their rhythm isn't nearly as fervent or eager as when Rich and I make love. As a matter of fact, it appears lackluster, but as his penis continues to thrust and invade her wet spot, I can see the sweat clinging to their bodies, making them meld together like glue. The temperature of my body increases along with my heart and pulse rates. I feel myself getting sick to my stomach and have the urge to regurgitate the food that I had digested hours before. The scream of terror that escapes my mouth breaks their rhythm. Rich turns his head and we lock eyes. Shock along with something indescribable fills his eyes. It is a stare that after ten years I have never seen before. In my heart, I want to believe that it is a gaze of regret. Guilt. Shame. Remorse. Sorrow. Pain. Lust, because he wants the body beneath him to be mine. Seconds passed and that look is replaced by an all-too-familiar look of pity and disgust, sinking my heart into the dark irises of Rich's eyes.

Vanessa is so caught up in the throes of passion she still hasn't realized we are there and locks her legs around Rich's calves to stimulate him to begin moving. But when he doesn't indulge her, Vanessa eases her body over to see what has stolen Rich's attention. Even in the dark, I can see the sinister smile that creeps on her face when she finally lays eyes on me. It is the same smug look that she wore at the restaurant that caused me to go off on her ass the first time. It is a look of victory. This is all a game to her as I stand on the sidelines like a spectator while she plays on the field having all the fun. She has my man now and there is nothing I can do. Or so she thinks, because in a flash I grab the cold metal from CJ's hand, aim at Rich, and pull the trigger twice. Before Vanessa can inch away from the crushing weight of his body, I pull the trigger one last time and the vain smile is now only a distant memory.

31

What Have I Done?

My head is pounding. I'm not aware of my surroundings and CJ is nowhere around. The last thing I remember clearly is pulling the trigger and watching Rich's body slump on top of Vanessa.

Where did CJ go so fast? One minute he was there and in a flash he was gone. It's almost like he vanished into thin air and now I'm left all alone to suffer the consequences of my actions.

The tears are sliding down my face, but I can't feel their dampness against my skin. I keep wiping my face, but there's no moisture and I become baffled. My eyes are filled to the brim with tears, but they aren't falling.

"Lawd, what have I done?" I bawl, but my cries fall upon deaf ears. Darkness surrounds me and the obscurity feels comforting. My mind begins to fill with thoughts of Rich and all of the good times that we shared and would no longer be able to, because of my jealous heart. If only I had given him the chance to come back to me. He would have eventually, but pride got in the way and I became impatient. I had to teach both him and Vanessa a

lesson. A lesson and a burden that would possibly never escape me and I would eventually pay a hefty penalty for.

My body is numb and I ache from the inside out. The feeling is nothing like anything I'd ever felt before. It is surreal and voices start to fill my head, but there's no one around me. The space I'm in is still dark and I feel trapped, but I'm afraid to make a move. I'm scared to move from that place and all I can will myself to do is to pray and ask for forgiveness. I need to be forgiven and I have no idea how I am going to face my family, Rich's family, my friends, or return to my job. What have I done and was it worth it? This misery is a greater abyss than before.

I'll drive myself crazy if I don't allow myself to think of happier times. The first time I laid eyes on Rich, I was with my homegirl and he was walking through Lafayette Gardens, looking like a black god with some chick on his arm. I dared not stare too hard, because if word got back to Colombo that I was peeping a next dude, it would've been my ass. Colombo had a quick temper and was incredibly jealous even though I had never given him reason to be that way. Still, my girl was clocking him and dissin' the girl that Rich was with. I listened casually as she scooped me on Rich. She clued me that she overheard he was going to be one of Colombo's runners. In my heart of hearts, that's when I knew trouble was going to start brewing. Colombo had a lot of boys and runners that came in and out of our lives, but I could tell Rich was special. Aside from that, he was the first person that I felt an instant attraction for and the last thing I wanted was for Colombo to pick up on my attraction to Rich. Colombo was always able to read me and if he thought I was lying, it was a wrap.

Almost a week later I had the fortune and misfortune of having my first encounter with Rich. Colombo, his boys Chief, Iron,

Butter, and I were in the house. I was supposed to oversee the girls as they bagged up the product while the guys tallied up the day's work. One or more of the girls was suspected of stealing, because we were supposedly coming up short on product. This reportedly had been happening for the past month. However, I never actually saw any of them mishandling the drugs. Still we kept falling short and I told Colombo that it wasn't the girls; it must've been one of his boys shorting him on the money side, because as far as I could see, everything looked good. The girls wore bathing suits and could barely conceal their tits and asses much less drugs. However, Colombo was determined to get to the bottom of the situation and randomly called each unsuspecting girl into the living room one by one. After I saw him and his boys doing a body search on the first girl, I became appalled and told him to stop being disrespectful. He ignored me and continued with his business. The second girl came out and they did a full body and cavity search. Colombo practically put his entire hand inside of her pussy while his boys copped free feels, parting her ass and lifting her top to fully expose her breasts. Just as I suspected, they found nothing and I was pissed and didn't want to subject the rest of the girls to their vulgar behavior so I told them to get dressed and go home.

Seconds after I gave the girls the order, Colombo and I got into a screaming match; he clocked me cold in my face causing my nose to bleed, and told me not to come between him and his business again. Shortly after, the third girl came into the living room. She appeared nervous, but I figured it was because the first two girls had reported how the guys had taken advantage of them. Colombo made her remove her top and bottom and told her to bend over. I got up to leave the room, but Colombo snatched me with the same hand he had just inserted into the girl's pussy and pushed me back down on the couch. I wanted to kill him, but knew if I tried anything he would kill me first.

The girl hesitated, her eyes staring in my direction as if pleading with me. I was in no position to help her as I steamed, thinking about how Colombo had disrespected me and possibly broken my nose. I turned my head when Colombo rammed his hand into her vagina. "Oh, God, please don't kill me," the girl pleaded.

My head whipped back around to see what was happening and Colombo removed two balloons from inside her. Hell and high water came to an impasse. I knew Colombo would have no problem killing her, and I wanted no part of what was about to go down. I tried to slither away. He practically shoved the balloons down my throat and I began to gag.

"This is what happens when you're not on your fucking job," he barked. "Tricks be stealing my product. All you have to do is watch them hos, but you so busy making friends you don't even see what's in front of your fucking face."

Astonished by the fact that he put the balloons that only moments ago were inside of her vagina in my mouth while his boys were rolling on the floor laughing, I became livid. I quickly spit them out and began to heave, forcing myself to vomit. When the shock wore off, I wanted to kill everyone in the room, including the girl for making me look stupid. I was upset for originally coming to her aid only to look like an ass in the end.

The girl tried to crawl away, but one of Colombo's boys kicked her to the floor and Colombo decided to get in on the action and began stomping her. She didn't even try to defend herself. She merely tried to cover her face as they kicked and beat her senselessly. I felt no mercy for her since she had brought this on herself.

By this time the other girls who had been in the back room became a captive audience. If they had had the notion of stealing anything from Colombo, they now knew better as they witnessed one of their coworkers being beaten to death.

When the guys were done with her and she was no longer moving, the girls ran back into the bedroom where they conducted their business. Colombo stepped over the lifeless body and headed to the back to deal with the rest of the women. I went in the direction of the bathroom to see the damage done to my face and to rinse my mouth. I didn't hear when Colombo entered behind me. He punched me in the back of the head, causing me to stumble closer to the sink and I held on for support. Before I knew what had come over me, I reached for the plunger beside the toilet and swung it at his head. I swung over and over, hitting his head and body a few times while he backed out of the small space in the bathroom. However, I was now at a disadvantage coming into the open area and he snatched the plunger from me and threw it across the room. He grabbed me and placed me in a headlock and was in the process of putting me to sleep when Rich came and pulled him off me. I don't know when he came into the apartment, but he was there. Colombo's boys were nowhere in sight, which meant they were probably harassing the girls. Rich wouldn't have been able to interfere if they were present. Still, if he hadn't come when he did, I don't know what would've happened. Colombo had beaten me in the past, but he never manhandled me the way he did that day.

"You betta get yo' hands off me," Colombo stated calmly. "If you wanna live, you'd betta back the fuck up."

"A'ight. I'ma back up, but why you wanna hurt yo' girl like that, man?"

"This here ain't got nuthin' to do wit you. I don't pay you to be up in my bidness. You understand, dawg?"

"I feel you. I'm not trying to step between y'all or nuthin'. All I'm saying is that you already got one girl out there half dead and now you about to do her too. I don't know what went down, but I'm just looking out for you."

Rich spit so much game to Colombo that after that I never received another beating like that again, until the day Colombo died. Rich not only saved my life once, but twice, and I repaid him by taking his life.

"How long has he been here? Huh? Get this trash out of my niece's room." The voice of my aunt Zenobia is as loud as a church bell at high noon. My head aches and I feel groggy, but I know without a doubt that my aunt is in the vicinity. As I attempt to open my eyes, everything looks cloudy and dark.

"Ma'am, please calm down. Ms. Daye has him listed as an emergency contact and he has a right to be here as well."

"He ain't got no got-damn rights! Get him outta here or I'm gonna call the po'lice. I'm this chile's next of kin. I'm her aunt and I want him out of here NOW!!! This negro got my niece driving crazy all times of the night and she nearly killed herself."

"Ma'am, please keep your tone down. Your niece is not the only one in this hospital. There are other patients that—"

"I don't give a damn about others. When you escort him out, I'll calm down."

"I'm just as concerned about Valentine as you are. That's why I'm here."

The voice is definitely familiar, but it can't be. It isn't possible for him to be here. This time when I open my eyes the vision is clear and I see a man in a white lab coat and a stethoscope, a doctor I presume. Aunt Zenobia is to my left and he is standing a few feet away from my aunt. None of this makes any sense to me and my surroundings are not in the least bit familiar.

"I'm going to have to ask you both to leave. The patient is coming out of her comatose state. We need to check her vitals."

"I ain't going anywhere. I need to make sure that Val is okay and I'm not stepping foot out of here until I'm sure!"

The man pushes some type of button above my bed and moments later two men in uniform enter the room. After much discussion both parties finally leave the room and the doctor and two nurses who have entered after the commotion stand by my bedside. He begins flashing a light in my eyes, while one nurse takes my blood pressure and the other changes my intravenous bag.

"Ma'am, do you know where you are?" he asks with a mild Indian accent.

"No," I answer, slightly confused.

"Do you know your name?"

Why is he asking me such stupid questions? I wonder.

"Yes, I know my name. It's Valentine Daye."

"Okay, great," he says, removing the light from my eye, satisfied with the dilation. "Well Ms. Daye, you are at New York–Presbyterian hospital. You've been hospitalized for twenty-four hours and comatose until now. You were in a very bad car accident. Do you remember the accident?"

"No. I wasn't in a car accident. What the hell are you talking about? Where's my aunt? Get my aunt and my cousin in here. I wasn't in any damn accident."

"Ms. Daye, please take it easy. You may have experienced

some memory loss. You've suffered a cerebral contusion and other bodily injuries, including a fractured arm, acute whiplash, and lower back disk injury. We need you to remain still. The injuries you sustained have caused your blood pressure to increase. Therefore, we need you to relax and we want you to know first and foremost that the baby is fine. Both you and the baby are going to be fine."

32

❧

What the . . .

What the hell is he talking about? This man is tripping. Did he just say baby? If I wasn't sure before, I'm positive now that I'm dreaming or Aunt Zenobia got ahold of me and allowed them to put me in some insane asylum.

First I wake up with a headache that no amount of aspirin or ibuprofen can possibly remedy. Then I think I'm hearing Rich's voice, but that can't be possible, because CJ and I knocked both him and Vanessa off. Then to top off the madness, this man whose name tag reads Dr. Pascal informs me that the baby is okay. He must have me mistaken for someone else. What the heck is he talking about? What baby? My ass is not pregnant and has never been pregnant. I'm on the pill and have been on the pill since I was fifteen. When he tells me that mess, I try to strangle him. I reach out and place my hands around his neck. Just before I begin choking the good doctor, I rip those pesky-ass needles from my arm. While the doctor is giving me his bogus-ass prognosis, the two nurses are poking and prodding needles into my arm and making me hella uncomfortable, so I snatch them the heck out.

Hours have passed, because the room is dark and I'm groggy as hell. They must've given me something to conk me out, because I don't remember much other than the doctor's face becoming bright red like a Christmas bulb, his eyes bulging from the sockets, and the nurses yelling. After that, everything is a complete blur.

When my vision finally clears up I see my aunt Zenobia fast asleep in the chair across from my bed. Her mouth is open wide enough for her to catch a few flies and I laugh at the thought. As kids, we used to put food in her mouth while she slept and she'd chew whatever we gave her in her sleep and never wake up. Those were simpler days.

"Girl, yo' ass is finally up?" Aunt Zenobia asks, getting up from her nap.

"Yeah, I'm up. I'm tired as hell though and my body aches all over."

"How you feeling?"

"Pretty banged up."

"That's what happens when yo' ass is speeding like a madwoman. You lucky you ain't killed ya' self. Shoot, that stupid-ass boy came running home high as a kite talking gibberish. The only thing I was able to get out of him was that you'd been involved in a car accident. He wouldn't tell me nuthin' else." Aunt Zenobia gets up and walks over to the bedside and leans on the railing. "So what in the hell happened? From what I understand the accident was way uptown, so how would CJ know before me or anyone else for that matter?"

The truth is I really don't know. My recollection doesn't include a car accident. It involves the death of Rich and Vanessa.

I remember being in the car with CJ and we were talking crap and then we went to the penthouse. My being in the hospital doesn't make any sense and I keep trying to put two and two together, but my answer comes up as five.

"Aunt Z, I really don't know what happened. I'm at a complete loss myself."

"Hmm, I'm sure you are," Aunt Zenobia says facetiously. She smacks her lips together as if she's just had a hearty meal. "Don't that man-stealing tramp live uptown? I heard the accident happened not too far from her Park Avenue address. Mmh-hmm! What business did you have up there at two-thirty in the morning?"

There is no use in responding, because Aunt Zenobia has already figured out half of the story herself. The part that she hasn't figured out is CJ. I refuse to give her any more ammunition, so whatever she conjures up in her head is good enough for me.

"Aunt Z, I'm feeling a little bit tired again. I'm drained."

"Yeah, I'm sure you are. Well, I'll let you and the baby get some rest."

"Baby? So it's true?" I ask, astonished to hear my aunt repeat what the doctor had told me earlier.

"Of course it's true. Your ass is pregnant! About three months. That doctor of yours has an attitude and wouldn't give me the full details. That's probably why you choked his ass up in here today and they sedated you. He probably deserved it. Anyway, Rich knows everything with his funky ass. I liked to whoop his ass up in here today. He rolls up in here posing like he a freaking television star, acting like he really cares. Whatever, playa playa! I raised so much hell, they finally made him leave. I knew when you woke up the last thing you wanted to see was him. Not after all the shit he's put you through. Oh, he had another thing coming. I'm yo' damn family, because when push comes to shove, we all you got."

All I hear is "three months pregnant." The rest sounds like Charlie Brown's teacher from *Peanuts*, "WHOMP-WHOMP-WHOMP!" I am really pregnant. What the hell am I going to do now? Am I really going to become a statistic? Single black woman with child, no husband, just another baby daddy. Don't we have enough of those already? This is exactly why I was faithful to the pill. Apparently, the pill hasn't been faithful to me.

I'm pregnant for the first time in my life by the man that I love and I'm glad to know he's not dead. However, we're not together anymore. He's moved on and has made it clear that he wants no part of me anymore. He's made a new life with Vanessa and though it's hard to accept I have to move on as well. I love him, but I have another life to be concerned with now, if I decide to keep the baby. It isn't too late; I still have options available to me.

A petite, freckle-faced, redheaded nurse enters the room cautiously. For whatever reason, she seems frightened. She removes the chart from the foot of the bed and remains at a safe distance. After reading the paperwork, she practically tiptoes to the machine with the IV bag.

"You can come closer, she ain't gonna bite," Aunt Zenobia snaps. "Why she up in here treating you like you got some type of man-eating disease?"

The nurse nervously changes the bag and pushes some buttons on the heart monitor machine.

"Aunt Z, its okay." I try to reassure the nurse. I know she's behaving that way because of my earlier attack on the doctor.

"Ms. Daye, is it okay if I take your blood pressure?" the nurse asks politely. I nod slightly and a sharp pain hits me. I use my free hand to rub the area.

"How is your neck feeling?" she asks.

"A little stiff," I reply as I try to stretch my head up to the ceiling.

"That's to be expected, but try not to move your head too much right now. The brace is there to support your neck injury, so don't put too much strain on yourself, okay?"

"No problem."

"Is there anything that I can do for you? Would you like a pain reliever to help you rest comfortably?"

"Yes, that would be good and some fruit if you all have some. I'm hungry."

"We can get you a meal if you prefer," the nurse says, finally relaxing.

"No, I'd prefer fruit if possible. I don't want to eat anything too heavy before going to sleep."

"Okay, I'll see what we can do for you," she responds and exits the room.

Once the nurse is gone, Aunt Z takes her post beside my bed again.

"Aunt Z, what am I going to do?"

"About what?"

"The baby. It's hard enough being single and now I'm alone and pregnant. I don't think I can go through with this."

"Girl, stop talking stupid. You ain't the first and won't be the last woman on this earth to have a baby with or without a man. Listen . . . half the time even if they are there, they ain't really there. Besides that, you got your family. Me and Shaquetta will be there for you. Besides that, you'll be set. That negro makes good money and will have to pay a good amount in child support. Sheeiit! I wish that had been me when I got knocked up with CJ and Shaquetta. They daddies weren't worth shit and it never made any sense to chase their sorry broke behinds down for child support."

"I know, but I always pictured myself with a family of my own. It was supposed to be Rich, me, and our babies. I don't wanna be a baby mama. I want the complete picture the way God meant for it to be."

"Well, as you know, God has a plan for all of us, and it may not be your plan, but you live by His will."

"His will or not, I'm not having Rich's baby."

33

❧

Business as Usual

"You had no right to do that, Mother!" Vanessa shouted into the receiver as she got up to close the door to her office. "I'm a grown woman, who can and will make her own decisions. You can't hire someone to spy on the man I love then degrade him and our relationship at our company gala. Haven't you learned your lesson with all that private-eye business?"

"Calm down, Vanessa!" Cornelia protested. "What did you think I was going to do? You can't parade that hoodlum around from one coast to the next in our family jet, and think I'm going to sit back and do nothing. Have you seen the tabloids lately? Your behavior is unbecoming."

"*Family* jet, Mother, which means it's my jet too. I can go wherever, with whomever I please. Grandfather Sirus told me—"

"Don't say another word. Not one. Now enough!" Cornelia lowered her tone. "Vanessa, I will not allow you to disgrace yourself and my father's good intentions with your selfishness. Father knows nothing about your little escapades with this man and I plan on keeping it that way. This kind of thing could ruin us all. You're going too far, Vanessa. Just too far! Jet-setting here and there, making news with this thug like you're some kind of cheap thrill. Can't you see he's using you?"

"You're wrong, Mother, Richard loves me. He gave up everything for me." Vanessa clutched the phone.

"Valentine Daye isn't much to let go of or have you forgotten? I've done some digging of my own. Both of them have very questionable backgrounds, Vanessa, and I'm not going to allow you to get hurt by this."

"Hurt how, Mother? Richard would never do anything to hurt me." Vanessa tugged at her vintage Chanel wool suit. Having been passed down from her mother's mother, she felt more like both of them today than ever before.

"Vanessa, I've watched you since Dexter's death, whoring yourself from one relationship to the next, trying to find something that died five years ago. I've stood back, promising myself that I would let you get all the hurt and rebellion out of your system as long as it didn't ruin your life or the family. I've been on my knees daily asking God to put a hedge of protection around you in this season, but now you've gone from bad to worse. You can't love this man. I won't allow it."

Vanessa lay her head on her desk. Combative words stormed her mind yet never made their way to her mouth.

"If you're not careful, these people will kill you. She's already assaulted you once. We don't know who she associates with and what they are capable of. I won't stand around and allow one of her thugged-out cronies to land you in the East River."

"What?" A faint whisper escaped. "Who? What . . . kill, Mother what are you talking about? Valentine may be ghetto but she's not crazy. Richard would never allow anyone to hurt me. He'll protect me."

"Protect you how? Did he protect you from the black eye you encountered? No! And he can't protect you from her. Can't you see she's a woman scorned? She'll stop at nothing to get him back."

"He's my man now. Don't you see, Mother? I've won!" Vanessa heard the words depart from her mouth. Concern flushed her face.

"I'm not sure Richard's the prize. And frankly, I'm no longer certain of the goal being true love. Vanessa, life and love are not a game. There are no winners here. These people are crazy, and too many people are getting hurt."

There was a long pause then Cornelia continued.

"My investigator claims there was an accident."

"Investigator? Are you still doing that? Mother, please! Enough with this." Vanessa's mind began to race at her mother's statements. "First Rachel and now Richard. Yes, he has a questionable past. And no, he isn't refined, but an accident, Mother, really! Will you stop at nothing?"

Vanessa could hear her mother sigh but before her mother could respond, she insisted, "I want to know everything you know. What else?"

"She's pregnant," Cornelia revealed.

Vanessa's stomach did a somersault. She knew Richard had still been messing around with Valentine when they first hooked up, but she never thought about the details of their relationship, which given his sexual nature should've been obvious. She wasn't naïve but the possibility of them starting a family never entered her mind.

"Are you sure?"

"My connections at New York–Presbyterian hospital where she's being treated confirmed it. I'll know more soon."

"Mother, how do you . . ."

"The how's of the situation don't matter, Vanessa." Cornelia's voice was haunting. "Now, you've got to do something about this. I will not have you in harm's way."

Vanessa slammed the files on her desk around, both angry and hurt by her mother's words and actions. Even though she was trying to protect her, she still didn't appreciate the blatant invasion of privacy.

"I've got to talk to Richard. Good-bye."

"Vanes—"

Vanessa hung up the phone before her mother could say another word. She took a deep breath, stood, and headed out of her office to Richard's.

"Ms. Knight! Mr. Jacobs just called and would like to see you in his office. He called while you were on with your mother."

Vanessa kept her head down, avoiding eye contact with her assistant. A glance in the wrong direction would show a tearstained face Vanessa had yet to blot back to perfection.

"I'm headed to Richard's office for a moment then I'll go up to see Mr. Jacobs. Let his office know I will be there in about ten minutes."

Vanessa took paced steps down the hall to Richard's office as if she were headed to death row. She was relieved when Richard's assistant wasn't at her desk since she wasn't in the mood for any small talk at the moment.

Knocking softly, Vanessa stood at the door for a moment with no answer. Gently she peeked inside to find Richard on the phone with his back to the door.

"I'll be back at the hospital just as soon as I can get away."

Vanessa's stomach soured at the thought of Richard's concern for Valentine. She knew it was ruthless of her to feel this way, but couldn't help herself. So what, she was hurt, Richard was her man now.

"I'll be there as soon as I can."

Vanessa quickly closed the door and scurried back down the hall. She would meet Richard as he came out, and hopefully read his expression and see what he would tell her.

As his door opened, Vanessa neared again. "Richard, I was wondering . . ."

His eyes were clouded with confusion and his thick brows were furrowed.

"Can't talk right now, Vanessa."

His words were short, and Vanessa didn't push. She just nodded and allowed him to brush past her. She wondered why he hadn't confessed what he knew about Valentine. Just when she felt they had gotten closer, this incident with Valentine made her doubt. As she watched his body fade down the hall, Vanessa stood motionless. With each breath she regretted ever allowing herself to fall for him. She didn't have the heart to move nor the mind to stand still. Within moments she walked without clear direction while trying to focus on whose office she was going to next.

"Jacobs," she thought aloud, keeping her other thoughts to herself. With the promotion and official line premiere just around the corner, Vanessa knew that worrying now could surely cost her later. She had to focus! Now was the time to put her best foot forward no matter how heavy her heart and steps were. As director of business affairs and strategic marketing at Jorge Jacobs and Richard's new woman, it was business as usual!

34

Liar, Liar

With her back pressed firmly against the personally contoured, cream-colored Omega massage chair in her meditation room, Vanessa tried her hardest to relax. With Mr. Jacobs breathing down her neck about launching proposals and print ads one week before the announcements for the new appointment of vice president, it was more than enough to drive someone insane. She and Richard had been working overtime to finalize the new line. And with all the distractions surrounding Valentine, and Vanessa taking the lead on most of the projects, it was becoming that much more challenging to feel like a team player.

"It'll all be worth it once this is over," Vanessa whispered to herself.

As Vanessa's feelings for Richard continued to grow, she knew there would be work with regard to bringing Richard up to a standard that her parents would accept. Vanessa wondered how long it would take Richard to tell her about the baby. It concerned her that he hadn't already mentioned it. With all she'd sacrificed by admitting her feelings for him there was no way Valentine could take Richard back from her now, he was in too deep. On the flip side, Valentine was a 'hood rat, and extortion was right up her alley. If Richard and Vanessa were to make a life together, Valentine could come around searching for her piece of Vanessa's pie. Richard would never make the money Vanessa was worth, and frankly with Valentine having a child with him, her ghetto mentality meant she'd probably use her baby as a pawn.

Vanessa smiled at the notion of taking custody—with her money and with Father's clout, she'd get it too. There wasn't a judge on the East Coast that her family didn't know or have ties with. Valentine could do all the work, and Vanessa could enjoy all the benefits of motherhood. Her smile widened momentarily.

"What the hell are you thinking about? I don't want her baby!" Vanessa screeched.

"Who are you talking to?" Richard asked as he entered the room.

Vanessa's eyes snapped open. "Richard, you scared me. When did you get home?"

"A few minutes ago. What were you talking about?" Richard asked, peeking around the empty room.

"I was just thinking . . ." Vanessa shuffled from the chair. "No one. It was nothing." Her breath was heavy as she fished for a change in subject. "Are you okay? You left work today in quite a hurry. Is everything fine?"

Vanessa saw Richard's bright eyes darken instantly. His posture stiffened and his eyes danced.

Speechless, he stood still.

Vanessa repeated the question.

"Just a client Mr. Jacobs wanted me to meet regarding the launching proposals and print ad campaign."

Liar, Vanessa thought to herself. Richard knew damned well Jacobs didn't ask him to take on that project. Little did he know she had been asked to personally oversee and handle that very same thing and they're scheduled to meet bright and early in the morning. Richard was not mentioned nor was he included. Vanessa didn't know whether or not to bust him now or see just how long Richard would continue to lie to her face.

"How is that going? I hear Mr. Garrett can be pretty tough." Vanessa smartly threw in the client's name to try and trap Richard.

Richard shrugged his shoulders. "It's nothing I can't handle." His eyes shifted forward.

"Did you meet at his office or at his favorite restaurant in Harlem?"

Richard rolled his eyes. "Damn woman, what's with the third degree?"

"Excuse me? Last I checked we did play for the same team. As your partner on this project, I just wanted to make sure that you didn't need any assistance."

"Right," he whispered. "I'm sorry, babe. Listen, I've just got a lot on my mind. I'm cool though." He leaned down and kissed her on the forehead.

The wetness from his lips sizzled through Vanessas. *I can't believe he's lying to me,* she thought. "Dinner?" she quizzed as he walked back toward the door.

"No, nothing for me, I grabbed something at the hos—" He stopped short. "I grabbed a hot dog while I was out."

"A hot dog." She rose to follow him. "Since when do you eat hot dogs?"

Richard stopped and faced her. "Since forever." He smiled. "I guess there are some things you don't know about me."

"I guess so," she said as she returned a fake smile, bypassing him down the hall. "You're full of . . ." she paused, "surprises."

Vanessa watched from the hall as Richard headed up the stairs. She leaned against the door frame of the kitchen in complete disbelief. She was torn with emotions as she fought off both hurt and anger. She was hurt because Richard didn't trust her with the truth and angry because he so blatantly and badly lied to her face about the entire thing. *Client, my ass!* she thought again as she walked into the kitchen to get her dinner. He'd pay for his lie, that was for sure.

Even though she dished her fair share of lies, Vanessa Knight couldn't stand to be lied to. She wondered if Richard was changing his mind about them. If she had made a mistake in allowing herself to fall for him. Like a light switch she knew when to turn on and off her emotions. If this was how Richard was going to be then she knew what she had to do. She opened the refrigerator taking out the grilled chicken, spinach, and artichoke salad she'd prepared earlier. As she reached for a bowl, her mind raced with thoughts of revenge. How she would punish him for his indiscretion was yet to be determined, for deep down she knew she loved him. But punished he would be.

She laughed as she poured balsamic dressing on her salad. "Hot dog." She chuckled, shaking her head. "Unbelievable!"

35

❧

Compromising Position

The hospital stench is starting to overwhelm my senses and my body is reacting. The least thing makes me hurl or want to hurl and suddenly I'm sensitive to anything and everything. The only good thing that comes out of me being bedridden is that I'm finally getting some rest and don't have time to be depressed. My room is flooded with visitors and flowers. Gina comes the second day after she finds out and spends the entire afternoon with me. Having her there is refreshing and feels like old times, like one of our girls' days out, except we can't shop.

Gina is extremely sympathetic and tries her best not to upset me by talking about Rich, but is ecstatic about the baby. She says it's the one good thing that came out of the relationship, but I disagree. What good is having a baby with the man you love when he's busy loving someone else? It'll be hard to see this child day in and day out and not think about Rich and everything that he has done to me. It will be impossible to erase that memory; especially if the child resembles the father. There is no way I can raise the child and get over Rich. If I want a clean slate, I'll have to remove the seed we sowed. I don't see a way around it and putting my child up for adoption is not an option. That would be equally difficult.

Later that evening, Oscar comes by and brings my beautiful goddaughter along with him for a quick visit and then they all leave together. I'm sad to see Gina go, but again I'm reminded that she has other obligations and a husband that cares for her.

The following day, Aunt Z and Shaquetta come by and help to clean me up properly. I don't know what the nurse thinks she's doing, but wiping down my legs and arms isn't much of a washup. Then my coworkers start pouring in one by one. Diane from the accounts receivable department drops by for a spell and shortly after Kristina comes by. As usual, Kristina talks a mile a minute and fills me in on all of the office gossip and who is doing who in the industry. She's able to distract me and even makes me laugh a few times. She's definitely "mouth almighty and tongue everlasting." However, she throws me when she asks me what's up with me and Rich.

"Are you two still together?"

I'm sure the look on my face is a dead giveaway, but I quickly try to compose myself and not be defensive.

"Of course," I answer. "Why would you ask?"

"Well, you remember that piece that was in the *New York Post* the other day?" She glances at me. I nod and she continues. "Word on the street is that he's hitting it with the chick that was in the picture with him. I heard that she is really big time."

"Where are you getting this information from?"

"Juicy Lips."

"What? You can't believe everything you hear from her. That's how rumors get started. And why would that be of interest to

Juicy Lips anyway?" I say, trying to breathe easy. Juicy Lips is *the* top female VJ and the biggest gossipmonger on radio. Coincidentally she happens to be my coworker, and if she is talking about this, I can only imagine the speculation of my peers at the station. Now that bastard Rich has got our business on Front Street and it's got me looking crazy!

"Well, insider information is being leaked out of Jorge Jacobs about the new urban clothing line and they're about to announce the new head of the division. It's been said that they think it could be Rich. Anyways, the insider is saying how Rich and the girl are always together. They stay late hours, come in together, and leave together. Of course, everyone at the office knows you're his wifey, so this only adds to the gossip. Juicy reported yesterday that 'one of our very own is betrothed to the infamous Richard Washington, more details to follow.' Those were her exact words."

"What? Oh hell no! Tell Juicy Lips to stay out of my business and keep my name out of her damn mouth. This is not a celebrity watch. Rich is not a famous person and neither am I. Juicy Lips is horrible. I can't believe she wouldn't speak to me first."

"I know, but they say Vanessa Knight is like the Paris Hilton of the black community. She's making big moves, has crazy bread, and is all over the society pages. Her name is everywhere. She's part of the *Who's Who* crowd. And since you've been knocked up in the hospital, Rich has been spotted with her everywhere."

"I can't believe this. It goes from bad to worse." I can no longer quell my anger as my face grows red and the room becomes increasingly hot.

"Val, I'm sorry to upset you, but I wanted you to know. I don't want the rest of the office to be stopping by, smiling in your face when everybody is talking about this stuff. I'm just looking out for you."

"Thank you, Kristina. I do appreciate it, but I really need to relax now."

"No problem. I'll be by to check on you again. Is that okay?"

"Yeah, it's okay." I smile at her. She means well and I know she doesn't mean any harm, but the bomb she dropped is a big one. In the office, I'm a very private person and now my business has become public domain. The listeners don't know who I am and could care less about me or my love life, but Rich and his connection to that woman have put my personal affairs on blast. So now anyone who knows me is aware of my business.

The past few weeks of my life have been filled with turmoil. All I want to do is get well and relax, but my mind keeps wandering to all of the events that led to this point.

My thoughts are interrupted by yet another visitor. I look up and to my dismay it's my coworker Ron. He has a huge bouquet of flowers and three pretty get-well helium balloons. I'm still so angry about the news from Kristina that I snap.

"What the hell do you want?" I ask, not bothering to hide my irritation.

"Well, hello to you too, Ms. Daye."

"Ron, what do you want? Why are you here?"

"Val, I came as a friend. What is it about me that you hate so much? I've never done anything but be nice to you, and you continually treat me like I'm nobody."

"Are you up at WFAT talking about me like the rest of the office too? All of y'all coming up in here smiling in my face while talking about me behind my back."

"Val, I can't win with you. I just wanted to spend some time with you and to see if you were all right. I can see that you're making out fine. Just tell me where you want me to put the flowers and I'm out."

Ron's right. He didn't do anything to deserve my ill treatment of him and in truth, I don't know why I resent him the way I do. Maybe it's because he gets under my skin and in some strange way is usually right. Somehow, he's always able to read my mood and pick up on personal things, like when Rich and I had a falling out he'd say, "Your man done messed up again, huh?" In a way Ron reminds me of Rich, because he's always with a different woman and that bothers me, because I know Rich always has other women outside of me. Ron's inability to settle down gets to me, though it's none of my business. And although he pays me nice compliments, a sexual innuendo is always attached.

Before Ron can walk out the door, I quickly apologize. I want to set things straight between us. The bottom line is that we work together and it won't be good if I continue to behave badly toward him, especially since we work in such close proximity to each other.

"Ron, I really appreciate you bringing me flowers and balloons. I'm sorry for jumping down your throat earlier."

"It's all good. I know you're experiencing a lot of pain, but you never did answer my question."

"What question?" I ask curiously.

"Why do you hate me so much?"

"You can't be serious."

"Dead serious!" Ron exclaims.

"I don't know." I suddenly become bashful and I can feel my pale cheeks becoming flushed with red.

"Ms. Daye, are you blushing like a schoolgirl?"

"Ron, shut up. That's why I can't stand you. You always have this way of reading me and sensing my moods."

Ron looks momentarily taken aback.

"What are you talking about?" he asks.

"Never mind," I say in an attempt to change the subject. "How are things going with you?"

"Things are good. The ratings have improved, advertisers are biting—so the good times are rolling—but things aren't the same since you left."

"Yeah, right. Whatever!"

"Seriously, no one's there to stay on top of Kristina, so she's been taking long lunch breaks and not taking messages. The office supplies are dwindling and the talent booker hasn't been booking any good people lately, so we know that you're the real connection now with the juice," he says, laughing. "And, personally I miss seeing your beautiful face in the office."

"You trying to make me blush again?" I say.

"Only if it'll make you smile."

"Ron, you are too much."

"So, what's going on with you? I see your arm is in a cast and you've got on a neck brace. What else did you manage to do to yourself?"

"Please, I had a concussion and I hurt my back."

"Ouch. You must be in pain."

"Only when the drugs wear off, which isn't too often. As soon as I feel an inkling of any type of ache, I press the call button and the nurse starts the bag over there." I point to the clear sack beside the intravenous bag. "And whatever the fluid is in there, it's the bomb." We both start laughing.

"That's cool. So what else is going on? Anything you wanna talk about?"

"No. Not in particular. Why'd you ask?"

"Well, you mentioned earlier about shop talk in the office. I heard some things, but I'd rather not listen to rumors. I respect you too much for that."

"You respect me or are you just nosy like the rest of those fools at the office?"

"Trust me, I don't involve myself in hearsay, but when it comes to you, Val, I become protective. There's something about you and this is not a pickup line. I'm genuinely concerned about you."

A lump takes hold in my throat, because I believe Ron. Honestly, I think deep down the reason I've been fighting him so long and hard is because there's something about him. I believe now that I'm scared of him, because there's a mutual attraction.

It's a bit risky, but I feel the urge to divulge everything to Ron for several reasons. I feel that I can trust him. I want to talk to someone other than my family to get a fresh perspective and to confirm that I'm making the right decision. And I want to talk to someone who won't pass judgment, and Ron has always been one to give me the benefit of the doubt. The fact that he's a man also helps. He'd listen objectively and without interruption.

It takes me three quarters of an hour to tell him the entire ordeal. I omitted the part about going to kill Vanessa and Rich. Details I needn't burden him with. However, I did tell him about the breakup and the baby.

"Are you sure you want to do that to yourself? Abortions aren't easy, Val. Trust me on that one."

"I know, but it's easier than having a daily living reminder. I just want to be able to move on with my life. Things are complicated enough."

Ron takes my hands in his and begins to caress them. He sees the look of anguish and confusion wash over my face. I want to be strong, but I'm torn. I've always wanted to have Rich's baby. This baby is supposed to be my pride and joy, but not under these circumstances. If I decide to have the baby, I'll still have to see Rich and that would be excruciating; especially if he's still with Viper Vanessa.

"You should really think this over some more and if it'll help, I'm volunteering to be the godfather."

My eyes light up at the prospect.

"Ron, you don't have to do that."

"I know, but I want to do that for you. If you'll have me, I'll be there."

"I don't know what to say." I'm truly at a loss for words. An hour ago, I wanted nothing more than for this man to leave my sight. Now I'm fawning like a schoolgirl.

"I won't decide today, but I'll let you know."

"Okay, I'm gonna get out of here now. I think I've worn out my stay," Ron says and I'm disappointed. I don't want him to leave. I was just getting comfortable.

"When will I see you again?"

"When do you want to see me?" Ron says as a smile slowly spreads across his face.

"Tomorrow, after work."

"Sounds good." My heart begins to pitter patter.

Ron bends down to kiss me on the cheek and I turn my head so our lips will join. His mouth presses against mine and I slowly part my lips to allow him entry. Our tongues waltz slowly. It's like being on a dance floor and suddenly holding your partner motionless as he gently toys with my tongue. The kiss is filled with passion and my mouth is hot as I hunger for more. Ron pulls away slightly to run his tongue across my lips and I open my eyes and try to catch my breath. I want our kiss to last forever. It has been so long since I've been kissed in such a sensual manner.

"Umph-hmm." We are interrupted by someone clearing their throat. I figure that it's time for the nurse to take my vitals again and I'm a little embarrassed at having been caught locking lips with Ron.

"Who the hell is this?"

I look up and am surprised to see him and then I become mortified because of what he's just caught me doing.

"All I know is that I want a paternity test. That baby probably ain't even mine," Rich says as he storms off, dropping the flowers and candy he had in his hands on the ground.

36

Mother Knows Best

"Has he told you yet?"

"No, and that's not what is bothering me the most, Mother. Why the need for discretion at this point? It's crazy." Vanessa combed through her newly streaked, bronze-highlighted mane. "It's just that I've put up with so much, and we've made such progress. I expected more from Richard."

"How could you, sweetheart?" Cornelia's voice curled with disapproval while she removed her Chanel sunglasses from her eyes. Fluffing the back of her newly bobbed copper-brown mane, she continued. "Richard can only give you what little he has, and what he has will never be enough. His upbringing won't allow the proper means of communication because he's never had to do it, dear. Street people play games. They manipulate the system to work toward their own advantage because generally they feel as if the world is out to get them. With a mentality like that, it's very easy to become selfish."

"How can you be so prejudiced against your own kind? It's like because Richard doesn't come from money or didn't grow up on the right side of the tracks, you judge him as if you're better. Richard has done so much with his life it's no different from Great-Grandpa Norman. He loves me, shouldn't that be enough?"

Cornelia lowered her head then sighed. "It should be, but unfortunately, honey, it just isn't. I know you feel as though Richard loves you. And perhaps on the surface you're correct. Yet, it takes more than love to make a relationship work, and you, my dear, have compromised so much to be with this man. God allows us to make choices—you can either choose right or wrong. I must say, Vanessa, since Dexter, you've made some very poor choices where love is concerned."

Vanessa's eyes began to tear with emotions. Her mother was right. She hadn't made the best choices with her love life. When you're young death isn't something you think about when considering a potential husband. And Dexter's death had been far off her radar of things that could possibly happen.

"I'm just going to be frank, Vanessa." Cornelia clutched the ends of the table and moved in closer. "You can't continue parading around town like some cheap slut, or sleeping with stray men that you aren't married to while bearing our family name. I'm not even going to get into what the Bible says about such behavior, but I will say that as your mother, I'm rather embarrassed by your behavior. We raised you to have more dignity and self-respect than this." Cornelia slowly leaned her body back into her chair as she lifted her glass of water and took a sip.

The table was silent for a moment, interrupted only by the waiter who requested their lunch order.

"I'll have the pear and cucumber salad and my daughter will be having . . ."

"The same," Vanessa responded with an almost unrecognizable whisper.

Vanessa did everything she could to keep from crying. She didn't know which hurt worse, her feelings or her ego that the dark truth was coming from her mother. *Slut* was all Vanessa could think about as she lowered her head in shame.

"Darling, would you like some tea?"

Vanessa forced the word no from her mouth, her heartbeat drowning out any audible sound. "I . . ."

Once the coast was clear and Cornelia could finish her conversation, it was too late. Vanessa's face was flushed with sadness. Her hard, put-together exterior could no longer withstand her now bruised inner emotions.

Comfort didn't come instantly from Cornelia as Vanessa waited for her mother to say something.

"I'm sorry, Mother," she managed to blurt out.

"No need for apologies now. The damage is done. All you can do is pick up the pieces, and put them back together correctly from here on out. How you act during a few seasons doesn't always reflect who you are, Vanessa. I know who you are, darling, and I love you. It's just high time you start acting like your true self again. Repent, forgive, let go, and move on."

Cornelia reached into her purse and handed Vanessa a handkerchief.

The silk was soft against Vanessa's cheek and smelled of lavender, just like her mother. Her eyes lifted a bit in her mother's direction. Sheepishly she asked, "Mother, have I really been that bad?"

Cornelia smiled. "I'd never let the world see you sweat, dear. Your behavior, like everything else, was perceived to be decent and in order. Now, I want you to get back with Stephen. He's good for you. Smart and affluent! If not Stephen, then you are free to find another, an acceptable suitor. But things must change and change now."

"But Richard . . ."

"What's left to say, dear? Richard hasn't been honest with you."

"He left her for me. Isn't that saying something?"

"What does it say to you? You've been second to that . . . woman, this entire time. And for what? He's handsome, yes, I get that. Promising career, okay. But your job is never to make a man. Either he helps to make you or you leave him alone. Do you actually think he's worth it?"

Vanessa took a deep breath, knowing what she had to do. The only problem was how she was going to do it.

If anyone knew how to settle things, she knew she was sitting directly across from one of the greatest masterminds of all times.

"Mother, I . . ." Vanessa cleared her throat. "I need your help."

Cornelia leaned closer, then reached into her purse, pulling out a piece of paper. As she handed it to Vanessa, she smiled slightly. "I knew I could trust you to make the right decision. I've written out exactly what you need to do. If you follow the list precisely, everything will work out just fine."

Vanessa's heart thumped in her throat. Her mother's words were both assuring and haunting at the same time. Not knowing what else to say, she responded, "Thank you, Mother. I always knew you'd be there for me. I knew you could help me regain control."

"Remember darling, the one in control . . ."

"Never loses control." Vanessa finished her mother's sentence.

Cornelia raised her glass. "Cheers."

37

Kiss My Ass!

Awkward is the only way to describe the situation between myself, Ron, and Rich.

It has been years since I've felt anything for anyone other than Rich. He is my heart, but he took my heart and trampled on it until there was barely any life left. Now that I've been resuscitated, he reenters and accuses me of infidelity. He has some nerve.

Initially I feel guilty and at least fifty emotions course through me when I first see him. I want badly to hold him again, kiss him, be held by him, hear him call my name like he used to, and talk to him. Then I come to my senses. He dogged me out and not the other way around. I'm banged up in the damn hospital because of his ass. Had he not stepped out on me and then turned around and left altogether, none of this mess would've happened. I've been nothing but the model woman to him for nine years. I put up with all of his crap and in the end he took the meanest dump on me and flushed my ass down the toilet with the rest of the shit.

When Ron realizes what happened he offers to catch up to Rich and explain, but I tell him not to, because as far as I'm concerned it's over. My hands are clean of that man. And my decision to terminate the pregnancy is final. There's no turning back. Love don't live here no more!

The following morning, my cousin Shaquetta comes dressed to the nines to keep me company and though I appreciate her trying to be by my side she annoys me and I can't wait for her visit to come to a close.

"You and Rich are going to make such a pretty baby! We got that good hair, and the baby may be a little chocolatey like Rich, but that's cool."

"Shaq, I'm glad that I got your approval and all, but I'm not having the baby."

"What? Girl, are you crazy? Pleez! Just because he ain't in the picture no more you're not having the baby?"

"Something like that," I say, wanting to change the subject. I realize that Shaquetta has a one-track mind and outside of shopping for clothes and men, we have very little else to discuss.

"Val, you make crazy money at the station, got a hot crib, and Rich would have to pay you a grip in child support, so it's not like you'd be down and out. You can still handle your business. Like Jay-Z said, *'money ain't a thang.'*"

I have to laugh at Shaquetta, because nine years ago, I would've been thinking the same thing. Straight out of the projects, my only concern was coming out on top. It didn't matter how, just as long as it happened. Now almost ten years later, my dreams of moving on up have come true. I have a good job, live in a doorman building, drive a nice whip, and I got some change in the bank. Even in my dreams I never pictured things to be this good, but here I lay and I made it happen. I don't want to hamper my life with a child that neither Rich nor I really want. He's already fast-forwarded his life with Vanessa and I want to be able to do the same. If Ron and I actually click, do I want to enter this relationship carrying another man's baby? Ron may actually be a stand-up type of dude, but he's definitely no Joseph and I'm not Mary.

"Why you over there cracking up?" Shaquetta asks.

"'Cause, girl, you're funny. Listen, I know you want to be an auntie and whatnot and between me and your cuckoo brother, it'll happen soon. But for now, I'm not sure this is the direction I want to go—"

Shaquetta cuts me off in midsentence. "But you're not getting any younger and this is a blessing."

"Listen, I appreciate your concern for my age and all, but I need you to respect my decision. There's still time for me to change my mind, but at this point I don't feel that I'm ready to be anybody's mother."

"Okay, cool. But at least think about it some more, all right?"

"I will. But now I need to get some sleep."

Shaquetta gets the hint and stands up to stretch before bending to retrieve her Dolce & Gabbana handbag and matching animal-print shoes.

Though I appreciate the brief interlude, I'm happy to see Shaquetta leave.

I'm able to get about two hours' worth of rest before Gina stops by.

Gina, being the good friend that she is, took yet another afternoon off to spend with me after I called and told her what had happened with Rich. It is such a relief to have her presence to distract me, because though my mind says one thing my heart has yet to catch up.

"So, you and Ron finally kissed?" she asks me excitedly as she settles into the chair.

"What do you mean, finally?"

"Oh, stop tripping. You and Ron have had this love-hate relationship for like forever. He's been chasing you like a dog in heat and you played the bitch to the hilt. The only thing ever stopping you two from hooking up was that dog Rich and now that he's out of the picture you two can 'get it on,'" she says, trying to impersonate Barry White.

"You definitely have an active imagination," I say, laughing, because it's true. However, I don't want to admit it openly.

"Well, I'm happy for you. You can finally move on with your life, because I think he's a good guy."

"What? You hardly know the brotha. Now, I may be willing to let him be my rebound guy or booty call every now and again, but we know that usually never really lasts."

"If you're talking like that, how could it? Just let things happen or simply allow him to be your friend. Don't jump into bed with him and if things progress naturally then so be it."

"Yeah, but I'm a little scared. Ron has had or probably still does have his stable of women. He likes to store women like a racehorse owner breeds horses."

"Maybe because he hasn't found the right woman yet."

"So, I come along and he suddenly changes? Gina, please. I think Rich is a fine example of men changing."

"First off, you shouldn't compare the two and who said Rich ever really wanted to change? You think cuz he's chilling with that chick and she got money that he's gonna change? I seriously doubt that. Look at Bobby Brown and Whitney."

We both burst out laughing and don't stop until long after the tears stop pouring from our eyes.

"You got me laughing so hard, my neck hurts, Gina."

"Okay, poor example, but think about it. Before Whitney, Bobby's career was in the toilet. He got with ole girl and it shot him up larger than life. Whitney had the money, the career, beauty, and he still had to get ass on the side, the left, and the right. Anywhere his ugly ass could get it. Money don't mean a thing."

"Halle Berry and Eric Benet," I blurt.

"Yeah, and Halle's tighter than a size-eight foot trying to get into a six." We both laugh and I feel good for the moment.

Gina gives me some real food for thought and shortly after our discussion, we chow down on the lunch she brought me from one of my favorite little spots on Fulton Street in Brooklyn called Soule. It's good to get something other than the preheated meals the hospital tries to pass off as nutritious food. After the meal, we pass out. I'm not sure how long we dozed off, but the phone interrupts our slumber.

"Hello," I answer, still groggy.

"Hey, Val. Wassup?"

I immediately come to when I heard his voice. My heart begins to race and I suddenly feel suffocated by the food that's still sitting on my chest.

"Nothing," I answer, waiting to follow his lead.

"Yeah, we need to talk," Rich says in a very monotone voice.

"About what?" I ask. Gina wakes up at hearing my voice.

"You know about what! Don't try to act stupid."

"Okay, first of all, you called me, so if you want to talk . . . talk! Second, I don't know who the hell you're calling stupid, but I will hang up this phone right now. Take that mess to your new bitch!" For once, my head is clear and my mind at ease. I still love Rich, but my heart has been trampled on enough. At this point, my mercury is well above 98.6 degrees and Rich is about to catch my fever.

"Hold up. Why you gotta be all that?" he asks rhetorically. "Anyways, I ain't saying you're stupid. All I'm saying is I need to holla at you for a minute."

I cover the receiver to whisper to Gina what Rich was saying and she tells me to continue, but not before coming closer to listen in on the conversation.

"You still there?" he asks.

"Yeah, I'm here. I'm listening. If you have something to say, Rich, say it. I don't have all day."

"Oh, is your new man there again?" he asks, placing emphasis on the word *new*. "Is that why you acting all funny now?"

"Rich, I'm not acting. I'm just giving you the floor to say whatever it is you need to say, because when I wanted your attention, you cut me off at the knees and left me to rot."

"See, now why you gotta go there? All I wanna know is if that's my baby."

"Ask him why he cares whose baby it is?" Gina whispers and I fan her away.

"You say something, Val?"

"Rich, you know what? You're real funny and I don't have time for this right now. You and the baby are the last things on my mind."

"So it is my baby?"

"What do you think, Rich?" I ask seriously. My mouth is twisted and I can't rotate my neck the way I want to without being in pain.

"I don't know what to think after I walk in on you and that clown kissing."

"First off, Ron is not a clown. He's a friend."

"Word? So now he's a friend? Where'd you meet this friend at?"

"You don't have the right to ask me questions anymore. You lost that privilege when you walked out of my life. And for the record, while we were together I never so much as looked at another man in a way that would've disrespected you. Last, I don't want you to call me anymore and as for the baby you don't need to worry about it. I'm taking care of everything."

"Well, don't be breathing down my neck for no doggone child support then, since you'll be taking care of everything."

The hurt that courses through my body could've shaken the earth off balance. It takes every ounce of strength for me not to snatch him through the phone and slap his simple ass.

Gina is in my ear telling me what to say, but I truly don't hear a word she's saying.

"You know I'm on the rise and I don't need no shit to get in my way right now. They're looking at me to be the vice president over at Jorge Jacobs, you know what I'm saying? Now if you had come to me correct, we could've dealt with this civilly."

"I can't believe I loved you the way I did. I gave you my every-thing and this is how you come at me? Don't step to you for child support? You're gonna treat me like I'm some two-bit whore on the Maury Povich show asking if you're the father?" Gina gives me a handful of Kleenex to wipe my face as the tears pour like a torrential rain shower. I try to hold it together so my voice won't crack. I don't want him to know I'm breaking down. "You done lost your damn mind following behind that woman. If I really wanted to, I could give you hell and keep your dumb ass tied up in the court system and you'd be giving me half of your new 'vice president' paychecks after I air your funky-ass draws before the judge."

"That's right, gurl. You tell him," Gina whispers, being part instigator, part cheerleader. I can tell she wants to snatch the phone from my hand to give him a piece of her mind too.

"Val, you don't wanna go there with me."

"Rich, you're right, I don't. I'm real tired and I've given up the fight, because you're just not worth it anymore. And if anyone's stupid, it's you. When I said I was taking care of everything I meant that I was aborting your baby. Yes, your baby, because I want no part of you in me. That trick you're with actually did me a favor and as far as I'm concerned, Rich, you can kiss my black ass!"

38

※

Don't Let a Good One Go to Waste

Vanessa walked through the front door to what looked like twenty dozen long-stemmed red roses. The room was dark and lit only by candlelight and the aroma of rosemary chicken filled the air. Vanessa was impressed.

"Richard," she whispered as she laid her bags down on the nearby chaise and headed toward the kitchen.

Al Green's "Let's Stay Together" played softly in the background as Richard sang along. Vanessa just stood in the doorway a while watching Richard cook, sing, and sample the food.

The conversation she'd had with her mother hammered in her head as she tried hard to stay focused on what she knew had to be done. It was hard though, especially since Richard stood in the kitchen looking even more scrumptious than the chicken he'd just pulled out of the oven. His rich skin glistened with light perspiration. The steam from the vegetables moistened his forehead with a delicious dew and he looked about as good as it smelled.

"My, my," Vanessa said, interrupting. "What's going on in here?"

"Just thought I'd do something special for you, since I . . ." Richard lowered his head. "I know I've been a little distant toward you lately. My attitude has been real messed up and you don't deserve that. It's just a lot has been going on and I've needed a minute to clear my head and put my thoughts together." Richard moved in close. Vanessa stood still, taking him and the entire atmosphere in. "You deserve the best, because you are the best thing that has ever happened to me."

The rhythm of Vanessa's heart remained steady in spite of Richard's words. As he kissed her, her mind thought of the many ways she should reject him. It was too late for an explanation now, almost a week had gone by since the accident and Richard hadn't said two words to her about Valentine or the baby.

In addition, she'd started to wonder if by not telling her about Valentine, his feelings for her were changing. Clearly, love couldn't be based merely on something physical. She knew if she and Richard ever had a chance, she'd need to trust him to always tell her the truth the first time around. Besides, the fact that they were from two different worlds made it almost impossible for her to give in to any kind of love she thought she felt for him. Yet even as her mind raced with thoughts of why this relationship wouldn't work, her body accepted his kiss and returned lips full of passion.

Within seconds a cloud of smoke emerged. The asparagus had steamed over.

"Smoky interruption, huh?"

Vanessa laughed as she took a deep breath, hoping to regain control of herself. Her legs wobbled a bit as she focused on Richard's tight butt and strong thighs. The cloud of steam drenched his T-shirt, causing the bareness of his skin to peek through. Vanessa couldn't take it.

She unbuttoned her blouse and before Richard could turn around her black, laced La Perla bra was exposing an alluring invitation.

Vanessa licked her lips then walked slowly over to Richard.

He smiled as he fanned the steam away. As she began unbuckling his pants, all her mother's words were immediately erased from her mind. She stepped back, watching as his pants dropped to his ankles. "Thank you for dinner."

"We haven't eaten yet," he said as he lifted the T-shirt over his head.

His penis hardened as Vanessa removed her chocolate skirt and nude hose.

"I made your favorite."

"I see," Vanessa said in between kisses.

"I was hoping we'd get to eat first. I wouldn't want it to go to waste."

Vanessa smiled. "I'm starving for something else right now." Her kisses grew deeper.

She leapt up on the countertop and placed him inside of her.

He moaned, following her lead. "What about dinner?" he whispered, switching his focus from food to flesh.

She gripped his skin with both her thighs and her hands, forcing him to go deeper. Her moans echoed throughout room. "Don't worry . . ." Her breaths were heavy. "I'm already full." She giggled, enjoying Richard inside her.

Vanessa forced any logical thoughts out of her mind, and let their moment of ecstasy take over. If her mother knew what she was doing, she wouldn't approve. Yet Vanessa couldn't help herself, she wasn't about to let a good one go to waste. Besides, how could Vanessa not reward Richard for all the effort he'd put into dinner? She was hungry for him, and constantly craved everything about him. In spite of her conversation with her mother, Vanessa wasn't sure if she was really ready to let Richard go.

Their breaths connected as his movement stopped. She pulled him as close as she could, causing an almost suffocating squeeze.

"Don't let me go, Vanessa." Richard's voice was faint.

Vanessa's body numbed at his words. *Had I said something out loud?* she thought to herself.

"What did you say?" Vanessa prayed she'd misheard him.

"I love you," he replied.

Vanessa leaned her head against his. Her heart ached and her mind raced with guilty thoughts.

"I love you too, Richard," she said, kissing the top of his head, fighting back the tears. She wasn't going anywhere, at least not tonight. As for tomorrow, it would just have to figure itself out.

39

"Who Should I Run To"

"Well, Miss Daye, your vitals are now stable and I can see that you've been taking our advice and relaxing. If you keep this up, you may be able to go home sooner than later," Dr. Pascal reports. We are on friendlier terms since my attack on him.

A smile burgeons on my face and words aren't necessary. For once in my life I'm at ease. Once I'm fully recovered, I'll make haste and take care of the next order of business. I know what I have to do and it isn't an easy decision, but abortion was truly my only option.

In truth, I wish things were different. A baby is supposed to bring you joy, but in my case it was accompanied by misery.

All my life I've heard of women who use abortion as a method of birth control and I'd shake my head in judgment at their stupidity or carelessness, but now I am one of them. Though I feel more like a victim who's been used, abused, and violated after the way Rich threw me to the side like trash. Besides, I took precautions against getting pregnant, but sometimes that's just not enough.

"Now, the nurses tell me that you had some questions about terminating your pregnancy. Is that true?"

Dr. Pascal's demeanor at that moment feels almost paternal and although my mind is already made up, I hesitate to answer. He comes across like an interrogator instead of my doctor and it makes me a bit uneasy. After all, it's my body and I can do with it as I like.

"Ms. Daye, I just want to offer you a word of caution."

I don't want to hear what he has to say, because I can already tell he is pro-life and we are headed in different directions as I head toward Death Valley.

"Okay, go ahead," I respond, giving the appearance that I half give a damn.

"You are in your fourteenth week of pregnancy, which means you are into your second trimester. From this moment on, your baby will grow quite rapidly and in the coming weeks your belly will quickly begin to swell. You should be aware that at this stage in your pregnancy, it's no longer a simple procedure."

"What do you mean?" Now he has my interest, because as far as I know, abortions are an in-and-out procedure with little pain. More agony than pain in the long run, but I'll have to deal with that in my own way.

"Well, when pregnancy progresses into the second trimester, only surgical abortion can be performed."

The look on my face has to be baffling, because he starts to speak slower as if I am hard of hearing.

You will now need to undergo a D and E."

"A D and E? What's that?"

"Dilation and evacuation is a combination of vacuum aspiration, forceps, and D and C . . . sorry, dilation and curettage.

"Ms. Daye, I don't want to bog you down with too much infor-

HE WAS MY MAN FIRST

mation, but if you want to know more, I'll have one of the nurses bring you a few pamphlets which can better explain everything. But I do want to ask you if you're familiar with endometriosis?"

"Endo-meet-me-who?"

"Endometriosis. Most women who have this condition are infertile, but you are one in a million and very lucky."

"Lucky?"

"Yes, lucky. I'll be by to check on you tomorrow and hope to have good news as to when you can go home."

"Okay," I answer, disheartened as he leaves the room. "Did he just say lucky?" I ask myself.

Fifteen minutes earlier I was feeling good and ready to take on any new challenge, but after the doctor scared me about end-o-meets-my-osis my mind begin to wander. This mess can't really be happening to me. The only thing I can do is look up and ask, "Lord, why have you forsaken me?" But the reality is, I am the one with plans to forsake the good Lord and He is going to have the last say.

My thoughts are interrupted by Ron, who comes bearing gifts. He must've gone home and changed before coming to see me, because he only wears suits at the office. He has on a pair of jeans that look as if they were made just for him and a plain white T-shirt that shows off his pecs and his nicely defined arms. I'm starting develop a new appreciation for Ron.

"How's my girl today?" he asks and kisses me on the forehead. I immediately begin to blush like a schoolgirl, which he is making me do way too often. One moment I'm sad and the next happy and giddy. Pregnancy is definitely shifting my moods of late.

"According to the doctor I'm good. Dr. Pascal just left and gave me, well . . . good and bad news."

Ron looks concerned as he places the bouquet of flowers in the water pitcher on the nightstand beside my bed.

"Nothing for you to worry about, so I'll start with the good news. I'm healing well and may be released the day after tomorrow. I'm happy about that, because I'm starting to feel like an invalid lying in this bed so long. In another day or so, I'll start to develop bed sores," I say to which both Ron and I laugh uncontrollably.

"Okay, so what's the bad news?" Ron asks once the laughter dies down.

"Hmm, well I'm much further along in my pregnancy than I thought . . ."

"Is something wrong with the baby? Did they do one of those monograms?"

"Boy, shut up! You're just as silly as me. No, they didn't do a sonogram. Now you gonna let me finish?" I ask and pause as Ron gives me the nod to continue.

"As I was saying, I'm about fourteen weeks pregnant and it wasn't my plan to continue with this pregnancy. I'm seriously contemplating terminating the pregnancy."

"But why? Why would you do that?"

"The most obvious reason, because Rich and I are no longer together. I don't want to be another statistic. I don't want to go at this alone or to be constantly reminded of what once was or what should've been."

Ron gets up from the chair and stands against my bed. He takes my hand in his. His hands are as soft as silk, but are firm as they cover my hand entirely.

"Listen and I really want you to listen. During my visit the other day, I told you that I would be there for you if you wanted me to. I can be your friend, but I'm gonna be honest, I don't know how long that can last because . . . well, Val, I have true feelings for you. Not to mention that I'm extremely attracted to you." He pauses and smiles. "Seriously, you've got a friend in me and I don't make offers like this often. Trust me, Val, for whatever reason I've been drawn to you since we first met. I'll admit it was definitely a sexual attraction, but over the years I've come to really respect you. I can be your friend and if you want more I can be that too."

My once heavy heart begins to feel lighter and the words from Ron's mouth are like music to my ears. In all of my life, that is probably the sweetest thing any man has ever said to me. He respects me and wants to be there for me. I feel a sense of relief that if I did decide to go through with this I won't be alone.

"Is that okay? I don't want to overstep my boundaries."

"Of course it's okay. Ron, my mind has been doing laps regarding the pregnancy and my situation with Rich from the moment the doctor gave me the news. I mean, deep down I'd love to have this baby, but it's hard. You know, it's just difficult." My words begin to sound choked up as tears stream down my face. "I feel so lost and I don't know which way to turn. Which way should I go and who can I run to? The easiest and safest route is the abortion."

"Val, don't cry. You don't need to stress yourself. I understand how you feel . . . scratch that, I don't. Still, I can imagine that all of this must be difficult for you and probably feels like everything is snowballing out of control. But don't let it overwhelm you, because you're strong. I know you're strong and if you need to turn somewhere, I'm right behind you and if you want to go somewhere, I'll take you and if you're wondering who you can run to, my arms are wide open."

If that wasn't enough Ron kisses the tears that bathe my cheeks and when he's done he positions his mouth atop mine and our lips meet. We share a kiss that makes my mouth dance and this time our kiss is uninterrupted.

40

❧

Decision Time

"Based on this budget Jorge Jacobs will save an average of seventy percent in both advertising and marketing, figures that almost triple from last year. As promised in my earlier projection of necessary client relations costs, our clients are much more comfortable keeping their advertising dollars here with us while we maximize those dollars with well-thought-out plans across the board that will benefit the masses instead of wasting those dollars on individual campaigns."

"I still feel that it's risky, Vanessa, to ask our key clients to come on board and partake in the same campaign."

"Well noted, Mr. Jacobs, yet this plan will not fail us. And the signed letters of intent from each of our clients should serve as solid proof that our key clients are more than comfortable with the mutual campaign. Rest assured, gentlemen, that I'm not in the business of taking such risk unless I'm confident of positive returns. I've personally handled each of these clients, creating the millionaire's club, assuring their comfort as well as Jorge Jacobs's. It's a sure win!"

"Impressive, Ms. Knight. The millionaire's club, I like that!"

"Richard has done a brilliant job at executing this strategy with the entire staff. This presentation is a collective effort of hard work and dedication from everyone."

Vanessa looked over to Richard whose face was flushed with gratitude. As she took her seat, Richard placed his hand on her knee and squeezed lightly. She smiled as she focused her attention on Mr. Jacobs.

"Great job you two," Mr. Jacobs stated as he rose from his seat and headed out of the conference room.

Once the room was clear, Vanessa leaned over to hug Richard. "We did it!" she squealed. "Oh my goodness, they just sponged it all up. I couldn't believe it."

"What can I say, you rocked it today. Besides reviewing the presentation, this was your baby. I'm proud of you, Vanessa."

Vanessa blushed. "I couldn't have done any of this without you. We make a cool team. What do you want to do to celebrate?"

"Yeah, about that . . . I kinda have something to do tonight. You know, finalize some things I've been working on. I'll be home a little late tonight, so don't wait up. You go 'head and get your beauty rest and we'll make it a wonderful morning. Breakfast at Sylvia's, your favorite."

Vanessa's excitement went from hot to cold in an instant. She wondered if Richard had plans to spend time with Valentine. Her thoughts were interrupted by Richards words.

"Sylvia's?" Vanessa's smile vanished. *Oh, no he didn't, I've never even eaten at Sylvia's!* Vanessa thought to herself. Her body felt hot as she tried to remain calm.

"I meant Chez Nous." Richard stumbled as he kissed her

lightly on the cheek while thumbing through his BlackBerry. "Babe, I'ma catch up with you later. I've gotta go. But I'll be back shortly."

"Richard . . ." Vanessa pressed. "Where are you . . . ?" But before she could finish Richard had walked out of the door.

Vanessa couldn't believe Richard was leaving after such a crucial presentation. He knew what lay in the shadows of this meeting and also knew what could happen if *they* didn't get the promotion.

Vanessa gathered her things and headed back to her office. The thrill from her boardroom performance quickly faded while suspicion enveloped her. She knew that page had come from one person only . . . Valentine! Vanessa had taken a backseat long enough, and with a baby on the way things between her and Richard would only get worse.

Vanessa reached into her pocket and pulled out the slip of paper her mother had given her. "*Follow my directions to a T,*" Vanessa remembered her mother saying.

Vanessa sighed.

"Cynthia, get me Stephen Douglas, please. And prepare a bottle of champagne to be delivered to the office address we have on file for him. I'm writing a note to be included."

Vanessa closed her door behind her as she waltzed into her office. Her next move was crucial if her mother's plan was going to work.

"Mr. Washington's office," the assistant answered.

"Hi, it's Vanessa, has Richard made it back yet?" Vanessa huffed, it had been over two hours since Richard left the office and Vanessa fumed with emotions.

"No, Ms. Knight, he hasn't. But he did send me an e-mail stating he wasn't coming back into the office this afternoon and to forward all calls to his cell. Would you like me to try him?"

Just as Vanessa was about to request to be transferred, Cynthia knocked on her door.

"Ms. Knight, Mr. Jacobs is here to see you."

Vanessa nodded, motioning Cynthia to send Mr. Jacobs in. "No, thank you. Just leave word for Richard that I called."

Vanessa stood as Mr. Jacobs entered her office. She was pissed that she hadn't a second to dust her face, but since his visit was completely unexpected, she wouldn't have been able to prepare anyway.

"Mr. Jacobs." Vanessa greeted him and extended her hand. "Did you have any further questions about today's meeting?"

Mr. Claude Jacobs shook his head then sat on the couch facing her desk. He extended his hand for her to join him.

Vanessa took her place in the chair facing the couch. "Mr. Jacobs—"

Mr. Jacobs stopped her. "Vanessa, you did a superb job today but I must admit . . . I was a little disappointed."

"Disappointed? I'm not sure I know what you're referring to."

"I've been watching you and Richard for the last couple of months, and whereas I can appreciate your friendship, I can spot a cover-up a mile a way."

Vanessa's heart felt as if it were going to pound out of her chest.

"It's one thing to be able to schmooze one's way in front of our investors and advertisers, but it will take more than that for someone to serve as vice president of business affairs and strategic marketing here at Jorge Jacobs."

"Mr. Jacobs, I can assure you that Richard and I . . ." Vanessa couldn't breathe. This was exactly what her father and mother had warned her about. How stupid could she be to think no one was ever going to find out about her Richard, she thought to herself. And to have worked so hard only to have it all go down the drain was more than she could fathom.

"Your esteem for Richard is complimentary to him, yet I know what's been going on. And I must say if I didn't know any better, I'd detect that there is something far more personal at stake here."

Vanessa felt faint as she searched her mind for just the right words to say.

"Mr. Jacobs. Richard and I have truly worked very hard at—"

"That's just it, Vanessa, I don't think you and Richard have done as much as you're giving him credit for."

Vanessa sat back in her chair. "I'm not sure I follow you."

"Let me just be frank. Etienne and our partners feel that as a team you and Richard should be a lot stronger. But your extraordinary efforts to ensure two multimillion-dollar accounts single-handedly haven't gone unnoticed. Your work on the gala exceeded our expectations. And your personal contacts are amazing. Based on your performance with this company during the last three years and considering your presentation today, the partners agree we'd like to offer *you* the position of vice president of marketing effective immediately. We'll discuss the logistics and all that comes along with the new role later."

Vanessa could not believe her ears. "What about Richard?" she asked, genuinely concerned.

"I went by his office to speak to him first, but he wasn't there. So you were my next stop. With the new title, I'll leave it to you to discuss the new developments. I'm assuming Richard will resume his title now, moving up to lead on all of your existing accounts."

Vanessa nodded in agreement. She was so excited she wanted to pinch herself to make sure she wasn't hearing things.

"Well?" Mr. Jacobs chuckled. "Say something."

Vanessa couldn't think of anything to say. She smiled then ran her hands across her face. As she repositioned herself on the chair, she shook her head. "I'm shocked and thrilled. Really! I guess the only thing left to say is thank you."

"Congratulations, Vanessa. You truly are an extraordinary woman." Mr. Jacobs made his way up from the couch and walked to the door. "I'm sure you have some celebrating to do. Good thing it's Friday, you can celebrate all weekend."

Vanessa's smile widened as she followed Mr. Jacobs closely. "I most certainly will do just that. Thank you again," Vanessa effused as she gently closed the door behind him.

With what seemed to be one huge step, Vanessa had made her way from the bedroom to the boardroom, literally.

Vanessa's first thought was to call her mother and inform her of the good news, but she stopped short, realizing her mother would only view this promotion as a distraction until she'd completed her assignment. Even with an incomplete agenda, Vanessa still had the urge to share her victory with Richard.

As quickly as the thought entered into her mind, Vanessa's fingers had dialed Richard's number.

"Richard—"

"Vanessa, let me hit you back."

"Excuse me!" Vanessa could not believe her ears. "Richard!"

"Vanessa, yo what the . . ." His words were both short and cutting. "Listen, I know what you must be thinking, but babe, it ain't what it seems. There's just a lot of stuff going on and I have to handle it."

"You're keeping something from me, I know it."

"No . . . it's not like that. I—"

Vanessa interrupted. "Richard, I don't want to hear it. Are you or aren't you still fooling around with that Valentine woman? This is un-freaking-believable."

"Vanessa, please, babe, you got to trust me. I'm not fooling around. I love you, I do. I need you to trust me. Val was in an acci . . ."

Vanessa hung up the phone before Richard could finish his explanation. Her heart was grieved but her anger took over. The fact that he was willing to offer an explanation was just a little too late. She was moved that he wanted her to know the truth but then again, she wasn't sure that she was getting the truth from Richard, mainly because he'd lied to her too many times before. She fumed at the thought of him cheating on her, even though she had started this whole relationship by committing the same act.

Now with the title of VP under her own belt, Richard was no longer an asset. In fact with a baby, and the constant nagging of Val and the anticipation of ghetto baby mama drama, Richard had just become a major liability.

41

Stranger in the Night

Visions of Ron danced in my head as I lay my head down to sleep. After practically professing his love he left with the hope that I'll think things over and give him a chance. Never in a million years would I have thought about Ron and me being a couple. Yes, I definitely find him attractive, but Rich was supposed to be the man that I married happily-ever-after. Though we haven't been happy in a long time. I realize that now, but I'm also feeling very confused.

My feelings for Ron are getting stronger, but I'm not in love. If given the chance, I'm sure I could love him but I don't want Ron to be the rebound guy either. He's too nice to get caught up in my drama and I'm smack in the middle of drama. At this point I could have my own VH1 reality show *He Was My Man First* and the ratings would be through the roof. My life isn't exactly a storybook, but it's definitely a page-turner.

It feels good to be wanted, but the fact is that I'm not in a place where I can make such life-altering decisions. Jumping from one relationship directly into another may not be the smartest thing to do. We work together, and that alone could cause a problem. Then there's the baby. I'm still undecided as to what I want to do. My conscience and my faith are telling me that terminating the pregnancy is wrong while the devil sits on the opposite side telling me to get rid of it.

Why did Rich have to be such an asshole? We'd been together for ten years and in all that time I'd never gotten pregnant and ironically that's when he decides to leave. I have to question if he really ever loved me. I mean really loved me, because you don't just walk out on someone when they're down or pregnant. That's not love, that's plain selfish.

Too many thoughts fill my head and I'm unable to sleep. The room is dark and the only sound to be heard is the heart monitor machine. The hospital personnel sits only footsteps away, but they are winding down for the evening and all is quiet. I decide to use this time to say a silent prayer for clarity.

Ten minutes pass and when I open my eyes I can feel a presence in the room. My door has been left slightly ajar, so there's a sliver of light peeking in. I try hard to adjust my eyes to the darkness. There's a figure in my doorway and my heart rate increases slightly, because if it was one of the nurses they would've turned the light back on. My hand quickly finds its way to the lamp on the nightstand beside the bed.

"Oh my goodness! What are you doing here?" I ask nervously.

"I just wanted to check on you."

"Why do you care?"

"Because I never stopped caring," Rich says.

He'd been standing in the doorway. I don't know how long he's been standing there, but he is the last person I expect to see tonight. Funny enough, I'm unmoved by his presence. I'm almost positive his new mistress has no idea where he is right now and he's creeping to come see me. How original.

My eyes show little to no emotion as I lay there motionless. I don't bother responding and have no intention of holding a pointless conversation with him.

"Val, I know some pretty harsh things have been said between us over the last few weeks and I'm sorry. I want you to know that I love you and I'll always love you. I never meant to hurt you. Ever! We had our good times and bad, and for years I've been asking you to soften up. But you've been so intent on maintaining this tough exterior and handling everything like Superwoman. All I ever wanted from you was to allow me to be the man, but you always find a way to undermine and emasculate me and it can't be that way. You always wanna tell me what to do, when to do it, and how to feel. You refuse to listen and everything always has to be an argument. We used to be friends, but it felt like once we started making money, that became more important to you. The job became your number one priority and I took a backseat. I don't mind you doing you, but you lost sight of us and the only time you ever paid any attention was when I stepped out on you. I'm not making excuses and it wasn't right, but it got your attention and then I'd become a priority again. Once you felt you had me back where you wanted me, you'd return to your same routine and that's what I became. A routine, but I wanted to be your man—your husband. Three years ago when I proposed to you, I was serious about you being my future. But you became married to the ring and the idea of being married.

"Now you're carrying my seed and I'm messed up. I'm really fucked up right now. My pops wasn't around like he should've been for me and I don't want to make the same mistake. I want to be there for my child. I'm torn, because I still love you. Still, I'm in a different place now and my future is looking real bright. When we last spoke you said you were gonna have an abortion. I just want you to know that should you decide to keep our baby, I'll be here for you."

Rich kisses me on my forehead, gazes into my eyes one last time, and then he leaves.

42

❧

To the Left!

"Yes, I realize what I'm asking, which is why I'm willing to pay triple the fee. I need everything out by seven P.M. My mother, Mrs. Cornelia Mitchell-Knight said you were the guy I should talk to and that no matter the request you would see to it that everything was handled efficiently."

Vanessa pressed the phone firmly against her ear as she moved from one corner of her living room to the next. "Thank you, Bruno, I'll expect your guys to be here in an hour. I assure you, this is not a big job. But I will need you to be as discreet as possible."

Vanessa hung up the phone and headed into her kitchen. She knew the mood had to be just right. Charles, one of the chefs from Mr. Chow's was busy at work in her kitchen.

"It smells divine in here," Vanessa purred as she passed Charles on her way to the refrigerator. "He won't suspect a thing."

"What's the occasion?" Charles questioned.

Vanessa smiled. "I was angry earlier but then realized that true love is about starting over with a clean slate. Tonight, I'm starting over."

"Mr. Washington is one lucky man."

Vanessa's smile widened. "He has no idea." She laughed out loud, sipped the water she'd just removed from the refrigerator, and then exited the kitchen.

Tonight she would let go of the past and once and for all move into her new future.

Vanessa's apartment was the ultimate setting for romance. She had perfectly recreated the atmosphere Richard had set the night before. She had warned the doorman of the night's events to ensure that there were no surprises. She lay in the bed full from dinner and an hour-long lovemaking session, pleased that everything had gone exactly according to plan.

"I'm so glad you changed your mind."

Vanessa snuggled into his arms. "I just realized that we'd been through so much together, that it'd be a waste to let anything else come between us."

"I love you, Vanessa."

Vanessa climbed on top of him and kissed him passionately. "Let's leave all that nonsense in the past. I'm ready to move forward with you."

"Babe, I just want you to know that you can trust me."

Vanessa kissed him again, interrupting his explanation. "Let's not talk about it."

The doorbell interrupted Vanessa this time as her lips parted from his. "One final surprise." Vanessa smiled as she lifted her naked body from his.

"You're too good to me," he cooed.

"Stay here. I'll be right back." She blew him a kiss while slipping her sex-sweaty body into a red silk robe.

Vanessa's robe resembled flames as she walked through her apartment. She opened the doors wide as if she was anticipating Santa Claus himself.

"Yo, what the fuck is wrong with my key? I've been out here for almost ten minutes."

"Richard!" Vanessa's face went from flushed to frustrated. "It's after midnight."

"And . . . I told you I was going to be late. Vanessa, what the hell is wrong with you? And what the hell is going on? The doorman was looking at me all crazy, talking about I can't come up and that he was calling security. My key doesn't work . . ."

"There's no easy way to tell you this, but love don't live here anymore."

"You bugging. What are you talking about? Love don't live here?"

Vanessa pulled the doors closed. "Richard, you're loud. I suggest you calm down."

"Calm down!"

"It's over! I can't take it anymore. You, Valentine, and now the ba—" Vanessa stopped short. "Let's just say, I'm done playing second fiddle to you and all your drama."

"I'm not with Val anymore. How many times do I have to tell you that! Are you outta your mind? Did you change the locks?" Richard continued to force his key into the lock.

"I changed a lot of things, Richard." Vanessa stood her ground.

"What do you mean, changed a lot of things? Where's my stuff?"

"Vanessa . . ." Stephen emerged from the bedroom wearing nothing but a smile. "I'm ready for my surprise."

Richard and Vanessa both turned their heads toward Stephen, who immediately covered himself when he saw Richard at the door.

"Baby, you all right? What the hell is going on?" Stephen asked, unsure of what to expect.

"Ooooooh hell no," Richard shouted.

Just as Vanessa turned her attention back to Richard, in a rage of anger, he punched the door, causing the door to knock Vanessa to the floor. "Son of a . . ." Vanessa pulled her body up and charged toward Richard. "You're a dead man. Are you crazy?"

Stephen rushed to Vanessa's side. She twirled from his grasp like a tornado and lunged at Richard.

"Vanessa? Richard? Your coworker?" Stephen's confusion was overshadowed by both Richard's and Vanessa's rage.

"You bitch! How you gonna play me like this? I told you it was over with Val, but you couldn't trust me. Could you?"

"Trust you?" Vanessa shouted back. "How dare you talk to me about trust!"

"And now you have this bastard in our house and in our bed? What, were you just gonna fuck him in my face?"

"Wait, you were living here?" Stephen questioned in an attempt to keep up.

"This is *my* house! There is no *ours*. You pathetic idiot! Stephen, call the police." Stephen's words and his defense of Vanessa got lost in the rage of the room and he vanished just as quickly as he'd surfaced.

"You have exactly two seconds to get the hell out of here. Or you'll find yourself in a worse set of circumstances than that ghetto 'hood rat tramp you're used to dealing with."

Richard's face was wet with both sweat and tears. "Vanessa," he whispered through gritted teeth. "Why? I gave up everything for you."

"You shouldn't have." Vanessa reached for the doors. "I had your things packed up and shipped back to Val's house. You belong there with her. You don't fit here with me." The sting to her face was way too familiar as she felt the side of her cheek swelling from the impact of the door. "Go home, Richard." Vanessa slammed the doors to her penthouse. "It's over!" she said, locking the doors.

As Vanessa cried, Stephen returned with the cordless phone in his hand. "Do you really want me to phone the police? What the hell is going on?"

Vanessa couldn't speak, instead she shook her head then buried her face in her hands.

"Give me a minute, please," she muttered to Stephen.

"Seriously Vanessa, tell me what the hell just happened. Who was that guy? Was there something going on between you two?"

"I'll explain everything to you. Just give me a minute. Please!" she shouted.

It took Stephen a moment to return to her bedroom. Vanessa silently waited for him to leave, determined not to say one word until he was gone. When the coast was clear she wiped the tears from her eyes and regained her composure. As she sashayed into the hallway bathroom, she looked at her reflection in the mirror and smiled. "Damn, I'm good!"

Her performance was every bit what her mother said it would be. And even though the scene was set up, the breakup and the emotions were real. Part of her actually felt bad for how she'd just treated Richard. Her falling in love with him, though genuine, was never part of the plan. Richard had become the closest thing to love she'd felt since Dexter. But with her getting the promotion to vice president, there was no room for him at the top. Her mother was right, the situation had gotten completely out of hand and she had long since lost control. Tonight was her first step in regaining control. Stephen was step two, and Richard would be a journey in and of itself.

Vanessa ran a cold towel across her face. She knew a serious explanation would be needed where Stephen was concerned. Vanessa loosened the belt to her robe and wiggled it off her skin. She walked out of the bathroom and made sure the front door was locked. As she prepared for Act II of her perfect performance she entered the bedroom. "I don't want to talk now," she said softly, making her way to the bed where Stephen waited. "Make me feel better," Vanessa said as she pressed her body against his, pushing him down on the bed. He tried to resist her kisses but Vanessa made sure her passion overpowered him. Regardless of what had just happened between her and Richard, Vanessa assured Stephen that all his questions would be answered. But for now, she wanted him without any further interruptions.

43

~

What's a Girl to Do?

Gina comes to the hospital along with Aunt Zenobia to pick me up bright and early Saturday morning. It takes at least two hours for them to get me cleaned up and ready and for the hospital to get my release papers in order. I tell Gina not to worry herself, but she insists on coming to tend to me. I'm happy and enjoy all of the attention everyone showers me with, but I'm not used to it.

My apartment feels foreign to me. It has been well over a week since I've last seen my home and the memories of everything come flooding back to me. Everywhere I turn, Rich is there. Our pictures adorn the walls, the rack with both of our bikes, his favorite mug on the dish drain on the countertop. If this is going to be my space alone, I'll have to do some serious redecorating. One of the first things I plan to do is change the second bedroom, which presently serves as Rich's office. I'll either make it into a guest room or possibly a nursery. My decision isn't final regarding the baby, but the more I learn about endometriosis, the more I realize that this may be my only chance at having a baby. Rich's appearance at the hospital is also playing a role.

"Girl, you haven't said a word since we arrived. What are you busy thinking about?" Gina asks.

"Probably that new young buck I seen running after her at the hospital," Aunt Zenobia replies, answering for me.

"Thanks, Miss Cleo," I say while laughing. "I can always count on you to know just what's on my mind."

"Sheeiit, the only things ever on a woman's mind is men, money, clothes, and more money and in that order."

"Aunt Zenobia, have you always been this crazy?" Gina asks, chuckling at my aunt's statement.

"If you only knew the half," I say. "Anyway, I was thinking about redecorating the place, you know? Maybe painting the walls, removing the pictures, and replacing them with some artwork and doing something different with the second bedroom."

"Painting, I like that. I'll come with you to pick out the colors and we can have a paint party."

"Y'all can have a paint party by your damn selves. I ain't thinking about painting nothing but the town red on my birthday next month. J-Boogie is gonna take me to one of them fancy restaurants in the city and then we gonna drive to the Poconos for the weekend. You saw those pictures where they have the heart-shaped hot tubs, unlimited champagne in those luxurious suites. I don't want nobody calling me unless the house is burning down. Sheeiit and they better not call me then either. They better call nine-one-one and have my stuff in order when I get back."

"See, Aunt Z, you ain't even right. I'm all banged up and you're not gonna come help your favorite niece out?"

"Girl, you better wait 'til your behind gets better or better yet, holla at your new man. I'm sure he'll be more than happy to help."

"Mmh, new man, huh? So you and Ron are really getting serious?" Gina asks.

I try not to blush, but being fair skinned doesn't help much and the grin that's tugging at my lips makes me lose the war altogether.

"Well, it's not official and I'm vulnerable right now. I don't wanna jump into anything so quickly. He's saying all the right things and making all the right moves, but it's just too soon."

"I hear you," Gina says, contemplating my words.

"What you hear, girl?" my aunt asks Gina. "Listen, that man wants your ass pregnant and all! You best get to shuffling before he realize that that baby ain't his. Shoot, who you know in this day and age willing to take on another man's child and he ain't even hit that yet? That negro don't even know if the coochie is any good. Coochie could be as old, sour, and funky as thirty-day-old milk."

"Aunt Z, you just wrong and showing out 'cause we got company."

"Well, in your aunt Zenobia's crazy way, she does have a point," Gina says as she gives me a steaming mug of tea and biscotti cookies on the side.

"So now you're agreeing with my crazy aunt? What is the world coming to?"

"Well, not about the coochie part." Gina pauses and chuckles. "Just that you may not want to be too hasty and turn your back on Ron. I know that you're feeling a brother. Don't think that I don't remember that night you two danced together at SOB's. I saw the chemistry working then and I can see it every time I mention his name. You're feeling him real hard."

"Whatever!"

"All I'm saying is don't let a good one get away."

"I know, I know. What's a girl to do?" I ask no one in particular.

"Speaking of, what are you going to do about the baby? What did that Dr. Rascal say about that disease you have?" Aunt Zenobia asks.

"Aunt Z, his name is Dr. Pascal." I correct her folly. "You make it sound like I'm freaking contagious or something. He said that I have mild endometriosis which is supposed to be really painful and usually causes infertility."

"Well, you're definitely fortunate," Gina replies.

"Infertility? Girl, God is trying to tell your simple behind something and don't be looking at me like, what? You need to have that baby. You are fortunate and the fact that you were able to conceive with all that going on goes to show that you are blessed. Don't throw away your blessing. You can throw away the man, but not the gift that God has given you. Your pregnancy is too far gone for that. Live and let live."

Aunt Zenobia has a way with words, but for once I know she's right. I may not have wanted to believe half of the things she's said in the past or follow her whacky advice, but this time she's right. In three more days I'll be fifteen weeks pregnant and whether Rich wants to be the father or not I have to be the responsible person. When I first found out I was pregnant Aunt Zenobia told me, "You ain't the first and won't be the last woman on this earth to have a baby with or without a man," and she was right.

"Ladies, it's been great, but J-Boogie and I have a date tonight and I gotta figure out what I'm gonna wear, go to the nail salon for my manicure and pedicure, and run a few other small errands."

"Okay, Aunt Z. Thank you so much for coming to get me from

the hospital this morning. Tell Shaquetta I'll see her later this week when she takes me in for my follow-up appointment."

"I sure will and if they have any openings at your job, Val, or your job, Ms. Gina, please let me know, because my child needs a steady paycheck, okay? She can't get over on her looks all of her life."

"I will," Gina answers and hugs my aunt.

"Listen, baby . . . your aunt loves you. If you need anything just give me a call and don't strain yourself. You be careful with that neck brace and cast on your arm. I laid out some clothes for you, unpacked your suitcase, and I'll be by tomorrow afternoon to wash your clothes and fix you something to eat or buy you something. I'll see how I feel."

"Thank you, Auntie." She hugs me gently and makes her way to the door. Gina follows her to lock the door behind her but when the door swings open, none of us expect to see what's on the other side.

44

❧

Forgive and Forget? Not!

There he stands in his entire splendor. I certainly don't expect to see him pay me a visit since I didn't tell him when I was leaving the hospital. However, it wouldn't be hard to find out that I had been released since the hospital personnel have to inform visitors when a patient has left.

He stole my breath away every time I laid eyes on him, but this time I don't know what to feel, especially after his last visit. I gave some thought to the issues he raised at the hospital. However, I decided to put him and his lackluster excuses on the back burner.

Rich doesn't look like himself and with each new day I realize that I'm not myself either. A lot has changed for good and for the better part of me. Growth is not only happening inside of me, but mentally I feel like I have shed a few layers of dead weight.

Aunt Zenobia jumps back as if she's seen a ghost and when the shock wears off, she quickly slams the door and locks it shut.

"Oh, hellllsss no!" Aunt Zenobia yells.

Gina appears just as shocked, furious, and disgusted. She takes a deep breath and turns her head toward me to check my reaction.

I try to maintain my composure and not reveal any emotion, but my heart flutters a bit. Though I'd only caught a glimpse of him when my aunt opened the door, I did notice that he appeared a little rough and unkempt, but as hard as he was probably working to get that new position, he probably came over here in a rush for something he'd left behind. I'm still angry, but curious to learn what Rich wanted.

"What the hell is he doing here? That negro was fixing to put the key in the door. Did you see that mess?"

"I saw that too!" Gina answers. "Val, did you change the locks? Who knows what he was gonna try to do to you. Thank goodness we're here. Do you think he had a gun?"

Aunt Zenobia pulls her cell phone from her purse and starts to dial. I still haven't said a word.

"Aunt Z, who are you calling?"

"I'm calling the damn police. We need to file a complaint and get an order of protection for yo' ass!"

"Val, do you think he knows that you're considering having the baby?" Gina asks, concerned.

"No, not since our last conversation," I answer and redirect my attention to my aunt. "Aunt Z, hang up the phone. I don't want to involve the police. I can handle it."

"Handle it my ass. Hello, I'd like to report a break-in. Yes, at . . . Val, what's your address again? Umm . . . Two-"

"Oh, my goodness, he probably does have a gun!" Gina says, panicked. "If he found out that there's a possibility of you having the baby, he may try to wipe you out so he can live happily ever after with that heiress chick."

"Yeah, umm . . . the address is Two-seven-five Clinton Avenue. The suspect is male; about six feet, two inches . . . yeah he's black . . ."

The incessant ringing of the doorbell brings me out of my stupor. My aunt is busy calling the police and Gina is creating scenarios that are straight out of a B movie.

"Aunt Z, hang up the phone and Gina, chill out. Now Rich can probably hear everything both of y'all are saying and then he will know about the baby. Now please relax, because you're both starting to stress me out."

Aunt Zenobia gives me the most unsettling look, but she finally tells the police to call off her request and that she knows the "perp." Gina stops running her mouth a mile a minute and takes a seat beside me. She begins to rub my shoulders while Rich continues to ring the bell and even begins banging furiously.

"I'm sorry, sweetie," Gina says, trying to pacify me. "What do you want us to do?" she asks, concern etched in her voice.

"Aunt Zenobia, I want you to go ahead and get ready for your date with your man and on your way out the door, leave Rich alone. Don't say a word."

"No. Mmh-mmh! I ain't going no-damn-where!" she says, placing her cell phone back in her purse as she walks toward the seat she just left.

"Please," I beg. "Don't change your plans because of me. Go ahead. Gina is here with me. Nothing is going to happen. You already called the police and they will not erase that call if something were to happen. They keep records of all the calls that they receive."

"I don't trust him, Valentine. That negro is a killa! A damn killa. I told you before and I'ma tell you again he is a straight up-and-down thug in a suit. Don't be fooled."

Gina looks confused, but she'll have to get an explanation some other time. I'm worn out from the two of them.

"Aunt Z, go and I mean it. Go now!" My free arm points her directly to the front door.

"Gina, you gonna be here, girl?" my aunt asks, frustrated as she shoots me dirty looks.

"Yeah, I ain't going anywhere. I had planned on spending the afternoon with Val anyway, so it's cool."

"See, Auntie? He's not stupid enough to try anything while Gina's here."

"You seem to be forgetting that that hoochie he's with got enough money to make all our asses disappear like we took a nice long vacation to Jamaica or some shit. Never to be seen or heard from again. When I leave here, I'm recording this on my video camera, writing it down, and putting it in J-Boogie's safe and I'm gonna tell Shaquetta, CJ, and some people at my job in case we start coming up missing. I don't trust no-fucking-body."

"Okay, Aunt Z, you do that," I say, tired of her ranting and raving. Rich is probably coming by to pick up the remainder of his stuff that he left behind. Since he and Ms. Knight have been living the high life, I thought that he forgot about his belongings. The same items I was planning to get rid of less than an hour ago.

Once again my aunt gets up from her seat and walks slowly to the door. At this point, I don't know if Rich is still there or not, because he's no longer ringing the bell or banging on the door. However, when my aunt opens the door, he's sitting on the floor with his back leaned against the wall across from my entryway.

My request to Aunt Zenobia falls on deaf ears as she steps to him and hovers above his head.

"If you so much as harm a hair on my niece's head, I will hurt you, boy. I will hurt you myself," she says and pats her purse as if she has a concealed weapon inside.

At that point, I want to laugh, but I don't want to chance Rich seeing that and taking it for a moment of weakness.

Once Aunt Zenobia walks off, Rich gets up from the ground and stands in the doorway.

"Can I come in?" he asks politely.

I remain seated on the couch and nod my head for him to enter. He comes inside and shuts the door and for a moment it feels like he's never left as I watch him turn both locks on the door and then walk toward me.

"Why don't you sit at the table over there?" I point, directing him to the dining room table.

"Hi Val. Hey Gina," he says in what appear to be an attempt to break the ice.

Gina merely rolls her eyes, sucking her teeth and crossing her arms across her chest.

"What can I do for you, Rich?" I ask in a very monotone voice.

"Nah, I just came by to see how you were doing. I called the hospital and they told me you had been released. I had planned to stop by again."

"Well, as you can see, my arm is in a cast and my neck is still a little messed up, but other than that, I'm good," I say and get up from the couch to walk toward the door. The back brace makes my gait a little stiff, but it improves my posture. "So if that's all you wanted to know, you can leave now."

"Val, why you gotta be like that? I can't pay you a visit? I can't holla at you?"

"Rich, seriously, your hollering at me days are long gone. Besides, last time we spoke you basically told me that I make you feel like less of a man. And you're in a different place now, so why aren't you at that place?"

"Do you ever forgive or forget anything? Damn!" Rich laments.

"Rich, you seem to have forgotten that I've forgiven, but then you'd turn around and do me dirty again. I'm not the one in the wrong here. You've treated me like shit for years. You walked over me like I was shit, talked to me like I was shit, and you held your head high as you left me for Vanessa."

"Why you always gotta take things so literally?" he says, doing a piss-poor job of pleading his case. Now he is starting to pique my curiosity, because the Rich I spoke to on the phone earlier in the week was cocky and self-righteous, unlike the Rich before me today.

"You know what, Rich, I wanna know why you're really here. Did your little girlfriend find out that I'm pregnant and you want to assure her that I'm really having an abortion? Is that it? Y'all wanna pay me off? Well I can't be bought."

Rich walks over to me at the doorway and I take it that he's surrendering and ready to leave, which is a relief. In truth, I don't know how much more of him I could stand.

To my surprise he bends down and whispers in my ear. "Can we talk in private without your girl being present?"

"What?" I ask, shocked. "No, anything you want to say to me, you will say in front of Gina," I say, loud enough for her to hear. "So if you have more to say, and you want to do it today, I suggest you say it now."

The biggest smile is plastered across Gina's face, replacing the smirk that had covered it moments earlier.

"Listen, I just want to apologize for the way I spoke to you earlier," he says in a fairly low tone.

"What? I didn't hear you." I turn my head as much as I can without straining myself and place my finger behind my ear for emphasis.

"I said I'm sorry for some of the things I said on the phone. When I stopped by the other day, I realized that although I said my piece, I failed to apologize."

"Yeah, whatever! You can take your lame-ass apology and save it for someone who gives a damn."

"Val, come on. Give me some credit. I came over here because I had some time to think about the way things went down and I realize I was wrong."

"Yeah, was that before or after I threatened to take you to court for child support? Are you worried that I'll tap into your new vice president's salary? Or is your trick concerned that if y'all get married that she'll have to give me some of her paper too? She probably sent your ass over here to make me sign some papers or something. Well, both of you can kiss my behind."

"So you decided to have my baby?" he asks, a little too excited.

"Now it's your baby?"

Rich falls before me on his knees and lifts my shirt and to my surprise begins rubbing my belly.

"What the heck are you doing? Rich, get up and get your hands off of me."

Before I know what's happening, Gina tips Rich over and he's on his side. "Get your nasty hands off of her," she yells.

"I want you to leave. I don't know what you're up to, but I need you out of here now," I say, confused.

Rich doesn't respond to the fact that Gina has pushed him or to my request. Instead he gets up and dusts himself off. Then he take my hand and leads me back over to the couch.

"Val, listen. I know I messed up and I'm sorry. I'm so sorry and I really just came by to ask you to forgive me."

"Why? Why do you care if I forgive you? Better yet, why should I forgive you after all of the awful things you've done to me?"

"Because you're better than me."

"It's a little too late for all of that. I really think you need to go now," I say, feeling like I'm on the brink of tears.

After all this time he finally comes asking for my forgiveness.

In the past everything simply went unsaid, then a bouquet of flowers would follow or some other small token and I'd always let him back in with a warm embrace. Then deep down I would hope and pray there wouldn't be a next time, but there was. There always was a next time and I didn't see how this time was going to be any different; especially since he was still with Vanessa. Did he somehow think that because I was having the baby that he could still get a little something on the side? Not a chance!

I snatch my hand from beneath Rich's and again order him to leave. I mean it with all my heart.

"Rich, please leave. I'll let you know if I decide to have the baby. I'm still thinking about it, but to be honest I'm at a crossroads. If I do, it'll be up to you how involved you want to be in your child's life. I won't interfere with that."

Rich looks at me intensely as if he has other questions to ask or more to say, but I believe he realizes that I'm exhausted.

He stands up and begins to walk slowly to the entryway. I follow behind to lock the door when he leaves. He turns the knob, and partially opens the door. With his hand still firmly on the knob he turns back to me.

"Val, I'm really sorry for all of the hurt and pain that I've caused you. I just want you to know that I've never stopped loving you."

Before I can get a word in he slips out the door and pulls it closed behind him.

45

❧

Extra! Extra!

Vanessa Knight named Vice President of Marketing at Jorge Jacobs

Jorge Jacobs announced today the appointment of Vanessa Knight as vice president of business affairs and strategic marketing and head of their new urban division. Ms. Knight's new position is effective immediately. This announcement also included the departure of co-director Richard Washington. No further information was provided as to the specifics of his departure.

Ms. Knight, who is fluent in both French and Spanish, has significant experience in the luxury goods industry having studied abroad in Paris for more than a year after graduating with honors from the Fashion Institute of Technology. Ms. Knight has proven a valuable asset to the Jorge Jacobs family.

"We are very happy to welcome Vanessa Knight to her new position as vice president. With her successful track record in the luxury goods and the urban development industry both domestically and abroad, we look forward to her contribution," said Etienne Jorge, Jorge Jacobs's founder and CEO.

"Over the past four years, I have strived to introduce the Jorge Jacobs's lifestyle to American consumers. I am a huge fan of Jorge Jacobs and I greatly appreciate the opportunity to oversee the company's marketing and new line development. With the new direction of Jorge Jacobs, I felt it necessary to put together a new group of leaders that will add a fresh new take on where we are headed as a company. With this new management team in place, I believe the Jorge Jacobs business will continue to grow," said Ms. Knight.

Mr. Washington was not available for comment over the weekend.

—*NY Fashion Journal*

46

First Order of Business

"Ms. Knight, please, I can't lose my job. I've got two kids, and my baby daddy left me six months ago. I won't be able to pay my rent if I'm not bringing home a check and unemployment won't cover it . . ." Chanel pleaded.

"You really need to calm down. Where's Richard?" Vanessa handed a tissue to Richard's very young and unprofessional assistant. Part of her found her little act amusing especially since she'd tried to be snooty in the past when Vanessa was looking for Richard and she wouldn't give up information regarding his whereabouts.

"He didn't come in yet. Did he say anything about me? I mean, if he's fired then am I automatically fired too?"

"Chanel, this is highly inappropriate. And until I speak with Richard, there is nothing I can tell you at this time."

Vanessa helped Chanel up and led her to the door. She indicated for Cynthia to escort her out of her office.

"Chanel, please inform Richard that I need to see him ASAP!"

"But Ms. Knight pleeeeeease . . ."

Vanessa closed the door behind her and stretched her neck. Even though it was stressful, she still felt satisfied. Vanessa had declined the corner office on the third floor with the other executives because she already occupied one of the best offices in the building. The lighting was superb and she liked the space allotted for her assistant, Cynthia. Besides, half of the furniture in Vanessa's office had been custom designed and she didn't want to have to redecorate another office, especially one of the same size.

"I'll need new stationery, buckslips, business cards—"

"Ms. Knight, Mr. Washington just arrived. Should I send him in?"

Vanessa looked at the signature crystal Tiffany clock on her desk and smiled.

"Please have him wait outside for a moment. I'll let you know when I'm ready for him. Oh, by the way, Cynthia, hand Mr. Washington the newspaper from Friday, please. Thank you."

Vanessa got up from her desk and walked toward the door to look out the side window. Richard accepted both the coffee and the paper from Cynthia as he made himself comfortable on the couch just outside her office.

He doesn't know! Vanessa said to herself as she giggled, waiting for a reaction. She stood anxiously awaiting him to read through the press release.

"Three, two, one . . ."

Vanessa scooted back behind her desk the moment she witnessed Richard almost spit out his coffee.

Within seconds her phone rang. "Ms. Knight, Mr. Washington says it's urgent."

Laughter almost spilled out of her but she managed to keep it together. "Cynthia, have him wait." Vanessa was short as she placed the receiver down.

Vanessa reapplied her makeup, assuring a flawless face as she allowed yet another ten minutes to pass before summoning Richard into her office.

"You can send him in now," Vanessa sang.

Richard's footsteps were swift and hard as his silhouette emerged toward the edge of Vanessa's desk.

She hesitated to acknowledge him as she continued to jot things down on her to-do list.

"Vanessa, you've sunk to a new low."

Vanessa held her finger up in midair, hushing Richard for interrupting her thought.

Once she finished with the last item, she rose from her desk, walked to her door, opened it slightly, and called for Cynthia.

"I've finished my list of things that will require updating to my new title. Please see to it that these items are ordered immediately. Thanks. Oh, and Cynthia, could you please confirm my call with *Women's Wear Daily*? If we could push the interview back thirty minutes that would fabulous."

Vanessa closed the door to her office softly and adjusted her black-and-red pin-striped Marc Jacobs skirt. Her crisp black button-down exposed subtle cleavage, while her matching blazer rested on the coatrack nearby. African black pearls kissed the skin on her neck while a stunning 3.5 karat ruby ring surrounded by diamonds and set in 18 karat gold donned her finger.

"Mr. Washington, as you probably already know, I've been offered the position of vice president of business affairs and strategic marketing. With this promotion comes immediate changes which are great for the company yet not so great for you."

"I thought we were a team. What? So all this time you were just using me? You bitch!"

"Tsk, tsk, Richard. I wouldn't do that if I were you. Especially since every referral you'll need will have to come from me. Have a seat."

"I'd rather stand."

"Suit yourself," Vanessa responded while crossing her arms and settling herself back into her chair. "I'm letting you go because I no longer need you. This is more professional than personal."

"I highly doubt that, Vanessa. This shit here is personal."

"On the contrary. This is business. You see, Richard, with me assuming the position of vice president, there is no room for you to grow with this company. In terms of position we were equal, but you'd be a fool to stay stagnant and work beneath me. You're far too talented for that."

"I've been a fool all right. A fool to think I could ever trust you. Val was right."

"Val? Valentine Daye knows nothing about me or this. If it weren't for her . . ."

"What, we'd be together?" Richard paced the floor. "I don't think so. What is it? Is it because I'm from the streets? A brother got a past? Your family didn't approve of me, did they? Shit started getting real with us and you what? Can't handle the pressure from your parents? That's what this is about. You're a puppet, Vanessa, and they pull the strings."

"I'm my own woman, Richard. This was never supposed to be about love."

"Did you love me?" He moved in close. "Because I loved you."

"But you still loved her and since I made VP there's no need for an 'us' anymore. It's over! I told you from the start. I don't share."

"I gave up everything for you, you spoiled, conniving little . . ." He pursed his lips together tightly.

Vanessa stood and walked toward Richard, placing her hand on his shoulder. He nudged back.

"You need not be testy, Richard, it's not becoming of you. Besides, my mind is made up, and as you see I've already taken the measures necessary to make my decision final."

"This has always been about Val, hasn't it?"

Vanessa pressed her lips together then raised her eyes toward his. "It's funny that you think this is about her. It isn't. It's bigger than that. However, you've been so stuck in the past that you couldn't see the future that was right in front of you. If the roles would've been reversed and you held this position, it wouldn't have been long before I would've had to leave anyway. It's in my blood to lead not follow. It's what I've been bred to be."

"Here we go on this whole breeding trip again. You know what? You're just like your mother."

Vanessa laughed. "You're right. I am."

Vanessa leaned against her desk, grazing so close to Richard that her perfume began to mask his own scent. "It's because of my mother that I'll allow you to leave here with a little dignity, because after that stunt you pulled on Friday, I should've had you arrested for assault."

"I didn't touch you. You got knocked down by the door, Vanessa, and I'm sorry about that. What did you expect me to do? You had dude walking butt-ass naked in our . . ." he caught himself, "in the house and you don't expect me to react? I ain't never been one to be punked. But I would never hit a woman."

"No, you'd assault them with lies and emotional hell."

"You knew what you were walking into when you hooked up with me. So don't go getting all self-righteous now, Vanessa. Val was there before and she was going be there. I wasn't sleeping with her anymore. I told you that."

"You're right. You did tell me. But it's what you haven't told me that brought us here."

"Vanessa, what are you talking about?"

"All of it. All the lies. Are you really that freaking naïve, Richard? For months you string along two women. While you were fucking me, I'm almost certain you were lying to her. So, what, now that the shoes are falling on your feet, you want to act all hurt? You had your share of making this bed, baby. Lie in it."

"Fuck you, Vanessa!" His voice cracked with emotion.

"I think I've let you do enough of that. Now it's your turn to be fucked. And how dare you come in here and act like you didn't participate in the creation of this chaos. If I'm a bitch, it's because you drove me to that point."

"No, this shit ain't new."

Vanessa shook her head. It didn't matter. "Listen, I've made some calls, there are some bids for you already. Ralph Lauren, Ecko, and Fabulosity are all interested in acquiring your services. I spoke to Kimora Lee this morning and they are in desperate need for someone to head up Fabulosity, her new kids' division."

"I don't need your handouts, Vanessa, I can take care of myself."

Vanessa flipped open her date book and began to jot some things down. "We've prepared a nice severance package that should tide you over for a while. You'll have until the end of the day to pack up your office. You may want to do something about your assistant, she didn't take the news well at all this morning and I've decided not to keep her any longer."

"So that's it? You're just going to run an ad in the paper, fire me and my assistant, and act like we didn't even happen?"

"What we had was fun. But now playtime is over. You have a lot on your plate, and frankly Richard, I'm full." Vanessa's stare was haunting. She didn't budge. "I have nothing further," she said, shooing him away.

Vanessa watched as Richard gathered his things and made his way to the door. A small portion of her wrestled with the thought of him leaving her life permanently. With him gone, there would be no more afternoon office romance and she'd never again kiss his tender soft lips.

"I'm sorry I hurt you, Vanessa," Richard said as he opened the door.

"You didn't!" Vanessa said dryly, knowing those words were a lie as soon as they departed her mouth.

She watched as he walked out of her office, closing the door behind him. Vanessa knew in her heart that Richard was sorry for his part in their pain. And she shared the blame too. She certainly hadn't acted like a saint, yet her relationship with Richard could not go on.

Vanessa reached into her purse and pulled out the note from her mother.

As careless as you were getting into this relationship with Richard, you have to be equally as careful getting out. This is about war, the war of love, which is never fought fairly. Do the following and allow Richard to be with the one who truly loves him . . . Valentine. Your bait . . . Stephen! The setup . . . dinner then destruction. Your delivery . . . heartless. Your destiny . . . freedom. He was her man first, Vanessa. With this baby, he needs to be her man last. I love you, Mom.

Vanessa slipped the piece of paper into her shredder and watched as the pieces, like her heart, were torn apart. She wasn't sure what hurt more, letting him go or feeling as if she had lost. Nevertheless, she knew what she did was ultimately the right thing to do.

"Ms. Knight," Cynthia interrupted. "It's Tara Simmons from *Women's Wear Daily* on line two."

"Thank you, Cynthia, I'm ready."

And that she was. With her new promotion and a clear conscience, Vanessa was ready for just about anything.

47

❧

Ain't Too Proud to Beg

"In case you're just tuning in, it's been one hell of a weekend. This is Juicy Lips with WFAT, 106.9 FM, always bringing you the juiciest gossip with my sweet and oh so juicy lips! From my lips to your ears and it ain't hearsay, it's Juicy-say!

"I went to one of the wildest industry parties this weekend and you'd never guess who rolled up in the spot with Vivica A. Fox? Since you weren't there I might as well tell y'all. Logo Benton, aka The Gift, the twenty-year-old rookie and number one NBA draft pick. Vivica . . . girl, don't put too much stock into that young'un! These women must be breastfeeding this young buck. He definitely has a thing for older women and he's taking them all for a ride on his big wheel. Anyway, I guess it's over between him and our very own evening shock jock, Noches Star. I guess its *buenos noches* for our star deejay Girl, if you didn't already know, now you know. Now that's Juicy!

"Now, the drama at WFAT continues, because I read earlier today in the *New York Post* that there's been a shake up and breakup at Jorge Jacobs, the fashion clothier. Oh yeah, apparently Ms. Vanessa Knight—you know, the heiress who has more money than she knows what to do with—was promoted to vice president of marketing. Now you know that sexy brotha she was frolicking around town with, Richard Washington, was engaged to one of our employees, Val. Now word on the street is that he left Val to hook up with ole girl, but when Vanessa Knight got her promotion, Richard was told to go, hit it deejay," *To the left, to the left. Everything you own in the box to the left.* "Okay, deejay, cut . . ." (Music abruptly stops.) "Val, *you can have another him in a minute, baby! We wish you well, girl.*"

My heart tightens and my head begins pounding after hearing Juicy Lips's commentary. After I turn the radio off, I feel an instant migraine pulsate my head. I make a beeline into the bathroom to retrieve some pain relievers and swallow at least four Tylenol tablets while gulping down tap water.

Once again, Juicy Lips allowed my name to pass through her mouth. I'm stunned at the news about Rich, but he got what he deserved. God never did like ugly. Seething mad, I promise that upon my return to work, Juicy Lips will be Fat Lips once I am done with her. I can't wait to get back to work and scalp her. She doesn't know me very well, but I will treat her like a street chick if she doesn't learn to respect my privacy. Now because of her blabbering, upon my return to work I'll be the talk of the office.

For the first time in many years, my mother comes to mind and I wish she were here to help me ease the pain surging through my body. She was the one person on earth who could make me feel better whenever I hurt. She knew all the right places to massage, whether it was my heart or an abrasion. She'd say the right things, cook the right foods, and hold me the right way. As I think about all of the things I miss about her, I begin to think of the things that I'll do for my child and the thought begins to lift my spirits.

The phone ring just as I'm about to pick it up to call Gina.

"Hello," I answer, only slightly upset now at Juicy Lips for airing out my business.

"Were you listening to Juicy Lips?" Gina asks.

"Yes, girl. I just heard her."

"I know you want to kick her ass for shouting you out like that."

"No doubt, but now it all makes sense as to why Rich was over here practically begging for forgiveness on Saturday."

"Girl, I wish I could've been a fly on that wall when that mess went down between him and Vanessa," Gina says. I echo the same sentiments.

"Gina, hold on. Someone is on my other line."

"Hello," I answer.

"Who gets the last laugh now?" my aunt hollers through the phone. She's a devout listener to Juicy Lips and she holds everything Juicy Lips says as truth. If my aunt has celebrity gossip, nine times out of ten she got her information from Juicy Lips.

"Aunt Z, I'ma have to call you back. I'm on the other line."

"Yeah, okay, but if I don't hear from you in ten minutes, I'm calling yo' ass back!"

"Gina, you still there?" I ask after clicking the line.

"Yeah, I'm here. So what you gonna do now?"

"What do you mean?" I ask, knowing full well what she's talking about. But for once in my life I have choices and the idea of hooking up with Ron is still weighing heavy on my mind. Yesterday Ron and I spent over an hour on the phone talking and laughing and the only reason I didn't let him come over was because I was afraid that Rich would make another surprise visit.

"You gonna take him back?"

"Gina, that's not even on my mind right now. I'm more concerned about getting better and preparing myself for this baby," I reply, half telling the truth.

"Okay, but you know I had to ask. Anyway, I'm so glad that you're going to have the baby. You're making the right decision whether he's in the picture or not."

"Yeah, I know. Deep down, I always knew. The fact that the baby survived after that nasty crash is a miracle in itself and I'd be stupid and a horrible person to do something like that. Look how banged up I got and the baby still made it through. It's just that I kept thinking about getting back at Rich by killing something that was his, but this baby is not about him. This baby represents new life."

"That's true. Well, you know I'm always here for you. I may stop by tonight after work, so let me know if you need anything before I leave."

"Gina, thank you for everything. I love you, girl, and I'll see you later."

After Rich left on Saturday I was so riled up and uptight that I had to leave the house. Gina and I went out and caught a movie and went to one of our favorite little spots, Soule on Fulton Street, to grab a bite to eat. When we returned the doorman told me that I had a delivery. Since I hadn't been home, they put the delivery in the basement and I still hadn't bothered to have anyone bring it up to the apartment. Yesterday no one was on call to retrieve the item and I was too tired to be bothered going down there myself and today was slipping into evening just as quickly.

"Hello, Roger . . . It's Valentine Daye in apartment four-B."

"Hi, Ms. Daye, what can I do for you this afternoon?"

"Yeah, I'm calling to see if anyone is available to bring up the package that arrived while I was out on Saturday?"

"Yes, I'll get someone and they'll bring your delivery up to you shortly."

"Thanks, Roger."

Less than two minutes later there's a knock at the door and the phone rings at the same time. *I knew the maintenance staff worked quick, but damn!* I think to myself.

I grab the phone on my way to answer the door. Without even looking at the caller ID I know it has to be my aunt Zenobia, because it was well over ten minutes since we'd spoken.

"Hello," I answer.

"Didn't I tell you to call me back, girl?" she exclaims.

"Yes," I answer as I walk from my bedroom through the living room to the front door. "And I was about to, but I had to handle something else really quickly. Hold up, Aunt Z, someone's at my door. Just a minute, I'm coming."

"Okay, so girl, didn't I tell you that negro was up to no good? He was a got-damn fool to let you go for that tramp. That dumb asshole got just what he deserved."

I hastily open the door for my delivery. "Aunt Z, I gotta go. I can't talk right now," I respond while trying to maintain my composure, but my breathing becomes shallow.

"Why?" she asks, ticked off that yet again I'm cutting her off.

"Because that dumb asshole you were just talking about is at my door. I'll speak to you later," I say and hit the end button on the phone before she can respond.

We stare each other down for what can only amount to seconds, but feels like five minutes. My look is full of contempt, while his is one of curiosity mixed with something else I can't quite place my finger on.

"What can I do for you, Rich? Shouldn't you be at work?" I ask, pretending to be clueless.

"I'm good. How are you feeling?" Rich asks, ignoring my question.

"I really don't care how you feel. But I am curious to know why you're stopping by here in the middle of the day."

"I'll answer, but can you at least invite me in first?"

I take two steps back to allow him entry and lock the door behind him. I watch as he strides over to the couch and takes a seat in his favorite spot. He loosens his necktie and removes his blazer as he waits for my next move.

"You need to stop doing these drop-bys, because last time I checked you don't live here anymore!"

Unlike Saturday, today he doesn't look like a man who's been beaten down. Although I know that he's been fired from his dream job at Jorge Jacobs, at that moment he exudes more confidence than I can ever recall.

"What do you want, Rich?"

"You want the truth?"

"Yes. The truth would be a nice change for once."

Rich removes his tie altogether and then begins cracking his knuckles, which is a nervous tic that relaxes him. Just as he gets comfortable there's a knock at the door.

"Hold that thought," I ask, relieved for the reprieve. This time I know it has to be the building custodian delivering my package. At least I thought.

To my surprise, several bouquets of flowers along with Ron stand behind the door. My mouth hangs open as I lean against the door to steady myself from the shock.

"Oh my goodness! Ron, I wasn't expecting you," I say, astonished.

"I know. I wanted to check on you," he says and bends over to peck me on the cheek. "You gonna let a brother in?" he asks with a huge smile on his face as he hands me the flower arrangement.

"Umm . . . well . . ."

The large bouquets don't allow him to see inside the apartment and my body blocks the door, limiting Ron's vision.

"Is everything all right?" he asks, concerned.

"Yeah, everything is good, my man!" Rich says as he steps beside me to open the door wider. He sizes Ron up with a once-over before facetiously attempting to give Ron some dap, which Ron ignores.

I'm glad that Ron came looking well dressed in a finely tailored suit, Gucci wing tip shoes, custom-made shirt with French cuffs, and a nice-sized diamond in his ear. His Patek Philippe watch glistens with diamonds around the faceplate, but isn't overt in display.

Ron's eyes go from mine to Rich and then return to me. His expression changes from happy to see me to disheartened, and I'm almost positive he can read the same from me as well. I'm caught in a very sticky situation. The new Val wants to kick

Rich out on his ass. Yet the new me is also carrying Rich's baby and at the very least I owe him the opportunity to speak his piece.

"Ron, I'm so sorry about this. Any other time, you'd be more than welcome, but you know we have some things to discuss," I say, pointing from myself to Rich.

"My man, next time you should call before making unannounced visits," Rich adds.

"Rich, if you could go back inside, I'll handle this," I say, doing my best not to explode and dis Rich in the process.

Rich gives me a look of surprise, but when he sees my face, he quickly heels and backs down.

"Don't take too long," he says as he leaves.

I place the flowers on the table beside the entrance and step into the hallway, pulling the door shut behind me.

"Ron, I'm so happy that you stopped by. None of this was planned," I try to explain.

"Val, no problem. You don't owe me an apology."

"I know. It's just that . . . well, I really care for you, but I have this ugly situation that I have to work through." My head tilts slightly toward the apartment to emphasize the point.

"Listen, and I mean this seriously. No matter what you decide to do, I'll still be here for you. The offer I made at the hospital still stands. It came from my heart and I knew going in that a sistah had a little baggage."

"A little?" I joke. A slight smile spills across Ron's face.

"Well, an entire set of luggage and some damn carry-on, but you're cool people and I'll always look out for you."

"Thanks, Ron," I say as we embrace and I inhale his manly aroma mixed with the familiar scent of Dolce & Gabbana Light Blue. It smells differently on Rich, but just as tantalizing on Ron and as I rest my head on his chest, I don't want to let go. His firm chest feels inviting and comfortable. However, once again our moment is interrupted.

"Ms. Daye?"

"Yes," I answer. I'm not familiar with this particular workman. I step away from Ron and he stands to the side to allow the men passage.

"We have some boxes for you," he announces. He's followed by another building maintenance man that I do recognize.

My eyes follow his toward the boxes, but I can't believe that all of this is for me. The maintenance guys have three wardrobe boxes and two smaller boxes in tow on dollies.

"Are you sure all of this is for me?" I ask incredulously, directing my question to the custodian I recognize.

"Yes. We're sure and here's an envelope that came with the delivery."

"Thank you," I reply and accept the packet. "You can place them in the apartment," I say, still unsure of what could possibly be inside.

"I better tend to this stuff," I say to Ron. "Today has been full of surprises. I don't know how much more I can stand." I chuckle softly.

"Just take it easy and use my number whenever you need to."

"Thanks." Ron pecks me on the forehead and I watch him head toward the elevator.

"Ron," I call out.

"Are you busy tonight?" I ask.

"No, why?"

"Would you like to come by later, say around seven-ish? We can order in and watch a movie, if you like?"

The elevator arrives.

"I'll bring the movie," he said as he steps one foot into the elevator.

"Great, so it's a date," I gush and blow him a kiss.

"It's definitely a date," he says, and the doors close.

The custodians have placed the boxes off to the right of the dining room and in part of the living room. As I reenter the apartment I begin to open the letter that accompanied the delivery. The envelope has a pressed seal for closure and a beautiful note card with the initials *VDK* displayed. The scent of vanilla wafts under my nose from the paper. I have no idea who this is from and quickly flip the card open.

> *Returning what is rightfully yours.*
> *Sorry for the trouble.*
> *Vanessa*

"No this bitch didn't!" I hiss as I head toward the boxes. Rich is so preoccupied with the beer in his hand and the television to even notice my return. "Rich! What the hell is in these boxes? It better not be what I think it is!" My temples begin to pulsate as I realize that the items in the cartons contain Rich's belongings.

Upon hearing my voice and seeing me frenzied, Rich simultaneously turns off the television and practically jumps off the couch.

"Baby," he says, grabbing my hands to which I resist. "Baby, I'm sorry. I'm really, really sorry." I continue to try to pry myself away from his grip to no avail.

"Now you wanna be sorry? After she played you? You wanna come crawling back to me? Damn, Rich let go of me!" I yell and he relents.

"I didn't know that this was going to happen!"

"Well, too bad. I guess you didn't know that you'd be out of a job either? Did you?" I ask, throwing salt into the wound.

Rich gives me a surprised but exasperated look. He goes through a string of emotions until he settles down with a look of surrender.

"That's right. I know you got fired, so I guess you're not getting that VP promotion you kept throwing in my face. I heard that your girl Vanessa got it. She really bent you over, didn't she? Took the position right from under yo' ass while she schmoozed you, screwed you, and then used you!"

"It wasn't like that!" Rich balks.

"Sure looks like it," I contest and point at the five boxes taking residence in the dining and living rooms. "You know what? You're starting to wear my patience."

Rich places his chin in the palm of his hands and looks up at the ceiling as if in deep thought. Carefully he chooses his words.

"Baby, please give me a chance to explain. You're absolutely right and I'll do whatever I have to if it means a chance to be with you again."

"You're moving real fast and slick. Besides, what makes you believe that I'd give you another chance?" I ask, infuriated.

"Because you've had a change of heart about our baby and right now that's all that matters to me. The chance to be with you and raise our child," Rich says as he tries to coax me toward the living room to take a seat. I reluctantly follow. I'm tired of arguing and even more exhausted from being on my feet.

"Val, if you were to slap me and spit in my face right now, I wouldn't react, because I know I deserve it. Baby." Rich pauses for effect and takes my hands in his massive palms. "All I want is a chance to right all of my wrongs. I'm not perfect and know that I've got a long way to go, but on my word, I promise I'll never break your heart again.

"I admit I was stupid for ever leaving you. There's no excuse for what I did and how I betrayed your trust and loyalty. You've been the only sure thing in my life. You believed in me when no one else gave a damn. You deserve so much more than I ever gave you. When I visited you at the hospital, I complained about the things that went wrong, but I didn't tell you the good stuff. Your strength sustained me during the rough times. Your faith gave me balance. Your smile makes my heart skip a beat. Your focus and determination fed my ambition and you helped build a better me. And your support helped me climb the ladder to success. I may not be at Jorge Jacobs, but trust me when I say RichWear will happen one way or another, and I need you. I want a second chance to prove that I can be the man that you've always wanted. I'm willing to go to counseling, if that's what it takes. I just don't want to lose you again."

As I digest Rich's words, which feel and sound sincere, I want nothing more than to believe him. On the other hand, there are years of damage caused mainly by Rich that has wreaked havoc on our relationship. Then he tries to use me as a scapegoat for his transgressions, claiming that I've emasculated him. I may have been feisty, but it was only because of the extenuating circumstances and provocation. I don't know if it's possible to start with a clean slate, due to the years of disrespect on Rich's part toward me. He treated me like a doormat and opening that door for him again may lead him to further step on and over me.

"Rich, I don't like the circumstances which caused you to come crawling back to me. I don't care for the way that woman decided that after she's had her way with you she feels she can just toss me her leftovers. I don't know if I can ever trust you again, and more importantly, I don't know if I can forgive you yet. This is all just too fresh right now and for the record the only reason I'm tolerating you right now is because of the baby. Whether I take you back or not, I do want you to have an active role in the baby's life," I say, slightly winded.

My eyes are welling with tears. I want to let go and let God, but the devil keep showing me flashbacks of every girl that Rich had cheated on me with: Qwanisha, Chantal, and the demon of all demons, Vanessa.

Rich kneels before me as tears spring from his eyes. He shuts them momentarily as if trying to cease their flow. Then he wipes them and takes a long exhale.

"Val, only time will tell and hopefully heal your heart, but I know you're a good woman. If I have to come back here every day and ask your forgiveness until you take me back, I'll do it. I want you back in my life and I'll do whatever it takes to get you back."

Later that evening when Ron comes over for our date, he arrives with all the trimmings. The latest flick featuring Idris Elba and containers of food from Soule. He didn't even know Soule is my favorite around-the-way spot, so I give him kudos for being on point.

Ron is trying his best to win me over and my soul needs the attention. I truly enjoy his company and the vibes feel good.

After years of devotion to a man who I allowed to treat me as he saw fit, it was time for a change. Unfortunately, the heart often doesn't listen to direction. It dances to a rhythm of its own.

48

❧

And He's My Man Again!

Patience. It was one of the many new exercises that Rich and I have been practicing for the past eight weeks.

Rich and I are definitely on the road to recovery. The one thing that I refused to do was make it easy for him to reenter my life. My conditions for his return were many, including counseling in the church with Pastor McCash. The bottom line is we need help! Our relationship is in ruins and without God and guidance we are doomed to make the same mistakes.

We sit silently and patiently in Pastor McCash's office waiting for him and his wife to join us for couples counseling. We have been seeing the McCashes twice a week for the past eight weeks and we are progressing mentally and spiritually. I know mending the relationship isn't going to be an overnighter. Too many things have gone wrong and too much damage has been done to our relationship for things to smooth over as easy as 1-2-3. Still, I am making a modest attempt to shift things in the right direction for the sake of our baby and because Rich is still a vital part of me.

As we sit in the small office space, my eyes glimpse the familiar wood-paneled walls that are covered with pictures of Martin Luther King, John F. Kennedy, and Jesus Christ on the cross. Rich and I have been there so often lately that if the room were a puzzle, I could put each piece in its rightful place without thought.

At the conclusion of each session, Pastor McCash gives us homework. While in therapy we talk about boundary issues, life transitions, communication, compulsivity, feelings, trust, infidelity, and sexuality enrichment. Then the homework starts and we have to list our goals for today, then for the next week and then for the next month. However, the last two assignments are the most difficult. The questions are simple enough, but complicated considering all that we've just been through. We have to be honest and place our feelings to the side.

Last week, Pastor McCash asked us, "Knowing what you know about your relationship, would you still get involved with the same person if you had to do it all over again?" Rich's response was short, sweet, and to the point. Rich said that I was the kind of woman that every man should look for. He discussed how I had been there for him from day one and was the reason he was able to turn his life around from a life of crime, but my downfall was my temper. Pastor McCash raised a brow and looked like he was about to agree. Mrs. McCash rested her hand on her husband's knee and he stopped him from making a comment. When the question was given to me, I was tempted to say no. However, my love for Rich was tried and true. My love for him at one point had bordered on obsession. However, this ordeal has taught me to invest more love into myself.

Although I said yes, Pastor McCash sensed my hesitation and encouraged me to elaborate on my feelings. I ran down a laundry list of incidents. It took at least twenty minutes and I held nothing back. When I was done, the room went silent. And although the McCashes tried to disguise their feelings, they couldn't mask the look of sympathy they felt for me. If Mrs. McCash and I were alone, I believe without a doubt she'd ask me why I had stayed so long. I have been through quite an ordeal with Rich.

After that session, Pastor McCash ordered that we do another four weeks and I agreed.

This week we were asked two questions: 1. Would you rather follow your heart or your head? 2. What do we consider most important in life? Both are simple, but not so simple questions.

Time and newfound wisdom have taught me valuable lessons. Ten years of being together with three of those years engaged was no longer cute. Yeah, I'm the one rocking the two-carat, princess-cut diamond and platinum engagement ring on my finger, but all of that is irrelevant if the marriage never takes place. We finally managed to set a date after completing twelve weeks of counseling. It's time that I take my rightful place and become his queen and it's partially my fault for allowing him to treat me like wifey instead of making him wife me.

My pregnancy has been going well. It's amazing. Rich accompanies me for my checkups. We can't believe the technology and how clear the images are of the baby.

Pregnancy is definitely an experience that I know I'll want to have again and again.

My first few weeks back at the office felt strange. Thanks to Juicy Lips, my business was fresh on everyone's minds and I could feel all eyes on me. It took everything in me to grin and bear it, but the new me sucked it up and before long things returned to normal.

Then there was Ron, whom I avoided for the first couple of days feeling that any interaction would be uncomfortable. Of course he wasn't having that. One day we had a brief encounter in the company lounge.

"If I could rewrite the alphabet, I would put U and I together."

That corny pick-up line caused me to burst into laughter. This was his way of letting me know everything was all right with us.

"So how are things?" Ron asked.

"We're making progress," I answered truthfully.

Ron had come to the apartment a few times and we bonded. If the circumstances were different, I'd definitely date Ron. He's a great catch and when he does eventually find someone I knew I'd be happy that he found happiness.

"I'm sorry to hear," Ron replied. "But you're looking good as usual."

Though he offered a smile with his remark, I knew he was being truthful.

"You know my offer still stands, so brother-man better not leave room for error." Ron laid his hand atop mine and gave it a quick squeeze. "If he messes up . . ."

"You'll be the first to know," I finished for him. "Thanks for being you, Ron."

"My pleasure," he said and strode off with his coffee in hand.

Rich is finally proving to be the man that I've always known he could be. Still, I'm not ready to let my guard down and I still have trust issues. Pastor McCash explained that it could take weeks, months, or years for me to overcome my fears, but if we continued on the path that we were on it would eventually happen.

The phone rings and breaks me out of my reverie.

"Hello, WFAT radio. This is Ms. Daye."

"Hey baby, how are you feeling?" Rich asks.

"The same as I did two hours ago when you called," I say, smiling and enjoying Rich's constant attention.

"I'm just checking on my girl. I just wrapped up a meeting with the dot-com department to discuss the soft launch of the company's new Web site and had a minute to call you."

Rich has finally received the vice president's opportunity he wanted so badly, but with an up-and-coming couture company, Touché. It took him two months to land the position after his dismissal from Jorge Jacobs, but he wasn't suffering given that he had received a very nice severance package. Now he makes more money than he had at Jorge Jacobs and he's afforded several luxuries.

"Well, I'm glad you did," I reply while answering a few e-mails.

"Good. So what are your plans tonight? You wanna grab a bite to eat after work?"

"Ooh, I wish you had asked me that earlier. I'm meeting with Aunt Z and Gina for dinner." They decided to team up for an intervention to prevent me from getting back with Rich. Though Gina and Aunt Z may not see the big picture, I believe that there is still hope for Rich and me.

They have my best interests at heart and I understand where they're coming from. But reflecting on my aunt's life and her struggle to raise two crazy children alone makes me rethink single parenthood. As for Gina, she lives a good life. She and Oscar are considering having another baby, purchasing a larger house, and placing Ashley in private school. Gina simply doesn't understand the real world and never had to walk a day in my shoes.

"Oh. Okay, that's cool." I can hear the disappointment in his voice. "So can I drop by later?" he asks.

"No, you better not. It'll be late by the time I get home, but tomorrow is Saturday so you can always take me out for breakfast instead."

"I'm game. I'll be by to pick you up around ten A.M."

"No problem. I'll see you then."

"Val," he say, pausing for a response to which I answer. "You know I love the mess outta yo' ass, right?"

I smile. "Yes, I know, Rich, and I love you too."

"So when you gonna let a brother move back in?" he jokes, but I know he's also serious. "It's been damn near four months already and I spend all of my time with you anyway."

"I know, but we still have a few hurdles to cross. But I promise you won't have to wait too much longer. Remember, Pastor McCash taught us to live our lives patiently."

"Yeah, but Pastor McCash got a wife lying up next to him every night, so I ain't worried about him. But a brother's got needs and this corporate housing situation ain't where I wanna be."

"Boy, you are crazy. I got work to do before I get out of here tonight, so let me go. I love you."

"I love you too, baby."

On my way out of the office, the front page of the *New York Post* catches my attention. There's a photo of Logo Benton posing for a jump shot. The headline reads, THE GIFT FROM HEAVEN. Earlier during Juicy Lips's broadcast, I heard her mention that Logo Benton had practically single-handedly taken his team to the playoffs. Below the large photo is another picture of him arm in arm with my archenemy, Vanessa Knight. I don't even bother to pick up the paper to read what that's all about. It's of no concern to me, and if they are a couple, she's his problem now.

Rich was my man first and he's my man again. Case closed!

As I head toward the elevator I say a silent prayer. My sole wish is that I never ever cross paths with that witch Vanessa Knight again.

And the church said, "Amen."